THE GIFT CASTLE

JUMPSTART DUCHY
BOOK 3

STEFON MEARS

Thousand
Faces
Publishing

Also by Stefon Mears

The Rise of Magic Series
Magician's Choice
Sleight of Mind
Lunar Alchemy
Three Fae Monte
The Sphinx Principle
Double Backed Magic
Mercury Fold (coming soon)

Cavan Oltblood Series
Half a Wizard
The Ice Dagger
Spells of Undeath

Power City Tales
Not Quite Bulletproof
No Money in Heroism

Standalones
Between the Cracks
Sects and the City
Prince of a Thousand Worlds
Devil's Night
Portal-Land, Oregon
Stealing from Pirates
Fade to Gold
With a Broken Sword
Twice Against the Dragon
The House on Cedar Street
Sudden Death
On the Edge of Faerie

Short Story Collections
Spell Slingers
Twisted Timelines
Longhairs and Short Tales: A Collection of Cat Stories
Confronting Legends (Spells & Swords Vol. 1)
The Patreon Collection, Vol. 1-8 (Vol. 9, coming soon)

Nonfiction
The 30-Day Novel and Beyond!

Spells for Hire Series
Devil's Shoestring
Zombie Powder
Spirit Trap
Dragon's Blood

The Telepath Trilogy
Surviving Telepathy
Immoral Telepathy
Targeting Telepathy

Edge of Humanity Series
Caught Between Monsters
Hunting Monsters

Jumpstart Duchy Series
Into the Torn Kingdoms
The Dragon's Gold
The Gift Castle
The Deadly Feast
The King's Test
Triumph in the Torn Kingdoms

Published by Thousand Faces Publishing, Portland, Oregon

http://1kfaces.com

Hardback ISBN: 978-1-948490-45-0

Paperback ISBN: 978-1-948490-34-4

THE GIFT CASTLE

FOREWORD

The man known as Aefric Brightstaff was not born on Qorunn. He was born on the distant world of Earth, where he went by the name Keifer McShane.

On Earth, he knew the world of Qorunn only through *The Torn Kingdoms*, the setting of his favorite roleplaying game. His primary source of joy and solace, following the untimely death of his wife, Andi.

When a Jumpstart crowdfunding campaign for the next edition of *The Torn Kingdoms* offered him the chance to become a duke in the world he loved, Keifer pounced on it. Imagined they would send him a patent of nobility. Ask his opinion about the non-player character who'd bear his name and title. Perhaps even allow him to include Andi as his duchess, when the books went to print.

He couldn't wait to become a part of the world he loved so well.

But he mistook it all for make-believe.

Keifer didn't expect the great Mage of Marrisford himself, the one and only Kainemorton, to show up on his doorstep.

Keifer didn't expect to be transported to Qorunn, where he would start life anew as an orphan boy on the streets of the fabled city of Sartis. That shining beacon on the southern sea.

Now known as Aefric, he grew into a powerful adventurer. Widely believed to be a wizard, he is in fact the first of the dweomerblood. It is said that magic itself flows through his very veins.

As Aefric, he mastered the fabled Brightstaff. He fought in the Godswalk Wars, and saved countless lives at the Battle of Deepwater, in the kingdom of Armyr.

In gratitude, King Colm of Armyr named Aefric Duke of Deepwater. And no sooner had Aefric taken possession of his duchy than he prevented an invasion by Armyr's southern neighbor, Malimfar.

Since then, he has worked to unite his vassals. To heal his lands and his peoples from the damage done by the Godswalk Wars. To fight off assassins, slavers and smugglers. To deal with foreign intrigues and the influence of the pirate queen, Nelazzi.

All while being pressured to marry, and sire an heir to one day inherit his duchy...

Keifer McShane. Aefric Brightstaff.

One man who has lived two lives.

This is book three of his story...

1

____

A HALF-DOZEN WARSHIPS GUARDED THE HARBOR OF THE PORT CITY OF Kivash. All of them great, three-masted beasts, and armed with ballistae. Soldiers in chainmail on their decks, with spears and swords, standing ready if needed.

And all of these warships flew two banners high and proud: the flag of the kingdom of Armyr — a golden oak tree on a field of forest green — and that of the duchy of Merrek — a gauntleted fist rising on a field of crimson.

From his relaxing wooden chair on the afterdeck of his two-masted schooner, the *Duke's Hand*, Aefric Brightstaff smiled at the sight.

Good to see that Duchess Ashling had been rebuilding Merrek's sea might, in the wake of the Godswalk Wars. If she could afford to keep six warships guarding this harbor, surely she had more than enough to see her trading vessels safely around the Risen Sea.

With Aefric on such good terms with the duchess, that meant more protection for his own ships as well. All to the benefit of Armyr.

"Six," Ser Beornric Ol'Sandallas said from a canvas chair, to Aefric's right.

Ser Beornric, captain of the Knights of the Lake — the elite of

Aefric's personal guard — had seen close to forty summers, but most of his bulk was still muscle. He had the rough features and old scars of a man who'd served as a soldier and knight for most of his life, but his black hair and bushy mustache were liberally sprinkled with gray.

He wore his full plate armor more often than not, though today he wore a dark red cotton doublet over a dark yellow tunic, dark brown breeches and new boots of strong leather.

"Exactly what I was thinking," Ser Yrsa said, from her canvas chair to Aefric's left.

Ser Yrsa Azenai, Aefric's general, was somewhere about a decade older than his own two-dozen summers. She was even taller than Aefric, and easily the strongest woman he'd ever met. Especially her hands and wrists. In battle, she made her twin huge, ridged maces cut the air like willow switches.

Her tightly braided blonde hair had red undertones — unlike Aefric's loosely worn locks, which were sandier in shade — and she never said or did anything to dissuade the rumor that the red in her hair came from the blood of her enemies.

As though her major scar wasn't intimidating enough on its own.

All knights and most soldiers had their scars. Aefric himself had picked up several during his adventuring days. But few had a scar so distinctive as the one on Ser Yrsa's face.

It began in the middle of her forehead, and slashed down through her left eye, all the way to her chin. A healer had saved her eye and her vision, but now that eye was red. Dark red for the iris, and pale red where most eyes were white.

A clear contrast to the dark gray of her right eye.

On some, that scar might've been repulsive. But with her strong features and deep confidence, Ser Yrsa wore the scar as comfortably as she wore her full plate armor.

She wasn't in armor today, either. They weren't expecting any trouble in Kivash. She wore a light brown tunic over dark brown breeches, along with her old campaign boots. Leather things that came up to her knee. They were heavily scuffed and scarred, but she swore she moved better in them.

"And what is it you're both seeing when you see those six warships?" Aefric asked.

"Duchess Ashling's expecting trouble," Ser Beornric said.

Ser Yrsa nodded.

"From Malimfar?" Aefric asked.

Up until this past spring, Kivash had belonged to the kingdom of Malimfar. But then Malimfar had tried to invade Armyr through the Indecisive River Valley, before being stopped by Aefric by means of a spell that almost killed him in the casting.

The single largest magical working of his life, stopping more than twenty thousand soldiers cold — literally, for he used ice magic — and the skalds had named the event the Battle of Frozen Ridge.

Frozen. Ridge.

Aefric supposed it could've been worse. But he wasn't sure how.

Either way, King Colm, working with Duchess Ashling, had gone on to march down the river valley and take Kivash from Malimfar, as both compensation and punishment for the attempted invasion.

"Possibly trouble from Malimfar," Ser Yrsa said. "No doubt they'll want to retake the port, when they can. But Duchess Ashling could also be worried about Nelazzi."

Nelazzi. The so-called pirate queen. Aefric would dearly love to go after her, especially since he'd recently proven that she was expanding her crimes to include slavery.

But the king had been most explicit. Aefric was not to hunt down Nelazzi without permission.

And that permission would not be forthcoming anytime soon. Not after those recent assassination attempts on Armyr's royal family.

Attempts that had not come from the obvious source: Malimfar. The crown's investigation was ongoing, and Aefric hadn't heard the latest—

No. Aefric had to stop himself there.

This trip was *supposed* to be vacation time for Aefric. A little break, and a chance to see about his gift from Ashling. Part of her thanks for the effort that stopped Malimfar.

Somewhere in this city, on a hill not very far from the port, sat a castle that she'd given to Aefric. Along with everything inside, and the hill beneath it.

Exploring a castle again. The thought made him smile.

Karbin should be with him for this. How many old keeps and ruins had they explored together, back when Aefric was Karbin's apprentice, and traveling with Karbin's adventuring party, the Last Sons?

Dozens at least.

But now Karbin was Aefric's court wizard. And he remained behind at Water's End to help Aefric's seneschal, Kentigern, get the new castellan, Ser Garnotin, acclimated to his duties.

Sers Yrsa and Beornric continued to discuss which was more likely to cause trouble at this point in the year: Malimfar or Nelazzi.

It was getting late into the summer, after all. The beginning of autumn was only three aetts away. And that seemed to imply something different to each of his two knight-advisers.

Knowing they could go on at length on this topic without resolving anything, Aefric tuned them out. Instead he watched as the warships waved both his ships — the *Duke's Hand* and the *Swift Wave* — past their line and into the harbor proper.

They weren't waving everyone past. Some ships got stopped and at least questioned. Possibly searched.

But then, those other ships weren't flying the banners Aefric's ships flew. Both Armyr's flag and his own Deepwater flag: the image of Lake Deepwater, with a sword sticking out, hilt first, on a background of navy blue.

What was more, the *Duke's Hand* also flew his personal standard — a staff with twin lightning bolts rising up from it, one to the dexter and one to the sinister, on a background of navy blue — indicating that the duke was aboard.

Busy place, the harbor. Some thirty ships of various shapes and sizes were either heading into port, out of port, or waiting for permission to dock.

And that didn't count the ships passing the port entirely and heading up the Indecisive River to some other destination.

Once upon a time, Kivash had been the only city here at the mouth of the Indecisive River. But before the Godswalk Wars had started, Merrek had been building up a town on the north bank — traditional Merrek territory, for the river had been the border between Malimfar and Armyr.

But now that Ashling controlled Kivash, she'd been visibly trying to blend her new city with her developing town.

The differences between the two sides, though, were still glaringly obvious.

To begin Kivash on the south side was easily five times the size it was on the north bank. Perhaps larger.

On the north side, the docks were small and made of beechwood. Aefric counted a half-dozen piers, only three of which saw current use.

On the south side stretched wide docks of bleached greenwood, with close to forty piers stretching out into the harbor. And nearly all of them busy with ships.

Beyond the docks, the north side and south side varied just as much.

The north side was mostly wooden construction, with few buildings taller than two stories. The only stone construction Aefric could see from the harbor looked to be a small, brown keep, somewhere about the center of town.

The south side, though, had a good deal of white stone in its buildings, some of which stretched as many as four or five stories.

And that wasn't counting the three castles, the freestanding tall, wide tower, the several temples. And of course, the series of domes off toward the far south, near the wall, which was also of white stone.

The north side looked like an afterthought. Which it was, really. Though no doubt Ashling was hunting for white stone to make both sides match.

She had her work cut out for her.

Aefric was about to call down, to see how long the wait would be, when a single-masted sailboat pulled alongside the *Duke's Hand*.

"Ahoy, *Duke's Hand*," someone called from the sailboat. "That old sea dog Sikel still your captain?"

"Who else?" Captain Sikel called back in a voice as big, rough and weathered as the captain himself. "Some sea devil spawn like yourself, Reyor?"

The two captains laughed. Captain Reyor looked to be even older than Captain Sikel, and maybe twice as roughly handled by the years and the weather.

"Not sure whose ass you kissed, Sikel, but I've got orders to let you skip the line. Follow me to the docks."

"*Swift Wave's* gotta come with us," Sikel called back. "Duke's men and all that."

Captain Reyor tugged on his thick, gray beard while he considered his answer.

"Don't have any orders about a second ship."

"So you think his grace is going to abandon his men?" Sikel said. "That sound like what you've heard about Duke Aefric Brightstaff?"

Captain Reyor frowned into his beard. "*Swift Wave* take orders from you, Sikel?"

"I'm flying the duke's personal standard. What do you think?"

"I think I need to hear an answer."

"Then scrape the barnacles out of your ears, Reyor. The answer's *yes*."

"Good enough for me," Reyor said, then raised an amplifying cone to his mouth and called to trailing ship. "*Swift Wave*, follow the *Duke's Hand* in." He lowered it and turned back to Captain Sikel. "I'll need you to sign something to that effect, once we dock."

"You gone remora, Reyor?"

"Tell you over drinks. Let's get you docked."

As the *Duke's Hand* was led through the harbor, Ser Beornric went down to the main deck to have a word with the six Knights of the Lake under his command.

He returned shortly and nodded at Ser Yrsa, who nodded back.

"Why do I feel as though you two are planning something?" Aefric asked.

"Because we are," Ser Yrsa said. "Does your grace wish to assert personal control over every aspect of his arrangements? Or would he rather display trust in his advisers?"

It was comforting to see amusement inside the challenge in Ser Yrsa's eyes as she asked that. It meant she really was coming to trust Aefric.

They hadn't gotten on well together, in the spring. What with his calling his forces to war and assigning Countess Faenella to lead them without so much as *informing* his general, let alone *consulting* her or offering her command.

The fact that he hadn't met Yrsa, or even known he had a general, was probably the only reason she hadn't either quit her post or tried to murder him...

Aefric gave her the answer she knew she'd get.

"Obviously I prefer to trust in my advisers," he said with a nod.

She cocked an eyebrow. Naturally, she chose the one split by her scar, emphasizing her red eye.

"And I trust your grace won't go flying off, leaving his guards behind?"

"I haven't done that in ... at least two aetts now."

"And when it's been at least a season, I'll ask less often. But I'll continue asking until at least a year passes between such incidents."

"Fine," Aefric said, raising an open hand in hopes that conceding the point was enough. "I *am* trying to move past my old adventuring habits."

"And we *do* appreciate it," Ser Beornric said, giving Ser Yrsa a meaningful look.

She nodded.

Oh, they were planning something all right.

Meanwhile, the *Duke's Hand* and *Swift Wave* weren't just guided to any old docking spots. They were guided to prime spots at the very foot of the pier nearest the river, with only one other ship — another two-master, though larger than Aefric's ship — between the *Duke's Hand* and the wharf itself.

From the way Captain Sikel raved, they must've been given a docking position second only to the duchess' own ship.

Which suggested that Duchess Ashling was here in Kivash...

The deckhands were tying off the *Duke's Hand*, and lowering the gangplank when Ser Yrsa took her turn to head down and see to arrangements.

Aefric stood and took the Brightstaff in hand, ready to head down himself.

"Tarry a moment if you would, your grace," Ser Beornric said, still seated.

Aefric gave his knight a questioning look.

"Please, your grace," Ser Beornric added.

Aefric sat. But he kept the Brightstaff in hand, instead of standing it beside his seat.

"Tell me," he said.

"Your grace must remember that, until the events of this past spring, Kivash belonged to Malimfar."

"You *are* expecting trouble."

"Not *expecting*," Ser Beornric said. "But it's better to be safe."

"Even though I had nothing to do with Kivash's capture."

Ser Beornric gave Aefric a frank look.

"All right," Aefric conceded. "It would still belong to Malimfar, had I not stopped their armies. But neither I nor any of my soldiers were here when Kivash was taken. Taken without bloodshed, I should add."

"Without a *fight*," Ser Beornric corrected, raising an index finger for emphasis. "Armyr caught them unawares, and they surrendered rather than risk being sacked. But that doesn't mean there's been no bloodshed."

Aefric frowned as he considered that.

"Ashling replaced the local leadership, didn't she? Their mayor. City council, if they had one. All her people now."

"Naturally," Ser Beornric said. "She needed people she could trust in the positions of power. Though the ones they displaced were most likely ransomed to relatives and left the city in safety. But what else do you think she's had to do?"

"Oh," Aefric said, wincing in realization. "She's rooted out resistance, hasn't she?"

"Speculation on my part — well, mine and Yrsa's, because I've discussed this with her. But we both think so. And neither of us think she's been gentle about it."

"Won't that strengthen their resolve?"

"Depends on a number of factors," Ser Beornric said. "Truth is, Duchess Ashling is likely quite effective at taking control of a populace. The Fyrenns have gained and lost a lot of land over the centuries."

Aefric sighed. "I imagine that many of the locals hate her right now."

"I expect they do," Ser Beornric said. "And will for some time. Kivash won't likely be settled again until at least the spring. And even if she then switches to the carrot instead of the stick, it may be some years yet before they come to love her here."

"Assuming they ever do," Aefric said. Shook his head. "And here I come, another Armyrian noble, and the man responsible for stopping their armies. Is that it?"

"More than that," Ser Beornric said. "You didn't just stop Malimfar's forces. You *froze* them. And not only their armies, but their mercenaries. Their supplies. Camp followers. Siege equipment. Everything."

"You make it sound as though I turned them into ice sculptures."

"As far as the skalds are concerned," Ser Beornric said, gently, "you did. Tales grow in the telling, your grace And the truth was impressive enough to begin with. The death count was ... not insignificant."

Aefric puffed out a breath. Being viewed as a hero was one thing. Being viewed as a villain was something else entirely.

"So they hate *me* here too," Aefric said. "And now you're worried about assassins."

"Some of them may hate you," Ser Beornric said. "Especially those who lost relatives at Frozen Ridge. Others will fear you. Either way, we are charged with your safety."

Aefric looked closely at Ser Beornric.

"You brought more troops than we discussed, didn't you?"

"No, your grace," Ser Beornric said. "We brought the forty soldiers Duchess Ashling recommended to hold and guard your new castle."

"Beornric," Aefric said in a warning tone.

"That much is true, your grace," Ser Beornric said. "However, it is also true that, in order to ensure your safety, I brought along the soldiers of your grace's personal guard, in addition to the Knights of the Lake."

Another two dozen soldiers then, all of them dedicated to Aefric personally.

"And you didn't tell me this because..."

"They are under my direct command, your grace," Ser Beornric said. "And your grace has assured me more than once that I have his full support in distributing and tasking your personal guard as I see fit."

"In other words," Aefric said, "you didn't want to worry me, and you didn't want me to cancel this trip."

"Between your duties and your researches, your grace has been working hard lately," Ser Beornric said. "A vacation was certainly in order."

"And I couldn't have simply retired to my hunting lodge for an aett or so? Perhaps with Byrhta Ol'Caran?"

"Undoubtedly that would have great restorative value for you, your grace," Ser Beornric said, smiling now. "But your grace did promise to come to Kivash and see your new castle. Not to mention that Duchess Ashling will take this visit as a kindness and a show of support."

Aefric laughed.

"Your grace?" Ser Beornric asked.

"Nothing," Aefric said, still chuckling. "It's just that, in my adventuring days, my forms of relaxation were often as dangerous as my work. I somehow thought that would change when I became duke."

"I suspect your life now is no less dangerous," Ser Beornric said frankly. "Though the nature of those dangers has shifted."

"Your grace," Ser Yrsa called up from the deck below. "A welcoming party arrives, flying Merrek colors."

"And this might be one of those dangers now," Aefric said, straightening his clothes.

There'd been some debate about how Aefric would dress when he arrived in Kivash. He was of the mind to approach this as exploring his castle. Strong cottons and leathers. But his valets had nearly thrown fits at the suggestion.

He was a duke, arriving in a newly Armyrian city, to lay claim to a castle. He had to look the part.

Worse, Sers Yrsa and Beornric — as well as Aefric's seneschal, Kentigern — had all agreed with the valets.

In the end, Aefric had surrendered that fight. Mostly.

He'd agreed to wear a fine silk tunic of sky blue, as well as the small gold brooch surrounded by sapphires that Ashling had given him. But instead of hose, Aefric had insisted on leathers. His boots had been a compromise. High leather so soft it was creamy, but good, hard soles.

The leathers, of course, were fine. But the silk was rumpled and a little sweat-stained from the long day at sea.

(Of course, his valet would have expected him to wear a different tunic on the water, and change before disembarking. But Aefric was still adjusting to the idea of changing clothes so often.)

He cheated, of course. He used a small spell he'd worked out in the early days of his apprenticeship, which freshened both his clothes and his person.

"All right," he said. "Now I'm ready."

THE SUN RODE HIGH AND BRIGHT IN THE RICH BLUE SKIES ABOVE, WHILE long white clouds chased each other east.

Warm winds blew across the deck of the *Duke's Hand* from out over the Risen Sea as Aefric crossed to the gangplank with Ser Beornric by his side.

Ser Yrsa was there and waiting, along with Sers Leppina and Arras, who wore their full plate, etched on the breastplate with the image of Lake Deepwater, marking them as Knights of the Lake. Apparently they were the two tasked to serve as Aefric's nearest guards today, which left him wondering where the other four were.

Ser Leppina stood almost as tall as Ser Yrsa, with an even stronger build, and a more pronounced tan. She wore her brown hair in a single long braid, that hung just past her ribcage.

Aefric had heard that she only cut her hair when someone bested her in single combat. Long as her braid was, that must have been some time ago now.

Which made Aefric wonder if she didn't count training bouts. Because surely she'd faced Ser Deirdre at some point...

Ser Arras, whose very dark black hair would likely have been thick and lustrous if she grew it out, kept it instead cut nearly battle-field short. Even so, it contrasted sharply with her skin, which was pale as any noble's.

Ser Arras had an aristocratic beauty that had led many to presume her the unclaimed bastard daughter of the late Duchess of Deepwater, Arinda Soulfist.

Ser Arras was also the only Knight of the Lake who fought with two longswords.

"Your guards are in position, your grace," Ser Yrsa said, "and the welcoming party awaits below."

Aefric nodded, and turned to look down the gangplank.

He immediately spotted Zoleen Fyrenn at the heart of the welcoming party.

Zoleen was Duchess Ashling's younger sister, and at least her equal in beauty of face and form. She wore her long copper curls down and wild today, hanging past her bare shoulders. Her dress was a lightweight chiffon and pale as sunrise, with a number of twists and straps that had to be a reference to a personal amusement they'd shared one night.

In fact, to judge by the smile on her full lips and in her sapphire eyes, she'd caught Aefric noticing those twists and straps.

She was surrounded not by other nobles but by pike-wielding guards in chainmail and Merrek tabards. No other nobles or ladies-in-waiting, but standing beside her was a magic-user Aefric didn't know.

He looked to be half-again Aefric's age, though he wore his years well. His pale skin had undertones of dark red. Or maybe that just came from his long, straight hair, which was so dark a crimson that he likely had some eldrani blood.

Yes. That would suit his fine features, as well, for he had a touch of the eldrani beauty. But either he aged more like a human, or he was much older than he looked.

He wore robes of olive green, and carried a gnarled, blackwood staff in which at least three gemstones had been set.

He also carried two wands at his belt.

Aefric could feel the magic of those wands and staff as clearly as he could feel that this man was some stripe of magic-user. Likely a wizard.

"Your grace," Zoleen said with a small bow, "welcome to Kivash."

"Thank you, Zoleen," Aefric said, giving her a smile he didn't quite feel as he started down the gangplank, accompanied by his knights. He hadn't forgiven her yet for something she'd done while visiting Water's End only a few aetts ago. "It's good to be here."

"Your grace," she said again, and unless Aefric was mistaken, she was emphasizing his courtesy just a little. "May I present Farondonic, apprentice to my sister's ducal wizard, Sirondfar."

"Your grace," Farondonic said, with a deeper bow. "I've long been an admirer of your work. Perhaps if we have time, your grace might favor me with a word or two about our shared Art."

"Perhaps," Aefric said, reaching the dock now to stand before them. "If time allows."

He noted that an enclosed carriage stood nearby and waiting. An enchanted carriage, much like the one King Colm had given Aefric. Horseless and luxurious, with room enough for eight inside.

This one, of course, bore the Merrek sigil on its ebony frame, rather than Deepwater.

Aefric also spotted soldiers of his personal guard out past the carriage, as well as protecting the other direction.

And that didn't include the forty soldiers he had, standing in formation and ready to move.

"Farondonic," Zoleen said, "You can await me back at the castle, I think. Should there be a need for magic to stand between me and harm, I've no doubt his grace will protect me."

"I am at your command, Mistress Zoleen," Farondonic said, and transformed himself to an owl and took to the air.

"Not bad," Aefric said, nodding.

"Oh, it looks impressive enough," Zoleen said. "But it leaves me forever wondering if he's hiding among the trees outside my window back at Fyrcloch, trying to catch sight of me at my bath."

"I should hope not," Aefric said, chuckling. "Have you spoken to Sirondfar about this?"

"No," she said, waving the idea away. "Not unless one of those owls gives me reason to think it's more than paranoia. Shall we?"

Aefric nodded, and one of her soldiers opened the carriage door.

"Ser Yrsa, Ser Beornric," Zoleen said, "I trust you won't mind riding up front?"

"At your pleasure, Mistress Zoleen," Ser Beornric said with a formal bow, and he and Ser Yrsa climbed up to where the drivers would sit, if the carriage needed drivers.

Sers Arras and Leppina took up posts one at each door. Merrek's soldiers, along with the soldiers of Aefric's personal guard, formed a wall around the carriage, with Aefric's remaining forty following in formation.

Though Aefric still didn't know where his other four Knights of the Lake were.

Aefric gestured for Zoleen to enter the carriage first, and followed her in out of the midday heat.

The interior of Zoleen's carriage had two long, well-padded benches, facing each other. They were upholstered in white silk, with the Merrek sigil in crimson.

She sat on the bench facing forward. Aefric sat opposite her.

Disappointment flashed across her eyes. Had she expected Aefric to sit beside her?

At her word, the carriage began to roll on its way.

"I trust your grace will forgive the size of his welcome party. I could have invited some of the local nobles, but I confess I wanted your grace to myself for at least the length of this ride."

"That's fine," Aefric said, honestly. "I'm not in a hurry to play politics."

Before she could respond, he gestured to the area around the carriage.

"You came with a good number of guards, though," he said. "Are things really so bad here?"

"It's more than are needed," Zoleen said. "Even without your grace's own soldiers adding to the number. But my sister is unwilling to risk anything happening to me."

"She's a good sister then," Aefric said. He drew a breath and added, honestly, "And I share her concern."

"Truly?" Zoleen asked. "Your grace does not wish to see me dead then?"

"Dead?" Aefric shook his head in disbelief. "Come on, Zoleen. That's not fair."

"Your grace withdrew his permission to address him by name," she said, pain quite visible in her eyes. "And banished me from Water's End. I've found it ... difficult to gauge exactly how far I've fallen in your grace's esteem."

"I don't know exactly either," Aefric admitted. "But obviously I don't wish you any harm."

"Your grace has not answered my letters."

"I told you. I need time."

She drew a deep breath. Slowly let it out.

"Your grace," she said, "I have discussed what happened with both my sisters at some length. Eppi" — meaning *Queen* Eppida — "thinks your grace overreacted. She agrees that I shouldn't have pressured the lers in Riverbreak to keep Byrhta Ol'Caran away from Water's End. But in her opinion, my actions only merited a small amount of personal censure."

"I see," Aefric said. "And did she have a suggestion?"

Zoleen's eyes twinkled. "She recommended a good spanking."

Aefric laughed before he could stop himself, which got him a broad smile and a raised eyebrow from Zoleen.

"I would be willing," she said softly. "If your grace favors the idea."

"I'll keep that in mind," Aefric said, still chuckling.

He'd been a noble here in Armyr for about a season and a half now, and he was still adjusting to what Armyrians referred as "the noble privilege."

In essence, the noble privilege meant Armyrian nobles were free to have sex with each other whenever they liked, in whatever way they liked, assuming no one involved was closely related, and everyone involved was willing.

There was no pressure to it, and refusal was never supposed to be taken as a slight or an insult.

Supposedly the noble privilege helped avoid jealousies and other evils of sexual frustration. And as long as one or both drank their nysta tea, there'd be no unwanted pregnancies.

That Queen Eppida suggested a spanking was no great shock. Aefric had learned firsthand that the woman ... had some kinky tendencies.

"What did Ashling have to say?" he asked.

Zoleen sighed. "She said I should have foreseen your grace's reaction. She insists that if I'd been listening when she told me about your grace, that I would have known better than to go behind your back that way."

"Is she right?"

Zoleen shrugged with one shoulder. "Ash ... can go on, sometimes. I developed the habit of tuning her out when I was a child."

Not that Zoleen was so very old even now. She was only perhaps half a year into her majority.

"And I confess," she continued with a smile, "I was more interested in hearing her talk about how handsome you are, and how puissant you are with magic. Her biased takes on your personality ... were less interesting."

She shook her head. "She really can go on, at times."

"I see," Aefric said. "And did she suggest a remedy?"

"She said I could try throwing myself at your grace's feet and begging for forgiveness, but that likely what I need to do is back off and give your grace time, then see if your grace might be willing to start anew."

"I'm not really comfortable with people throwing themselves at my feet and begging."

"I'll keep that in mind," Zoleen said, teasing Aefric with his own phrase. "Personally, I'd prefer the spanking."

Aefric chuckled, but then Zoleen's expression got more serious.

"Your grace," she said. "I know now how wrong I was. I might not've understood when your grace banished me from Water's End, but I've had a great deal of time to think, and I've realized where and how I erred."

"Where and how?" Aefric asked.

"While my thoughts were only on the ... distraction that Byrhta Ol'Caran could have presented, I did not consider the whole of the situation. My actions kept two fiercely loyal vassals, Byrhta Ol'Caran, Baroness Regent of Riverbreak, and Vercy Ol'Karmak, future Baroness of Riverbreak, away from Water's End at a time when they could have been impressing his majesty with tales of how well your grace has run his duchy."

Practically the same words Aefric had used, during his explanation of why he was so angry, just before banishing her.

Not exactly enough to merit forgiveness. Especially since she still seemed to be missing the point.

But perhaps she'd been tuning him out as well...

"But even without factoring in their importance as vassals," she continued, "I still should not have done what I did."

She shook her head, lips a tight line, but gained a haughtier look as she continued.

"It's no exaggeration to say that Byrhta Ol'Caran may be the most beautiful woman walking the surface of Qorunn," Zoleen said. "And yet, the fact remains that she is the daughter of your grace's own vassal. She has no title of her own, nor a powerful family supporting her. She lacks even an impressive dowry to recommend her to your grace for anything more than the bliss moment.

"I, on the other hand," she continued, "am a Fryenn. Sister to the Duchess of Merrek. Sister to the Queen of Armyr. I have the family and position to make a good match for your grace. And while my beauty does not compare to that of Byrhta Ol'Caran, your grace has demonstrated quite amply that he appreciates both my beauty and my company."

The carriage rolled to a stop.

"I should have trusted in my own appeal," Zoleen said, "rather than trying to remove unworthy competition."

Aefric sighed.

"Your grace," Ser Arras called into the carriage. "We've arrived."

"Zoleen," Aefric said, "while I confess I don't care for your characterization of Byrhta, you've missed the most important point."

Zoleen frowned, with a slight pout that Aefric suspected was deliberate.

"I have?" she asked.

"Think back to what I told you before I sent you away. Assuming you didn't tune *me* out as you do Ashling." He moved toward the door. "Thank you for the ride."

Zoleen still hadn't spoken again when he stepped out of the carriage.

Aefric wondered what it said about her that she'd missed the most important point.

Right now, Aefric couldn't trust her.

2

———————

ZOLEEN'S CARRIAGE ROLLED OFF ALONG THE COBBLED STREET INTO THE midday heat. Slowly, so that her guards could keep pace on foot.

On foot. That was odd. Why not just bring horses for her...

Oh. Of course. They were pikemen. Fighting with a pike from horseback would take training most soldiers wouldn't have.

And the carriage could have only gone so fast anyway. The street was certainly busy enough, with traffic both on foot and ahorse, including hand-drawn carts and horse-drawn carriages.

No other magical conveyances nearby.

Aefric was drawing a lot of attention, though. Not that this was a surprise. He was the only person in the area surrounded by nine knights and more than sixty soldiers.

Wait.

Nine knights? The Knights of the Lake were seven, including Ser Beornric. Ser Yrsa made eight, and the ninth—

"Your grace." Ser Deirdre Ol'Miri dropped to one knee — as she always seemed to insist on doing, even though it wasn't appropriate. She gave Aefric a rakish smile. "Welcome to Kivash."

Ser Deirdre wasn't just any knight. She was a dweomerblade, one who trained in a way that interwove both magic and martial skills.

Where the other knights around her wore full plate (excepting Sers Yrsa and Beornric today), she wore leathers of deep maroon red.

Where the others favored broadswords or longswords (maces in Ser Yrsa's case), Ser Deirdre wore a rapier and dueling dagger.

And she'd more than earned the confidence in her bearing. Aefric wasn't sure he'd ever seen her match with a blade.

Ser Deirdre was also startlingly pretty, with her burgundy hair bound in a braid most of the way down her back. And her jade green eyes always seemed to sparkle with a joke she hadn't let the world in on.

"Rise, Ser Deirdre," Aefric said, one eyebrow high. "I wasn't aware you'd be meeting me here."

"I am here at the request of your grace's general," she said, clearly enjoying herself. "She wished me to check the lay of the land here in Kivash, before your grace set boot upon cobble."

"Anything I should know?"

"Many things, I suspect. But about Kivash, they believe your grace could stop the sun in the sky, if he had a mind to."

Damn it. That statement should have irritated Aefric. After all, it implied that they were even more afraid of him than he thought.

But Ser Deirdre, she had this way of making him laugh. Even when she said things that shouldn't be funny.

He held back from laughing this time, but he could tell she saw the laughter in his eyes, and the sight widened her smile.

"But all appears to be secure around your grace's new castle." She stepped back and gave a wave of her arm, as though presenting the castle to Aefric herself.

Aefric knew from the drawing he'd been given that the castle had two walls. One around its perimeter, and the other in closer to the castle itself.

At the moment he could only see the one.

Down here at street level, the outer wall stood roughly three times Aefric's height, and likely of a decent enough thickness. The outside was impressively smooth. And also looked to have been recently washed, because it wasn't notably dirty. A tricky thing, with white stone.

No guards visibly patrolled the wall at the moment, which he found interesting.

Had Ashling's soldiers already been removed?

As for the castle itself, what little Aefric could see from his current angle, it also looked to have been built from that white stone.

He found himself wondering where they quarried it. In case he needed more...

He could sense a touch of magic from the iron gate in front of him. Nothing too impressive. A strengthening charm, and a little something to keep away rust and decay.

It was a solid, rectangular gate, with a small sliding window at about head height.

"Not very convenient for deliveries," Aefric said.

"There's likely a secondary gate for such things," Ser Yrsa said. "Small, so that no more than one could come through at a time."

"Well," Aefric said, "let's see if anyone's home."

Ser Yrsa drew one of her maces, and used the butt end to hammer on the gate.

Two crossbowmen aimed down from atop the walls.

"Who knocks?" one asked.

"His grace, Ser Aefric Brightstaff, Duke of Deepwater, Baron of Netar, and Hero of the Battles of Deepwater and Frozen Ridge."

Aefric wasn't sure how politic it was to mention the Battle of Frozen Ridge, but wasn't going to correct her.

The crossbowmen looked hard at Aefric, and took note of the Brightstaff in his hand.

It was a distinctive weapon. Carved from a single branch of white thunderwood, with a brown leather wrapping for a grip. Embedded in its top, a yellow diamond as big as the last joint of Aefric's thumb.

"I hope your grace will forgive the challenge," the crossbowman said, "but I and mine were told to ask to see some lightning. Not that we want your grace blowing down his own gate. Just to avoid the risk of impostors. Kivash ... remains unsettled at this time."

Aefric tapped the butt of the Brightstaff on the cobbles and caused white lightning to play along its length.

"Sufficient?" Aefric asked.

"Welcome to Castle Hrafnvigi, your grace."

The iron gate swung open with impressive silence. Clearly someone had oiled it in anticipation of Aefric's arrival.

Thirty-six soldiers stood in formation in the center of the road, which sloped up the hill to another white stone wall. The other four soldiers appeared to be coming down from their posts on the battlements.

All around the road grew grass, yellowed from the heat of summer.

"Don't fret the yellow grass, your grace," the one crossbowman continued, as he approached. "First rain'll green it right up again. Good, strong roots."

"Thank you…"

"Pakes, your grace," he said. "Sergeant Pakes. And I stand ready to turn over the keys, if your grace stands ready to receive them."

Aefric's instinct was to step forward and take the keys himself, but he and Ser Beornric had already discussed this.

Aefric nodded.

Ser Beornric stepped forward.

"Squad!" Sergeant Pakes snapped.

All forty of the duchess' soldiers saluted, their right fists high in the air.

Aefric acknowledged their salute with a nod, the way he'd been told.

Sergeant Pakes handed Ser Beornric a ring of keys.

Ser Yrsa stepped forward then, and began discussing the way the keep had been guarded and the sergeant's observations and suggestions, while Aefric and his Knights of the Lake — along with Ser Deirdre — started up the hill to the keep.

THE HILL INSIDE THE OUTER WALL HAD A DECENT SLOPE, AND NO COVER. Anyone getting past the outer wall would be an easy target for archers on the interior wall.

The interior wall stood about the same height as the one down at street level. Its gate wasn't iron, though, but thick oak. Unscarred, as Aefric ran his fingers across it, and old enough that likely no one had assaulted this castle in the last ... fifty years or so.

"The gate's likely unbarred," Ser Beornric said. "Shall I see it opened?"

"Not yet," Aefric said. He turned to look back down at the street.

Inside the wall, he could see his own soldiers talking with Ashling's. And the soldiers of his personal guard had spread out, and were moving in small groups around the interior of the outer wall, and checking out the hill itself.

Out beyond the wall, Aefric could see the river, the harbor, and a great deal of the local neighborhood. As well as more than a few of his new neighbors.

A few of the locals were watching him from across the street, and from windows, but most of life in Kivash was moving on.

Aefric took a slow walk around the inner wall, with the others following. The inner wall was just as smooth as the outer. If anything, it might have been smoother under his fingers.

The wind felt good up here. Not quite so warm, under the midday, late summer sun.

"Your grace," Ser Beornric said softly. "You haven't eaten since dawn. If you aren't ready to go inside, we should probably find a restaurant."

"I've gone longer than this without eating," Aefric said absently. It was true, though, that he could barely taste the lingering remains of the spicy sweet nava fruit he'd finished his breakfast with back aboard the *Duke's Hand*.

As he made his way around, he glanced down the hill, and out across the city. Getting used to the feel of the place. Something was...

Magic.

Aefric could sense magic from within his new keep. Possibly wards. Possibly something else.

And not just within the keep. He could sense magic from a tower nearby. Or at least within about catapult range.

He looked around and spotted it, off to the east. Looked to be freestanding, rather than part of a castle. Four stories tall. Crenellated top, and the crenellations were triangular, rather than rectangular.

Triangular windows too. From this angle, the windows seemed to spiral up, instead of being regularly spaced on each floor.

The design looked ... familiar.

Aefric had seen a freestanding tower like this before, with crenellations and windows like those. Some time ago.

And there must've been a good amount of magic to that tower, if Aefric could sense it so clearly from here.

There was something more, within that sense of magic from the tower.

Almost as though someone inside it felt Aefric's regard...

"Problem, your grace?" Ser Beornric asked.

"Not ... at the moment," Aefric said, shaking his head, and bringing his attention back to his surroundings.

"Ah, the tower," Ser Deirdre said. "Knew your grace would notice that. Stands out, doesn't she?"

"She?" Aefric asked.

"I always assume buildings are female," Ser Deirdre said with a shrug. "After all, people are always trying to get inside them."

Aefric hung his head for a moment. He would not reward her by laughing at that. Not so much as a snort. Even though it was the kind of humor he'd heard often in his adventuring days.

He would *not*.

"Deirdre," Ser Beornric said in an exasperated voice, "*this* is why the nobles don't like that you're part of his grace's court."

"Anyway," Ser Deirdre said, unabashed, "I checked it out. There's magic to the tower itself. And it's owned by a local wizard. Goes by Relimmorea. Lived here close to a hundred years."

"Think she'll be trouble?"

"Keeps to herself mostly," Ser Deirdre said with a shrug. "May be nonpartisan. Kind who doesn't care who runs the show, long as she isn't interfered with."

"Thank you," Aefric said, then continued on his circuit of the wall.

He spotted the other gate in the exterior wall. The one Ser Yrsa said would be there. It was iron, reinforced by three iron bars, and only wide enough for one to enter at a time.

No second gate in the interior wall, though. Anyone who came through the secondary gate in the outer wall would have to take the small path up to the interior wall, and follow it around to the main gate.

By the time Aefric completed his circuit and stood once more before the heavy, oaken gate, he was confident that none of the other buildings in the area were close enough or tall enough to help anyone who wanted to assault Castle Hrafnvigi.

Defensible enough a position, even in what was functionally an enemy city. The hill beneath his new castle wasn't very decorous, though. Especially as badly yellowed as the summer heat had left the grass.

Aefric turned his attention back to the heavy, oaken gate.

"All right," Aefric said. "See it open."

He could have opened it himself with a small spell. Possibly a gesture, if it was unbarred. But he knew that would lead to a lecture from Ser Beornric about safety and protocols and likely a few other things.

Ser Beornric nodded to tall, dark-skinned, shaven-headed Ser Temat, who stepped forward, longsword in hand.

Ser Temat had a scar *almost* as distinctive as Ser Yrsa's. His cut a wicked, jagged line across his neck.

Sword at the ready, he pushed on the gate.

It swung open soundlessly.

Inside was a decent-sized courtyard. Not big enough to host a tourney or anything, but big enough to give his soldiers room to train.

And that training would be on level footing. The hill looked to have been downright decapitated, leaving the surface flat and even.

Two other buildings inside that interior wall. A stable to Aefric's left. To his right, a barracks tall enough to function as an expansion to the battlements.

From the smell, and the soft whickering, there had to be horses in those stables.

Ser Temat moved in cautiously, accompanied by Ser Micham, who also had his longsword drawn and ready.

Ser Micham had earned his weathered skin by spending a good deal of time at sea, while growing up in Ajenmoor. He kept his brown hair and beard fashionably trim, making no effort to cover the half-ear he'd lost to a borog's spear during the Godswalk Wars.

"Is this necessary?" Aefric asked, referring to what he considered an excess of caution. "Odds are good that Ashling's soldiers slept in those barracks, so they should have found any traps the previous occupants might've left in the courtyard.

"Safety first, your grace," Ser Beornric said, without taking his eyes off the two lead knights.

Ser Beornric nodded. Sers Vria and Wardius drew their swords and moved in.

Ser Vria looked too small and pale to be a knight. Adding to that the eldrani beauty of her features, her golden eyes, and the hints of orange in her hair, it was no wonder that many underestimated her.

At least, until they faced her and learned the error of their ways.

Ser Wardius was rarely underestimated on the basis of appearance. He was a wiry kind of tough, and the most heavily scarred knight Aefric had ever met.

Ser Wardius not only had jagged scars on both cheeks, but had lost the tip of his nose, as well, and the small finger of his left hand.

The two of them went south around the main castle keep, while Sers Temat and Micham moved around the north side.

"Check the stables and barracks," Ser Beornric said then, and soldiers of Aefric's personal guard — two groups of four, with spears in hand — moved to obey.

Aefric had been too focused on the castle. He hadn't realized that any of his soldiers had approached. But now he saw the rest of his personal guard there and ready, in case of trouble.

"Think anyone will give us a fight?" Ser Deirdre asked.

One of the soldiers called back from the stables.

"Found someone!"

Ser Deirdre rubbed her hands together. "Good. I haven't had a fight in days."

WITH THE ANNOUNCEMENT THAT SOMEONE HAD BEEN FOUND IN THE stables at Castle Hrafnvigi, a lot of things happened at once.

Sers Arras, Leppina and Beornric all stepped in front of Aefric. Ser Deirdre dove, rolling forward and to one side in the dry dirt of the courtyard. Likely so she'd have more room to maneuver.

Eight of the soldiers of Aefric's personal guard ran in to help at the stables. Another eight formed up behind Aefric, guarding his back.

The other four soldiers, along with the other four Knights of the Lake, continued their part of the search of the courtyard.

Aefric's soldiers emerged from the stables...

...with a lad no older than a page walking at spearpoint.

Poor kid looked terrified. His arms couldn't hold his hands any higher than they were. His eyes were so wide Aefric half-expected his eyeballs to just fall right out and bounce away.

The boy was in brown roughspun: tunic, breeches, and shoes. His clothes were dirty. His skin was dirty. His mousy brown hair was unkempt.

Aefric gave Ser Beornric a droll look.

"Better safe than sorry," Ser Beornric said softly, though even he sounded embarrassed at the amount of effort that had gone into capturing what appeared to be nothing more than a stable hand.

"What's your name, boy?" Ser Beornric said sharply, once the boy in question was no more than a half-dozen strides away.

"Gosser, ser," the boy said, twitching as though he wanted to bow, but was afraid to lower his hands.

"You can put your hands down, Gosser," Aefric said.

"But I wouldn't make any sudden moves," Ser Beornric said, then glanced at Aefric. "The best assassins don't look dangerous, your grace."

Gosser nodded, and slowly lowered his hands, though he didn't stop trembling.

"What are you doing here?" Ser Beornric asked.

"Begging your pardon, ser," Gosser said, bowing now, then straightening up quickly, in case bowing was wrong. "I was just tendin' the horses like I always done."

Ser Beornric looked at one of Aefric's guards. Nodded. The soldier turned and ran back down the hill.

Aefric hoped sarcastically that the soldier had been sent to check Gosser's story with Ashling's soldiers, and not to summon rein-forcements.

"You worked for the previous lord of this castle?" Ser Beornric asked.

"Most o' my life, ser," Gosser said. "I was born in the kitchens, but have no hand for it. But the horses love me. And I love them, ser."

"Is that why you didn't leave with your lord?" Aefric asked.

"Yes, ser," Gosser said, "er, yes, um, my lord?"

"Address him as 'your grace,'" Ser Beornric said.

"Yes, your grace," Gosser said quickly. "Me mum wanted me to come south with her and the others, but I just couldn't leave the horses. They'd've died without someone feedin' 'em, cleanin' up after 'em, and lettin' 'em stretch their legs now and again."

"How many horses?" Aefric asked.

"Twenty, your grace," Gosser said. "I'd be more 'n happy to tell all about their names and habits. If'n your grace'll let me serve him, 'stead o' killin' me."

"You don't mind that I'm an Armyrian duke," Aefric asked, "rather than a Malimfari noble?"

"Your grace keeps me safe and fed," Gosser said, "and lets me look after the horses, and I'll serve 'im good and proper."

He nodded eagerly.

"What does keeping you safe entail?" Ser Beornric asked. "Do you have a room in the keep itself?"

"No, ser," Gosser said. "Got a little room next to the storeroom in the stables. 's all I need, ser."

"Ser Beornric," Aefric said, "I'm not inclined to think this boy's an assassin."

"Neither am I," Ser Deirdre announced. "He doesn't have the balance for it."

"I'm inclined to agree," Ser Beornric said. "Though with your grace's permission, I'd like to hear the report from the duchess' soldiers before we welcome him."

They waited briefly for Aefric's soldier to run back up the hill. Wasn't even panting for breath. Ser Beornric was keeping Aefric's personal guard in good shape.

"Your grace," the soldier said with a bow. "Sergeant Pakes confirms that Gosser was here when Ashling's forces moved in. Says the boy caused them no trouble, and has done an excellent job of tending the horses. The sergeant recommends keeping him on."

"That's settled then," Aefric said, gesturing for his soldiers to lower their spears. "Welcome to my service, Gosser."

"Thank you, your grace," Gosser said eagerly. "Can I introduce you to the horses now?"

"Later," Aefric said. "First, how well do you know the castle?"

"Hardly at all, your grace," Gosser said with a shrug. "Kicked me out o' the kitchens when I was a lad. Been in the stables e'er since."

"All right, then," Aefric said. "Show my soldiers around the stables and tell them anything you think we should know about the stables, the castle, the castle grounds and Kivash itself. Otherwise, I'll leave you to it."

"Yes, your grace," Gosser said with a bow so fast and deep he staggered a step. "Thank you, your grace."

Gosser led four of Aefric's guards back to the stables.

"I know this looks excessive," Ser Beornric started, but Aefric spoke over him.

"That's all right. I have more experience exploring ruins and evil strongholds than recently occupied castles, but I expect the dangers can be much the same. Traps and hassles left by people who don't particularly want me here."

"Just so, your grace," Ser Beornric said.

The four guards returned from the barracks then.

"Enough bunks for forty, total," one guard said. "Including officers' quarters and a private mess stocked with plenty of food."

"We should stop and eat something," Ser Beornric said, and Aefric realized that likely none of his knights or soldiers had eaten since *he* had last eaten.

"All right," Aefric said. "As soon as we're all together. It looks as though Ser Yrsa is finishing up down there."

"And here come the rest of the knights," Ser Deirdre said, Then, louder, she addressed those approaching knights: Sers Temat, Micham, Vria and Wardius. "You missed the fun. We captured a stableboy."

"Did he give you much of a fight, Deirdre?" Ser Vria asked, which got a round of laughter from all the knights, including Ser Deirdre.

"No surprises in the rest of the courtyard," Ser Temat said. "Two gardens in the back. One for roses, and the other for vegetables. At least, that's what I think they were. Someone tore them up pretty badly."

"Sheesh," Ser Deirdre said. "Did they salt the soil, too?"

"I don't think so," Ser Wardius said. "They just didn't want us to enjoy what they'd grown. Didn't even take any of it with them. It was all scattered around the ground. Roses and vegetables both."

"I don't think they were allowed to take anything but what they wore," Ser Beornric said. "And they may have been searched to make sure they didn't try to make off with gold, silver, or jewelry."

"Seems a bit excessive," Aefric said.

"Terms of surrender," Ser Beornric said, as though he didn't consider it excessive at all. "We can check with the duchess' soldiers, but I'm pretty sure the nobles were offered their lives and the chance to leave for the ransom of the castle and everything in it. Including wealth."

Down below the iron gate closed with a *boom*, and Aefric heard the scraping of bars being set.

Ser Yrsa came up the hill then with thirty of the soldiers who would be stationed here, with the remaining ten starting their first shift of guard duty.

"Now," Aefric said to Ser Beornric, "we can eat."

THEY DIDN'T TAKE TOO MUCH TIME WITH LUNCH. SOME OF AEFRIC'S soldiers had done their share of field cooking, so they were the ones chosen to roast a few chickens and soften some wheat rolls with heat and butter.

They offered to try to do something with the vegetables in the barracks root cellar, but their main idea was a stew, and that would take too long.

They did break out a cask of day beer, though, which was very well received. Good and crisp as any IPA Aefric had enjoyed as Keifer, back in Oregon.

This day beer even had a touch of raspberry to it. Not so much as to distract from the taste of the beer itself, but more as an undertaste.

The beer helped make up for the fact that the roasted chickens were on the bland side, and those rolls had clearly been trending towards stale.

Nevertheless, now fortified with food, Aefric's party split into three groups.

The soldiers who would remain here as castle guards began settling into the barracks.

The soldiers of Aefric's personal guard began going thoroughly over the courtyard, and establishing a rotation for their own rest while they were here.

Aefric and his knights — now including Ser Yrsa once more — approached the main doors of the castle itself.

The double-doors came together to form an arch twice Aefric's height, and together they were just about as wide. They were made from beechwood that had been bleached so white they seemed to fit in with the stonework.

Ser Beornric took out the keys.

"Not yet," Aefric said, and began leading his knights on a circuit of the keep itself. Checking out the smooth white stone. Noting the height of the nearest defensive wall, over which, here atop the hill, he could see only sky in all but two directions, where he could see the turrets of other castles in the distance.

That wizard's tower was not visible from here. And the two white stone castles that Aefric could barely see, those likely included the one Ashling had claimed for herself and the one she'd given to King Colm.

The windows of Castle Hrafnvigi itself started at the third floor. Smallish, arched things, with closed shutters. Below the third floor, only arrow slits.

Whoever had designed this castle had certainly been concerned about defending it. But the lack of natural light was disappointing.

Aefric had been spoiled by the huge windows of his apartments at Water's End. But then, that castle was large and grand enough to make this one look like a grass hut.

Castle Hrafnvigi had crenellated towers at each of its four corners, as well as crenellations along the top of the keep that implied battlements there as well.

In the back of the keep, near the two gardens, was a single door of bleached beechwood. It was locked, and Aefric left it that way for the time being.

Sad, the state of those gardens. They hadn't just had their plants yanked out of the ground. Oh, no. The soil had been hacked at viciously with hoes, and the remains of the plants left to rot on the torn dirt.

The gardens looked as though they'd been murdered by a spurned lover.

Aefric shook his head as he surveyed the carnage.

"Ser Yrsa," Aefric said, "do you think Baron Osmaer would be willing to come down and see what he can do with this?"

"I'm sure his lordship would be pleased to right these gardens," Ser Yrsa said, "and bless them in the name of the Green Lord."

Aefric nodded and turned back to the castle then...

...and spotted something his knights had missed in their survey of the grounds.

"What have we here?" he said, approaching a spot along the stone of the wall that looked *almost* the same as the rest. But not quite. There was something...

"I see it now," Ser Vria said. "I think that's a hidden door, your grace."

"I think you're right," Aefric said. And sure enough, he could just trace what looked like the outlines of a door.

"How do you see that?" Ser Yrsa asked. "Looks the same as the rest of the wall to me."

"Look at it from the corner of your eye," Ser Deirdre said, apparently able to see it now herself.

"Nothing," Ser Yrsa said.

"I don't see it either, your grace," Ser Beornric said, getting agreement from Aefric's other knights.

Aefric stilled his thoughts.

There it was.

"Magic," Aefric said. "Just a hint. A whisper. And subtly woven, so that even an experienced magic-user like myself or Ser Deirdre had to practically stand on top of it to notice it."

"And Vria here has those eldrani eyes," Ser Deirdre said. "Useful as they are pretty. Bet they get you into all kinds of trouble."

"Now and again," Ser Vria said, fluttering her lashes.

"We have to swap stories later," Ser Deirdre said, while Aefric focused his attention more sharply on the door.

Yes. It was a door. And yes, magic was involved in hiding it...

And *also* in locking it...

Yes.

There. Slipping and sliding along the borders of the door. Traces of power that hid the grooves ... that bound the door closed ... that would not yield without...

"It's a password lock," Aefric said. "Anyone who knows the password can open it."

"We'll need a guard stationed inside," Ser Yrsa said, "once your grace moves in."

"No," Aefric said. "Comes to that, I'll spend the time to change the password. Speaking of which."

He looked at Ser Beornric.

"Have to assume the previous owners have keys," Ser Beornric said, grimacing. "I'm sorry, your grace. I should've thought to bring a locksmith."

"No need," Aefric said. "There must be one on the north side of the river who was never Malimfari."

"Deirdre," Ser Yrsa said.

"I'm not one of your soldiers, you know," Ser Deirdre said casually.

"Ser Deirdre," Aefric said, turning to face her. "Right now I must consider the security of my new castle compromised. For all I know, the departing nobles tossed full sets of keys to prominent local thieves and agitators. By now, copies could be in the hands of everyone in Kivash who means me ill.

"I know the skills you possess at studying a city and its people," he continued. "I know you can find me a trustworthy locksmith, to ensure my safety. And once we have finished clearing this castle, I would appreciate your beginning the next day by doing so."

"Your grace does know how to flatter a girl," Ser Deirdre said, smiling and fanning herself with one hand. "As though I could resist those big blue eyes. Of course, your grace. I'll see to it at my first opportunity."

"Thank you, Ser Deirdre."

She said something else as he turned away. Her words were too soft for him to catch, but he heard Sers Vria and Arras snort with laughter.

He considered asking what was said, but decided he was better off not knowing.

There wasn't much else of interest to be found during the rest of Aefric's circuit of the castle, leaving him and his knights once more standing before those white beechwood double-doors.

Ser Beornric started toward the doors, keys at the ready.

"A moment," Aefric said, holding up a cautioning hand.

Ser Beornric frowned and stepped back.

Aefric closed his eyes and extended his free hand toward the double-doors. Stretched forth with his senses...

Yes. He was right.

The doors in this case were easily seen. No attempt had been made to hide them. But that just left more subtlety for the magic of the wards that guarded them.

Anyone who tried to open those doors right now, while those wards were in place, would trigger...

What kind of response?

Aefric drew a deep breath. Eased his mind outward through the flows of magic inherent to Qorunn, and from there into those subtle wards.

How many times had Aefric done this over the years? While exploring lost tombs and ancient ruins, even while breaking into the castles and keeps of fell necromancers and demonolotrists and the like?

Too many to count.

It didn't take him long to determine that the trap here was quite simple, and explosive. It had some power to it, too. Enough to kill everyone and everything within about five paces, and wound badly about three times that distance.

But all the effort had gone into powering the fiery explosion and hiding the ward. Nothing had been put into protecting it from a magic-user paranoid enough to check even an innocent-looking door.

The spell hinged on a password: *raudrtonn*.

Aefric could disable the ward simply by speaking that word. But the ward would have been left in place, and he had no intention of letting anyone stumble into something so dangerous.

So Aefric went over the structure of the spell three times, until he was certain of what he was seeing.

The entire ward hinged on that one word, which wove its way through the spellwork, leaving the structure weak just behind it.

Simplicity itself then, to strike just behind the moving word with a jolt from the Brightstaff.

He flared pure emerald power at the right spot.

The ward collapsed.

Aefric double-checked, to make sure there hadn't been another ward hiding underneath. He'd seen that once in the tomb of that hideous undead wizard Nevca.

Nevca had layered his wards four levels deep, which made the two times that the wards went *five* layers deep all the more dangerous...

"All right," Aefric said, letting out a deep breath. "Ser Deirdre? Would you like to attempt something dangerous?"

"Always, your grace," she said, stepping forward.

"Return to the hidden door in back, and try the password *raudrtonn*. See if it admits you."

"At once, your grace," Ser Deirdre said, and turned to do so.

"Micham. Wardius. Accompany her," Ser Beornric said, which got a snort of dissatisfaction from Ser Deirdre, but if she hoped that Aefric would overrule Ser Beornric, she was in for disappointment.

"All right, Ser Beornric," Aefric said. "*Now* it's time to open the door and see what we have here."

3

Aefric was more excited than he expected to be, as Ser Beornric stepped forward to unlock the bleached beechwood double-doors of Castle Hrafnvigi.

Aefric could feel that old twitching in his guts, and it wasn't from his roasted chicken lunch. It was the same twitching he'd felt during his adventuring days, every time he was going to begin his descent into some new hazard.

Hardly the same sort of circumstances, though.

Back in his adventuring days, the group would have been small. No more than four or five, himself included. Usually one or two who were good with swords, another who specialized in subtlety and swiftness, and, when possible, a cleric of some stripe or other.

Though true clerics had never exactly been *commonplace*.

Aefric was hardly surrounded by an adventuring party now. Five of his Knights of the Lake, including Ser Beornric, plus Ser Yrsa. All of them the type most comfortable fighting from the front lines, in heavy armor.

And this was hardly his usual adventuring circumstance. A hot summer afternoon in the middle of a bustling port city. Looking to enter not some lost tomb or ancient ruin, but his own castle.

Well, a castle he'd been *given*. It wouldn't feel like *his* until he'd at least been through the place. Made sure it was safe. Seen what all he could find within.

And yet, there'd been enough tension so far to help juice his old adventuring instincts. Warships in the harbor. That talk with Zoleen. Finding that secret door at the back of the castle. Disarming the trap-wards here at the front.

And those last couple of things were the closest Aefric had come to the kind of exploring he thought of as real *adventuring* since before the Godswalk Wars.

Ser Beornric hesitated with the keys just short of the lock.

"Your grace," he said, frowning, "might there be some more mundane trap waiting for this key?"

"Not likely," Aefric said. "The magical trap I disarmed would have been enough to fry any mundane trap they set up, which would be counterproductive. But I can check, to be certain."

Aefric had been hesitant to check, because he'd been trying to maintain a certain sense of decorum since becoming a duke. And the method he'd developed for checking, well, it always made him smile like a fool.

There was something about the process that just appealed to the child in Aefric.

He brought the Brightstaff in front of himself, held it with both hands, and gazed through its yellow diamond at those double-doors, while whispering the right words of power.

Through the facets of that yellow diamond, he saw five different images of the double-doors.

All of them were clear and yellow.

Had there been a trap on one or both of those doors, or the frame itself, of the ground in front of them, at least one of those images would have glowed red around the trapped area. The more of the images that glowed red, the more dangerous it was.

The images were entirely yellow.

"Clear," Aefric said, lowering the Brightstaff again.

"What's that you're humming, your grace?" Ser Yrsa asked.

Humming?

Oh.

Aefric started laughing.

He hadn't cast that spell since before that moment this past spring at Kainemorton's tower when he, as Aefric, became aware that he had also been Keifer, and gotten all those memories available to him consciously once more.

The tune Aefric found himself humming while casting that trap-detection spell had been from a children's show Keifer used to watch on Earth, when he was young. At one point each episode, the hostess who would pretend to look through a faceted magic lens and see some of the children who were watching the show. She would call out the first names of children she claimed to see.

And while she did that, a tune played. The tune that Aefric hummed, every time he cast his trap-detecting spell through the Brightstaff.

"It's nothing," Aefric said, still smiling. "Just a song I heard a child. Not sure why it came to mind now."

"But the doors are safe?" Ser Beornric asked.

"They're safe," Aefric confirmed with a nod.

Ser Beornric unlocked the doors and pushed them open.

The creak of those doors was like a homecoming to the adventurer in Aefric. And so was the dusty darkness they revealed.

"Should've brought torches," Ser Yrsa muttered.

Aefric gave her a droll look.

"Forgive me, but Brightstaff or no, your grace is not leading the way in."

Aefric continued giving Ser Yrsa that droll look as he crouched and picked up a pebble from the ground. He wrapped it in a spell of light, and tossed it past the doors and into the castle.

"All right," Ser Yrsa said with a nod, "I hadn't considered that."

Aefric chuckled and clapped her on the shoulder.

The pebble now lit up a dusty antechamber, perhaps five good strides long and seven across. Here the white stone floor was dirty.

Another set of double-doors, the same size and look as those Ser

Beornric had just opened, stood waiting on the other side of the antechamber. The rest, Aefric couldn't see from where he stood.

"Vria, Temat," Ser Beornric said.

Swords drawn, the two knights cautiously stepped in.

"Single doors on each side," Ser Vria said. "Should we try them?"

"Let me check them first," Aefric said. "Just to be safe. Once we get past these, unless I tell you otherwise, any unlocked door should be fine."

Aefric stepped into the antechamber and verified that no traps, magical or otherwise, barred those interior doors.

Ser Yrsa gently cleared her throat.

"Fine," Aefric said, stepping back out into the early afternoon heat.

"Small cabinet, right-hand side," Ser Temat said. "Tapers, flint, lamp oil, and some other things that servants might need in a pinch."

"Door on the left is a cloak closet," Ser Vria said. "Lots of cloaks. Some boots. Couple of hats and canes. Fancy stuff. Malimfari style."

"Door on the right opens into a hallway," Ser Temat said. "Looks to go about thirty feet down to a door and a left turn."

"And the double-doors?" Ser Beornric asked.

Aefric heard those doors creak open. If anything, their complaint was louder than that of the main castle doors.

"Great hall," Ser Vria said.

Ser Temat tossed the lit pebble into the hall.

"High ceiling," Ser Vria said. "Six chandeliers. Red carpet running to a pair of thrones on a dais at the end. Tapestries on the side walls. Can't tell what they are yet. Chairs and benches along the sides too."

Aefric looked at Sers Yrsa and Beornric.

They looked at each other.

Ser Beornric nodded.

Ser Yrsa sighed and said, "Very well, your grace."

Aefric stepped into his new castle.

As soon as Aefric entered the great hall of his new castle, he issued a word of warning for his knights to guard their eyes.

He lit up the diamond atop the Brightstaff.

The little light he'd put on the pebble was nice. Helpful. But this was more like daylight within the hall, and gave him a real view of his surroundings.

He realized immediately that living at Behal and Water's End was spoiling him.

Back when Aefric was an adventurer, he would have considered this great hall clean. It hardly had enough dust to taste on the air. And not enough to make him sneeze, even if all of his knights ran around the room kicking up all they could.

And they certainly had room to do so. The hall was a good hundred feet long, and about half as wide and tall. Most of it open space right now.

Still, compared to what he was used to in the old days, this dust was nothing. He'd been through old ruins and tunnels and more where the dust had been thick enough to swallow the soles of his boots. Where it fell in strands and webs from the ceiling in mimicry of the work of spiders.

And once he and his party began moving through such places, it would be as though a fog had set in. He'd have to wrap a wet scarf around his face, just to breathe clean air.

And yet, as Aefric looked around at the the great hall, the finely carved chairs and benches along the walls, the run of red carpeting down the center of the white stone floor, even the two wooden thrones on the dais, he found himself sneering a bit at how filthy it had gotten over the past season.

He wanted to summon his *wizard's valet*, an invisible motive force that could perform a wide variety of basic tasks, such as cleaning.

That spell even had an advantage over the simple cleansing spells Aefric had developed during his apprenticeship. The *wizard's valet* could follow him through the castle, cleaning in his wake.

He knew that Ser Beornric would ask him not to cast that spell.

Would ask that Aefric let the mess remain until the newly hired servants arrived to begin tending the place.

Wouldn't do for them *not* to have a mess to clean, on arrival. Might make them feel unnecessary.

So Aefric turned his attention to the décor.

The walls and ceiling were plastered and painted a dark, smoky gray.

The tapestries were typical fare. Scenes of battles on land and sea intended to convince the viewer that the castle's previous owners were famous for their martial skills.

The heroes depicted in those tapestries, men and women both, shared common family traits. Raven black hair and eyes, pale skin, sharp noses.

The artist was a little too ... enthusiastic with his or her portrayal of spilled blood for Aefric's taste. The tapestries in here would all have to go.

Six wheel-style iron chandeliers hung by chains from the ceiling, all of which looked as though their candles had been changed not long before the castle was abandoned.

Aefric sent the light from his Brightstaff to the chandeliers, evening the bright glow throughout the room, and allowing his knight-advisers to look at him without squinting.

"Six exits, your grace," Ser Beornric said. "Four regular doors, two double-doors, split evenly along the long walls."

"Does that including any exits behind tapestries?"

Ser Beornric's hesitation told him that no one had checked for that. But then, his knights might have had plenty of experience with battles and politics, but this kind of exploring, that was new to them.

"Check the tapestries," Ser Beornric said, and Aefric fought down a smile.

"I want to see these thrones first anyway," Aefric said, continuing down the red carpet.

Speaking of tapestries, a large one hung on the wall behind the thrones. Nearly as wide as the dais itself, and just as tall. Golden background, depicting a waraxe in dark red, dripping three drops of blood.

Lovely. If this was the family sigil, then Kivash was likely well rid of them. And did they have to make the sigil so *large*? That axe was twice Aefric's height. Easily. Maybe three times.

Compensation for a noble family fallen on hard times, after the Godswalk Wars?

The thrones themselves were relatively simple in design. Some dark hardwood. Good, thick arms and legs. Low, padded backs upholstered in black leather, as were the seats.

Something glinted in places though.

As Aefric walked closer, he could sense old magic. Nothing active. Just the remains of some old spells.

Likely spells that had been cast often, over a stretch of time.

Spells cast on the ... left-hand throne, from Aefric's view.

The glinting came from rubies in gold settings, at the end of each arm of each throne, and arrayed across the top of the backs of both thrones.

Decent sized rubies, too. Each of them about as wide as the nail on Aefric's small finger.

There.

The ruby at the end of one arm on the left-hand throne. The ruby that would be under the occupant's right hand.

Aefric could feel traces of magic from that ruby, left by many, many castings...

"No luck," Ser Deirdre called, swaggering into the great hall, flanked by Sers Micham and Wardius. "I tried every pronunciation I could for the keyword, and even tried adding a breath of power. Whatever password it wants, *raudrtonn* isn't it."

Aefric looked up, only half-aware she'd spoken, and not quite comprehending her words yet. His focus was too much in the old magic for that. But he nodded, knowing those words would make sense in a moment, and turned his full focus back on those traces of spellwork.

The spells would sweep out in a cone in front of the ruby, angled slightly to Aefric's right. Covering the area ... yes, the area in front of both thrones for about ... six or seven paces.

It was sensory magic. Magic intended to detect...

Something ... something about thoughts?

No. Not thoughts. Lies.

Spells of lie detection?

Aefric whistled, without thinking.

If he was right, whoever cast those spells was attempting a very difficult task.

Part of the reason that the justiciars of Taesark were both revered and feared was their ability to ferret out truth, even from those who had heard only lies.

Trying to sense truth from falsehood by spell alone was a tricky prospect. What if a person believed a lie while speaking it?

Aefric had known several men and women through the years — skalds, mostly, but he wouldn't be surprised if Duke Wylyn shared this trait — who could convince themselves that a lie was true. For a period of time, at least.

Would the spell see through that? Would it detect falsehoods themselves, or instead seek out attempts at deception?

Because sometimes people told the truth in deceiving ways...

"Your grace?" Ser Beornric asked, stepping in close. "Are you all right?"

"Excuse me," Aefric said, coming back to himself and awareness of the room again.

Huh. Significantly cooler in here than outside. Was that just because the doors had been closed so long that the stone acted as insulation? Or was there another factor?

Aefric shook himself. Once he started speculating, it was all too easy to just keep going.

And he understood now what Ser Deirdre had been saying about the password on that hidden door at the back of the castle.

"I'm fine," Aefric said, giving Ser Beornric a smile to ease the worry in those brown eyes. "Just investigating traces of old spells. Someone was trying to use magic to detect lies."

"Good luck to them," Ser Deirdre said. "Your grace knows how hard that is."

Aefric nodded.

"Here," Ser Vria said, from behind the great sigil tapestry at the back of the dais. "A door. Not concealed like the one by the gardens. Just hidden by the tapestry. Not locked."

"Where next, your grace?" Ser Beornric asked.

"Wait," Ser Yrsa said. "Your grace said that any unlocked door should be safe enough, yes?"

Aefric nodded.

"Then in the interests of time, may I suggest we split up? Teams of two knights. First the left-hand doors, then the right hand."

"And you expect me to remain here?"

"I'm not so big a fool as that, your grace," Ser Yrsa said with a grin. "I would suggest that your grace would proceed through the door behind the tapestry, accompanied by myself, Ser Beornric, and, I imagine, Ser Deirdre."

"I would be most pleased to do some exploring with his grace," Ser Deirdre said, which got snorts of amusement from a few of the other knights.

Interesting that his knights felt free enough for such laughter here. So different from at Water's End, where politics often required them to hide their thoughts behind stoic masks.

Here, they were acting as though they were out on campaign. Eyes and posture constantly alert for danger, but quick to share a laugh.

Of course, given the political climate in Kivash, that might not be far wrong. Certainly Ser Beornric didn't censure them for it.

"I always appreciate your sword by my side, Ser Deirdre," Aefric said — specifically ignoring any other meaning to her phrasing — "but if we're going to split the group, I'll need you to act as a rover. First to pass down each hallway, and the last to check each room. Ser Vria *may* notice magic along the way, but you *will* notice it. And I need you doing that."

"Of course, your grace," Ser Deirdre said, sounding serious for a change.

"Ser Arras and I will accompany his grace, I presume," Ser Leppina said to Ser Beornric. "We were tasked to active bodyguard duty from dawn to dusk."

"And if we leave the castle today, you'll return to that," Ser Beornric said. "For now, I think Yrsa and I should be able to guard his grace through an unoccupied castle."

"Besides," Ser Yrsa added. "I suspect that if we try to surround his grace with too many knights, he'll feel a bit *constrained*."

That got a few more chuckles from his knights, and this time Aefric joined in.

"One thing," he then said, forcing everyone to be serious again. "With the possible exception of Ser Deirdre, you're all new to this kind of thing. I'm not. So let me give you some advice."

He looked at each of his knights in turn, to make sure they were all paying attention.

"Don't give anything just a glance," he said. "Tap walls and floors with the pommel of your sword, or at least your dagger. Search desks. Search cabinets and any other furniture you run across. And check behind and underneath them, behind tapestries and paintings, under rugs. Everywhere you can think of.

"Assume that *every room* hold secrets, and your job is to find those secrets. We know this castle has at least one truly hidden door, and so far, one concealed door. Those will not be the only doors not easily found. So look sharp."

"Aren't hidden and concealed the same thing?" Ser Wardius asked.

"Not quite," Aefric said. "At least, not to an adventurer. *Hidden*, or *secret* — you can use either — applies to a door designed not to look like a door. Like the one we found near the gardens. Or maybe a bookshelf that moves if you pull the right book, revealing a hallway behind it."

Aefric pointed to the tapestry behind the thrones.

"Back there is what we call a *concealed* door. It's just a door some-place people might not think to look for a door. Understood?"

His knights all slapped the hilts of their weapons in accord.

And with that they split up and began their search.

Aefric had to fight down a flutter in his stomach. Splitting up while exploring was one of the original *don'ts* of adventuring.

But this wasn't that kind of exploring. The castle should be safe enough.

Shouldn't it?

AEFRIC HAD BEEN INTENDING TO GIVE MAGICAL LIGHTS TO EACH SET OF knights before they went off to explore the first floor of the castle, but Ser Yrsa pointed out that there were oil lamps in the halls, and plenty of tapers in that cabinet in the antechamber.

Aefric did light the tapers by magic, but it was still disappointing. Made what they were doing feel less like one of his old adventures.

Then again, maybe that was a good thing. The party was splitting up, and they certainly weren't expecting to find monsters, curses, tomb guardians or anything along those lines.

He did light the Brightstaff's diamond before he and Sers Beornric and Yrsa opened the door behind the huge tapestry at the back of the great hall's dais.

Both knights had their weapons in hand, though Ser Yrsa drew only one mace drawn for the moment. She was the one who threw open the door, while Ser Beornric held back the tapestry.

The door opened into a short, white stone hallway. A little tight, but not too bad. Not like some of the half-size halls Aefric had seen behind concealed and hidden doors in the old days.

"There are lamps," Ser Yrsa pointed out, sitting in alcoves along the walls just inside the door.

"We have light already," Aefric said. "Why waste fuel?"

"Because your grace will be following us," Ser Yrsa said patiently. "And we may want some light at the front."

"Oh, for crying out loud," Aefric said. "If I had a copper for every time some warrior complained about light—"

"You could buy your own castle?" Ser Yrsa said dryly.

Aefric had to laugh at that. "Point taken."

He wrapped Ser Beornric's sword in light, the way he'd wrapped the pebble earlier.

"Happy?" Aefric asked.

Ser Yrsa looked at the ridged ball at the end of her heavy mace.

The *unlit* ridged ball.

"Fine," Aefric said, and lit her mace up as well.

"Thank you, your grace," Ser Yrsa said with a small bow.

"Can we begin now?" Aefric asked, dimming the light of his Brightstaff down to a similar level as the sword and mace.

"Steps down," Ser Beornric said. "Looks as though it goes down a level. Proceed or come back?"

"Proceed," Aefric said.

Ser Beornric descended the stairs. Ser Yrsa moved to the top of the stairs.

"Doors ahead," Ser Beornric called up, stepping just into the hall. "Facing each other. Which do you want first?"

"Let's see where the hall goes," Aefric said. "I have a hunch."

Ser Yrsa took her turn down the stairs, followed by Aefric. Even down here they were using that white stone for everything. Must be a big local quarry.

The doors Ser Beornric mentioned were all at the tops of small sets of stairs, as Aefric expected. He'd even be willing to bet he knew what kinds of rooms were on the other sides of those doors.

Eight sets of facing doors total, down the hall, each with its own set of stairs.

The end of the hall ascended another flight of stairs to a ninth door. On the landing beside the door, an ascending spiral staircase.

The door had no handle.

"Good," Aefric said, nodding. "I thought that was where this would lead."

"The escape route," Ser Yrsa said. "They could flee from behind the thrones, or any of eight ... what ... offices?"

"Might be the family chambers are all along this corridor," Ser Beornric said. "Builder seems to have been paranoid enough to have put them in the center of the first floor. Probably fake chambers on a higher floor."

"Maybe," Ser Yrsa said. "Though those spiral stairs have to go somewhere important."

"True," Aefric said. "Either way, one thing bothers me about this."

"They've got a hill," Ser Beornric said. "So why have their escape route take them only out of the castle? Why not dig a route down to the harbor or something?"

"Exactly," Aefric said.

"Not the harbor," Ser Yrsa said, contemplatively. "The river. It's closer by several hundred yards. And the family could have a holding along the riverbank without drawing attention. Could look like a warehouse or office or even an inn. Some part of the family business. Maybe even do some trade. But it's actually there to guard the exit of the passage, and keep a boat ready if they need it."

"Which begs the question," Aefric said. "What's the deal with this door?"

"They're a martial family," Ser Yrsa said. "You saw those tapestries. The design of the castle and grounds. Could be this door isn't for escape, but for assault. A sally port, basically, in case anyone breached the outer walls."

"Good thought," Aefric said. "But we won't know until we check out the other rooms here."

"Before we do," Ser Beornric said. "We should investigate that spiral staircase."

"I'd rather stick to the first floor for now," Aefric said.

"I don't mean going up the stairs," Ser Beornric said. "I mean that landing. After all, this door doesn't lead down to the river."

"So maybe there are more stairs, hidden," Aefric said. "Good thought. Maybe we'll make an adventurer of you yet."

The three of them moved onto the stone of the landing by the spiral staircase.

Sers Yrsa and Beornric tapped on stones with the butts of their weapons. Aefric did as well, here and there, with the Brightstaff. But he also checked for magic, and finally dismissed the Brightstaff's light so he could look through its diamond, hunting for traps.

No traps, so Aefric shifted mental gears and used a similar technique to scan for hidden doors.

Well, not for *hidden* doors per se. Specifying that would have added a layer of complexity to the spell without adding any benefit.

Properly speaking, Aefric's spell detected doors in general. Not windows. Only openings designed to be used as entrances and exits.

It was a question of intention in design. Even a hidden or concealed door was still designed with the intention of admitting people through it. Even if it only admitted those who knew how to find it, or knew the password, or who passed any other restriction.

A door was a door was a door.

And there was no door on that landing.

"Sorry," Aefric said, interrupting the tapping of his knight-advisers. "No door here."

"You're certain?" Ser Yrsa asked.

"I know a spell that will find almost any door. Concealed, hidden, or otherwise."

"Why are you only just using it now?" Ser Beornric asked.

"It's bad to get into the habit of relying on it," Aefric said, shrugging. "While I'm using that spell, I can miss all kinds of other things. Traps, enemy magic and other dangers. Might not even notice someone coming up behind me."

"Could still be worth using here in the castle," Ser Yrsa said. "Low risk factor, especially with us here."

"True," Aefric said. "But only in places we think likely to have a hidden door. Otherwise, I want all my senses available."

"Fair enough," Ser Beornric said.

"And this landing was worth checking," Ser Yrsa said to Ser

Beornric, then turned to Aefric. "Since we're at this end, shall we take the other doors in reverse order?"

"Makes sense," Aefric said.

The approached the last set of facing doors. Ser Beornric went up the stairs to his right.

"Locked," he said. "Is it safe?"

Aefric checked. "No traps."

Ser Beornric pulled out the ring of keys and began testing.

He tried each key in succession, going through the whole of the ring.

None of them turned the lock.

Ser Beornric sighed impatiently. "May I break it down, your grace?"

"Not necessary," Aefric said, and with a gesture cast a simple spell that undid basic locks and bindings.

He nodded at Ser Beornric.

Ser Beornric tried the doorknob.

"Still locked," he announced a moment later. "Your grace."

Aefric frowned. Cast a more advanced and complex version. One that would have undone dozens of locks and bindings in an instant, no matter how complex or interrelated.

Aefric had never seen any lock or binding meet that spell without surrendering.

In fact, it was a derivation of this spell that Aefric had once used to rapidly undress Zoleen without harming her gown. When they were on better terms.

"Still locked," Ser Beornric said, frowning now, and wonder in his voice.

Aefric's turn to frown. There was no magic to that lock, or anything about that door...

Aefric shook his head. No. It couldn't be.

He cast his spell to detect doors, then sighed.

"It's a fake," he said. "It's not a real door at all."

He swept his spell-aided gaze through the Brightstaff's yellow diamond and down the hallway, then shook his head in disbelief.

"In fact, *none* of the other doors in this hallway are real."

AEFRIC AND HIS TWO KNIGHT-ADVISERS TOOK A LITTLE MORE TIME going slowly down that strange hall filled with fake doors.

And they were all fake doors. Aefric double-checked them each with his door-detecting spell. And as he did, either Ser Beornric or Ser Yrsa tried the handle, and put a shoulder into the door. Just in case.

But they all seemed to be fakes. Their best guess was that the walls had been chiseled out just enough to frame out the appearance of a door, but that behind those "doors" was nothing but solid stone.

Aefric had seen that kind of thing only once or twice, back when he was young, and still traveling with Karbin's group, the Last Sons.

Given what Aefric had seen back then, there might not even be rooms on the other sides of these fake doors.

When they reached the foot of the first stairs they'd come down, the ones behind the thrones in the great hall, they looked back down the hallway.

"So we have an apparent escape route, that only leads out of the keep itself, not off of the grounds." Ser Beornric said. "Along the way there are fake doors, but a real set of spiral stairs."

"Unless the stairs don't go anywhere," Ser Yrsa said. "We didn't check."

"All right," Aefric said. "So what's the point of this design? What's their goal?"

"I have an idea," Ser Yrsa said, "but first I'd need to know if those spiral stairs go where I think they do."

"All right," Aefric said, "let's check."

As they made their way back down the hall — still moving cautiously, just in case — Aefric considered lighting up the Bright-staff again.

Decided against it. He had enough light to see by, from the spells he'd put on Ser Beornric's sword and one of Ser Yrsa's maces.

He did smile, though, that they had him at the back of the marching order. In his adventuring days, he would have been in the middle, with a warrior of some stripe at the front and another at the back.

After all, attacks could come from anywhere.

But then, the only people likely to approach Aefric's back right now were his own knights.

He kept checking, though, out of long-established habit.

They reached the far end of the hall, ascended the stairs to the handle-less door that led to the gardens. Just to their right was the spiral staircase, going up.

Ser Yrsa led the way this time, staying five stairs ahead of Ser Beornric, who insisted on being five stairs ahead of Aefric.

The stairs were wide enough for two, and broad enough to go up and down quickly.

"Door here," Ser Yrsa said from the next landing. "Real door."

Before Aefric had gone another step, Ser Yrsa was back at the top stair and coming down.

"Exactly what I thought," she said, prompting Aefric and Ser Beornric to head back down. "Guard station."

Once all three of them were back down in that hallway, Aefric asked, "So what does that mean?"

"The hallway's a trap," Ser Yrsa said. "Someone comes after the lord and lady of the castle, they flee from their thrones through the door behind the tapestry. Straight shot to the back of the castle, where guards will be waiting to protect them."

"Meanwhile," Ser Beornric said, coming around to the idea, "the invaders are delayed by fake doors, and pinned in on both sides by guards. And even if they reach the back door, they won't know the password to open it. Smart."

Aefric agreed ... and he didn't. Most of that sounded right. And yet...

"One thing," he said. "That exit still bugs me. There's no reason to assume that there'd be safety behind the castle, just because invaders come through the *front*. There might be fighting on all sides."

"If the invaders have enough soldiers, maybe," Ser Yrsa said, while the three of them started back down the hallway. "But most of the time, the attackers will pour in through one entrance. They manage get in through the front, they'll all come in that way."

"Efficiency and coherency matter during a battle," Ser Beornric said. "By going straight out the back, a warlike lord and lady would be able to rally any remaining troops outside the castle itself. And the gardens would make for an easy rallying point."

"I suppose," Aefric said, still frowning. "But you know, we never checked the first landing."

"We checked all the fake doors," Ser Yrsa said. "And their landings."

"No," Aefric said, trotting now and forcing the other two to keep up. "The landing just behind the concealed door. We never checked it. And I bet..."

He quick-stepped up the stairs to that first landing, behind the concealed door, which still stood open.

Eager to see if he was right, Aefric didn't take any time with tapping. Went straight to his door-detecting spell.

And there he saw it, glowing green through the yellow diamond atop the Brightstaff.

A trap door, hidden among the stonework, just beside the doorway.

"Here," Aefric said, feeling around for the catch he could see but not quite see. The spell found doors, after all, but not specifically handles or catches.

There. A spot under his fingers gave with a click, and the trapdoor sprang open.

A strong, silk rope hung down from its center.

Beneath it, a small room lit brightly by magic.

A ladder down the wall, presumably for coming back up. Down at the bottom, a large, comfortable-looking couch. Several large cabinets along the walls, as well as a pair of well-stocked book-shelves.

A painting of a schooner sailing the Indecisive River hung on the wall above the couch. Three casks stacked in a corner, with the top one on its side, a tap in place.

"Clever," Ser Yrsa said, "Grab the rope and jump inside, the trap door closes behind you. Then you relax in safety while your soldiers repel the invaders."

"Only admits one that way though," Ser Beornric said, frowning.

"Unless the first one down takes the ladder and the second the rope," Ser Yrsa said. "There's room enough down there for two, if they're friendly."

"You know we have to check it, right?" Aefric asked.

"I'll take the ladder," Ser Yrsa said, hanging her mace from her belt.

"As will I," Ser Beornric said.

"I'll use magic," Aefric said, "if it's all the same to you."

"I'll come down last then," Ser Beornric said, "and test the rope. Best to be sure it holds, and I'm heavier than both of you."

Ser Yrsa climbed down. Aefric floated gently down by magic. And Ser Beornric hooted as he jumped in, clinging to the rope with both hands.

The trapdoor closed with impressive silence.

"Huh," Ser Beornric said. "I expected a *boom*. I must admit, I'm a little disappointed."

"Not magically silenced," Aefric confirmed.

"Impressive engineering then," Ser Yrsa said. "Makes sense though. No good hiding down here if everyone hears the door slam."

A thorough search of the room turned up spare clothes and supplies of very high quality, as well as a variety of easily preserved foods.

Weapons and armor, too. Two sets of fine, gold-washed chain-mail. Sword belts with short swords. A pair of fine bows, with sixty arrows in quivers.

"So they'd be ready if the invaders found the trap door," Ser Beornric said with an appraising nod.

The books were all works of poetry and fiction, mostly about love or war or both.

A quick check of the top cask revealed a thick, dark beer that was pretty tasty.

No other magic down here than the perpetual light. No hidden exits or other caches.

The phrase *safe room* came to mind, but Aefric didn't bother speaking it aloud. He knew the term from Keifer's vocabulary, but hadn't ever heard it spoken here in Qorunn.

"All right," Ser Yrsa said. "I trust it now makes sense, your grace?"

"Yes," Aefric said. "The lords of the keep lead invaders behind the tapestry and into the hallway. They escape to safety down here, while up above the hallway serves as a killing zone, with the castle soldiers hitting the trapped invaders from both sides."

"Clever," Ser Beornric said. "And vicious."

"All right," Aefric said with a smile. "Let's see what the others have found."

AEFRIC, AND SERS YRSA AND BEORNRIC CAME OUT FROM BEHIND THE tapestry to find Ser Deirdre, leaning against the back of both thrones, her arms stretched wide and her maroon leather boots crossed at the ankle.

The Knights of the Lake were gathered around behind her, with Sers Arras and Micham shooting her disapproving looks. As though even leaning against the backs of what were now Aefric's thrones was improper.

Ser Yrsa cocked a split eyebrow at Ser Deirdre and cleared her throat.

Huh. So that *was* considered a big deal. Aefric wouldn't have thought so. This was hardly the ducal seat, after all, and she wasn't exactly sitting on the throne.

But from the looks all the other knights were giving her now, *inappropriate* might've been an understatement.

Ser Deirdre straightened up, unabashed, and gave Aefric a broad smile.

"Please forgive the impertinence, your grace," she said without the slightest hint of sincerity in any of her words except his honorific. "But I wished to be certain your grace's attention first came here."

"What have you found, Ser Deirdre?" Aefric asked.

"Here," she said, crouching down and pointing.

The hind feet of the thrones were locked into place, in the stonework beneath.

"So they didn't move the thrones," Ser Leppina said. "From what I've seen, the previous owners seemed arrogant enough to have their thrones in place even while hosting a formal ball."

"A fair conclusion," Ser Deirdre said, one index finger raised, "but the wrong one. Watch."

She ran her hand over the stonework of the floor between the hind feet of the right-hand chair. The one that had once held spells intended to detect lies.

"Ah," she said. "I knew the catch would be here somewhere."

She pressed a spot on the floor.

The throne tipped forward until its arms hit the stone of the dais. The bottom of the trap door had a handle, not a rope this time. And underneath it was not a short drop of ten feet or so into a lit room, but a sliding shaft that led off into darkness.

Small whistles and mutters of appreciation from the knights.

"Very good work, Ser Deirdre," Aefric said, and she preened a bit at the praise.

"Now *that*," Ser Yrsa said, pointing to the shaft with her mace, "will lead to an escape tunnel."

"I believe you're right," Aefric said. "And it's probably not the only one."

"It's not," Ser Temat said. "Vria and I found a shaft like that in an office, down the right side of the keep."

"Lots of interesting stuff in that office," Ser Vria said. "Looks to have kept all the castle's accounts and records. And there's a concea—I mean a *secret* door in the back wall."

"We couldn't open it though," Ser Temat said, sounding disappointed.

"Wasn't magically locked," Ser Deirdre said. "They had me check."

"Good finds, all the same," Aefric said, giving Sers Temat and Vria a smile. "In fact, let's get everyone's reports, staring with the left side of the first floor."

"We found servants' quarters," Ser Arras said, including Ser Leppina in her report. "Simple beds. Simple chests full of simple clothes. Nothing hidden or concealed, except the sorts of small treasures that the poor servants should probably have gotten to take with them."

"She means a silver-plated comb here," Ser Leppina said, "a pewter bracelet with a garnet in it there. That kind of thing. Little of it worth much, apart from sentimental value."

"The hall did lead to the kitchen, as well," Ser Arras picked up. "That was more interesting. Big enough to cook for maybe ... sixty?"

"I thought eighty," Ser Leppina said.

"Eighty then," Ser Arras, said, shrugging one shoulder of her full plate armor. "Some of the food's turned by now, but there's still plenty good in the pantry. And the stairs down look like a wine cellar and probably more storage, but we didn't check."

"Figured we should get permission to leave the floor," Ser Leppina chimed in.

"And you were right to do so," Aefric said. "Just in case. Anything else?"

"Not really," Ser Arras said. "Staircase going up, but that's it."

"Bedding for how many servants?" Ser Yrsa asked.

"Thirty or so," Ser Arras asked Ser Leppina.

"Sounds right," Ser Leppina agreed. "Not private rooms though. Six rooms with five bunks each, and oak chests for personal belongings."

"The main castle servants then," Ser Beornric said. "We'll likely find some better servants' quarters on an upper floor for your grace's valets and the like."

Aefric nodded, then turned his attention to Sers Wardius and Micham.

"We had the double-doors on that side," Ser Wardius said.

"A music room with a harpsichord," Ser Micham said, "as well as three harps set up as though they're always there and ready."

"Out of tune though," Ser Wardius said. "The harps, I mean. The harpsichord's fine."

"Closet in there," Ser Micham said, "with more instruments."

"After that, a sort of family museum," Ser Wardius said. "Two large rooms on either side of the hall. Both decorated with weapons and armor, paintings, tapestries, sculptures. A few important edicts. That kind of thing."

"Magic light always on in those rooms," Ser Micham added. "And we found a hidden ... no, a *concealed* door behind a tapestry. It was locked, so we didn't try it."

"After that, four guest rooms," Ser Wardius said. "Pretty nice, considering they're single-room affairs. Copper tubs and wash basins. Feather beds. Calinwood armoires, and the like."

"I *thought* I found a hollow spot along the outer wall in those rooms," Ser Micham said.

"You *did* find a hollow spot," Ser Wardius confirmed. "Just because we couldn't find a catch or groove or anything, doesn't make that wall solid."

"No, that makes sense," Aefric said. "There's probably a series of hidden passages in this castle, like the servants' backways at Water's End and Behal."

"Or at the very least," Ser Yrsa said, "a spyhole, for watching guests."

"Ugh," Aefric said with a grimace. "You think so?"

She gestured to the ... aggressive tapestries decorating the walls of the great hall. "Don't they seem the type?"

"I suppose they might," Aefric said.

"That's all we found on the left side," Ser Wardius said.

"We found several rooms used for storage," Ser Temat said. "Furniture for this room, for different kinds of events. Small stages. Tables and chairs. A lectern. That kind of thing."

"Hard to check for secret passages in those rooms," Ser Vria said. "We'd have to start moving furniture, and that would take a while."

"Yeah," Ser Temat said, shaking his head. "I don't know what organizational system they used, but it doesn't make sense to me."

"We'll leave that for the servants to straighten out," Aefric said.

"The end of that hall led into the kitchen as well," Ser Vria said. "Arras and Leppina were already in there, though, so we left them to it. Which was pretty much all there was to see down our hallway."

"Your grace already heard about the magic light in the museum rooms," Ser Deirdre said, picking up her turn. "Apart from that, two of the weapons on the walls have magic to them. A spear and a gladius."

"Gladius?" Ser Beornric asked in disbelief. "No one's used a gladius in five hundred years."

"Not in this part of Qorunn, at least," Ser Yrsa agreed.

"Must by why it's on the wall and not in a scabbard," Ser Deirdre said, shrugging one shoulder.

Interesting that her leathers didn't creak when she moved.

She turned her attention back to Aefric.

"Their magic isn't exactly impressive. Hardly noticeable. Given how old that gladius must be, they're probably fading."

"The spells would only fade if the enchantments were done wrong in the first place," Aefric said.

"Again," Ser Deirdre said, "probably why they're hanging on walls, and not in hands." She shook her head. "No other magic on that side of the castle."

"All right," Aefric said, "let's go see about these hidden doors and magic weapons."

Sers Wardius and Micham led the way, and Aefric had them lead to the guest rooms first. While they were doing this, Ser Beornric sent Sers Vria, Temat, Arras and Leppina to check out the stairs leading down from the kitchen.

Aefric asked Ser Deirdre to accompany them, checking for magic.

The guest rooms were on the low end of nice, when it came to accommodations for nobles, just as his knights had described them.

The copper for the tubs and basins was finely hammered. The calin-wood armoires well built and polished.

The walls and ceiling were plastered and painted a dark red. The floor wasn't plastered, but the much of the white stone was covered with rugs of woven rushes that had long-since lost their sweet scent.

No windows but arrow slits, which Aefric just found weird for guest rooms. Even the room he'd been given at Forest's Edge by recalcitrant Count Ferrin had good windows.

Then again, that room hadn't been on the first floor, either.

Ser Deirdre was right that there was no magic in here. Candles and oil lamps for light, ordinarily, though at the moment the spells on the weapons of Sers Yrsa and Beornric cast more than enough light for the guest rooms.

The hollow spot that Sers Micham and Wardius had spoken of was within arm's reach of the armoire. So Aefric looked where his knights hadn't thought to, and found the catch just behind the armoire, near the floor.

A panel of wall silently slid aside, revealing a narrow hallway running both directions.

"All right," Aefric said. "Once we're ready to continue, I'll want everyone following these secret passages, opening every door they can find. The hidden doors will be much easier to find from that side."

"Good," Ser Yrsa said. "That tapping on walls thing was going to drive me mad."

"I'll remember that," Aefric said with a smile. "Now. Let's see about those weapons."

THE TWO MUSEUM ROOMS MADE AEFRIC FEEL WISTFUL.

Not because of the contents. They were uniformly martial. Each painting and tapestry depicted some great battle or other. Often victories, but apparently the Hrafntonn family — their names were on little placards below each piece of art — even commemorated great defeats.

And like the tapestries in the great hall, the art did not stint on blood.

Even the sculptures were not simple busts of great members of the Hrafntonn line. They were full-body works, complete with armor and weapons.

No, it wasn't the nature of the work that made Aefric feel wistful. It was seeing all of it so clearly in the bright perpetual light of the spells here.

Dusty. Forgotten.

Aefric might've found the art as distasteful as the dust on his tongue, but no doubt every piece of art in here evoked pride in the Hrafntonn family.

"Your grace," Ser Beornric said. "Did you wish to see the concealed door or the weapons first?"

"The concealed door," Aefric said. "Better find out if it leads to the same secret passage as the ones in the guest rooms."

"Doubtful, your grace," Ser Wardius said. "It's on the wrong wall."

Sers Wardius and Micham moved aside a tapestry featuring a vicious battle with those hideously fishlike humanoids known broadly as the sea devils.

They were right. This was on a short, side wall. Not the long wall, where the secret passage was. Plus, it was visibly a door. Regular brown oak, against the dark smoke gray paint on the plaster of the walls.

Hardly the sort of thing used to hide the entrance to something like a servants' backway.

Aefric used the Brightstaff to check it for traps.

"Clear," Aefric said to Ser Beornric, who began trying keys.

He grunted in surprise when one of them turned in the lock.

The knights readied their weapons, just in case.

Ser Micham pushed open the door.

Storage room, with more armor and weapons. More paintings. Even a few more sculptures.

No magic in there. And Aefric gave the room a quick spell-check to determine that there were no doors in there, secret, concealed or otherwise.

"All right," Aefric said. "The magic weapons are across the hall, I take it?"

"Yes, your grace," Ser Micham said. "This way."

If anything, the art on this side of the hall was even bloodier. Aefric didn't waste time studying it. He already had an idea about what he wanted to do with the contents of these two museum rooms, and it didn't involve studying the art.

The spear and the gladius, though, drew his attention immediately.

The spear was old enough that its haft was worn down, and its head was fashioned from bronze, not steel.

The gladius was steel, but it was visibly old steel. Before more modern techniques had refined the process.

And yet, both the spearhead and the gladius looked razor sharp and ready to do damage.

But that shouldn't be the case. Not if they were old magic weapons that hadn't been enchanted right in the first place. They should have been notched, or at least scuffed.

His knights clucked disappointment in the two weapons. Muttered about archaic designs, and the drawbacks they personally saw in each.

Aefric considered the possibilities. What it might mean that these two weapons looked old in some senses, but battle ready in others...

Aefric tuned out his knights. His gut fluttered with excitement. He fought to tamp it down. Yes. If he was seeing what he thought he was seeing, these two weapons were a find. But still.

He had to be sure.

Aefric slipped quickly into the kind of meditative state he'd never normally trust while exploring a strange keep. But this keep was unoccupied. if his knights couldn't keep him safe here, where could they?

He slid his awareness out of himself and into the flows of magic inherent to Qorunn. And from there into...

...yes. The spear first. It was older. It was more likely...

No.

No conclusions. Too early for conclusions. What mattered now was investigation.

He followed the flows of magic first around the spear, starting from the spearhead and then down along the haft.

The feel here was right. The natural magics of Qorunn moved around this spear *almost* the way they'd move around a normal weapon.

Almost. But not quite. Here and there, they bent towards the spear. Flowed along its length. Shifted through it, even.

Good. Very good.

And once Aefric's attention returned to the spearhead, he noticed that the shifting and flowing was more pronounced here. As though the local magic were ... not *pulled*, per se, but *inclined* to move through the spearhead, rather than around it.

Oh, this was looking even better.

Aefric finally moved his awareness inside the spear itself. First along the haft, for comparison.

And here, most notably, Ser Deirdre was right. The haft felt almost as though it had no magic at all. So little that a rushed magic-user might overlook it completely. And an apprentice definitely would.

Yes. Exactly what Aefric was expecting there.

Now into the spearhead...

Hah!

There was no core of enchantment here at all! Oh, magic was flowing through it. Not a lot, true, but some. But not because some magic-user had lain spells upon it, casting them during the forging process so that weapon and spell became one.

Oh, no.

Nor were these dweomerblade weapons, which came to develop

enchantments through their constant use in spellwork that suited their design and purpose. Developing as their wielder developed.

Uh uh.

If Aefric was right — and he'd need probably a full day of study to be sure he wasn't missing something — this spear was *becoming* magical.

Slowly, yes. Very, very slowly. And yet, without the spells or even the guidance of a single magic-user.

This weapon's history and regard were so strong that, over time, the ambient magic of Qorunn itself had begun to enchant it.

If Aefric was right, given another hundred years, this spear would be superior to any mundane spear, no matter the brilliance of its design, the quality of its materials, or the skill of its maker.

Three hundred years, and other magic spears would be hard pressed to stand against it.

Five hundred or a thousand years? This spear might become a thing out of legend.

Aefric forced himself to calm.

But by the time he confirmed that the same was true of the gladius, he started babbling like a loon before he was even fully aware of his surroundings again.

"...don't you understand?" he said, not yet checking to see who might be listening. "This family is so warlike and so reverent to its past that this reverence is literally making two ordinary weapons magical!"

The audience turned out to be all his Knights of the Lake, plus Sers Yrsa and Deirdre.

"Over the course of a *thousand* years," Ser Yrsa said. "Your grace will understand, I trust, if I care little about a weapon that won't see any power at all until *centuries* after I've died?"

All of his knights seemed to agree. Even Ser Deirdre.

"I should've brought Karbin along," Aefric grumbled. "*He'd* get it."

"The stairs in the kitchen," Ser Yrsa said, "appear to lead down into storage cellars. Nothing more interesting than that."

"Though the quality of some of the alcohol is interesting to *some* of us," Ser Deirdre said. "They have entire *casks* of ishka, your grace. Still aging. They must have a distillery nearby."

"As well as plenty of wine, beer, and more," Ser Yrsa added.

"Yes, but the *ishka*," Ser Deirdre said, earnestly enough that Aefric laughed.

"Well," he said, "we'll see about the ishka later. For now, let's go back to the great hall, and hear about the right side of this castle."

BACK IN THE GREAT HALL, STILL LIT BY AEFRIC'S SPELLS ON THE IRON chandeliers, the knights arranged seating, along the right-hand wall. Ornate single chairs for Aefric and Sers Beornric and Yrsa, and two elaborate benches for the other knights.

Furnishings that *looked* great, but weren't as comfortable as the ones he was used to from Water's End.

The spot his knights had chosen was central along that wall, which made it conveniently close to all three passages leading out into that part of the castle.

Unfortunately, this also left them under a particularly graphic depiction of some Hrafntonn patriarch or other holding up a pair of longswords while standing on a pile of dismembered and disemboweled borogs.

Blood was everywhere. On the swords, the armor, all over the corpses and whatever hilltop lay beneath. Even the skies above seemed to be bleeding, though that was probably just because the sun was setting in the scene.

The face of the patriarch, of course, was clean except for a single artistic streak of blood on his cheek, that clearly wasn't from any wound of *his*.

Aefric had to fight down an urge to set fire to the damned thing.

"All right," he said. "Who wants to go first?"

"Why don't we, your grace," Ser Yrsa said. "The others should know what we found. It might even shed some light on their own discoveries."

Aefric nodded, and let his knight-advisers describe everything they'd found on the other side of the concealed door behind the dais. The false doors. The stairs up to a guard post. The handle-less door at the back, which had to be the same as the hidden door they'd found beside the gardens.

And perhaps most important, the hidden room, where the lords of the castle could hide from invaders.

Unfortunately, nothing about that concealed passage seemed to resonate with anything the others had found.

"We found a guard post," Ser Micham said, including Ser Wardius with his report. "Just inside the first door. After that, the hall looks like a guards' area. A couple of small quarters with two bunks each, and wooden chests. A pretty good-sized common room with couches and a round table. Cards, dice, that kind of thing."

"After that, a small armory," Ser Wardius added. "Decent selection of weapons and armor. Opposite that there's even a small forge. Though it doesn't have nearly enough ventilation."

"That's because the forge is enchanted," Ser Deirdre added lazily. "Sucks away the smoke and fumes." She smiled at Aefric. "Nifty bit of work. I think they may have a bound air elemental handling things. But if so, it must be *tiny*. Can't get a fix on it."

"I'll check it out in a bit," Aefric said. "What else?"

"Oh," Ser Deirdre cut in before Sers Wardius or Micham could. "I should point out. Magic-user who did the work on the forge didn't cast those light spells in the museum."

"That *is* interesting," Aefric said. "More recent work?"

"Can't be sure about that," Ser Deirdre said.

"All right," Aefric said. "Now I'll definitely look forward to checking out this little forge. But what else is down that hall?"

"Stairs down," Ser Micham said. "We didn't follow them, but I'm betting that's where the castle cells are."

"I agree," Ser Wardius said. "The door to those stairs is thicker than most, and has a bar."

"Plus," Ser Micham added, "why else have all those guards there?"

"Any secret or concealed doors?" Ser Beornric asked.

"If there are, we didn't find them," Ser Micham said, shrugging apologetically. "Only hidden thing I found was a stash of love letters under the mattress of one bunk."

"I found a few other things, with the most interesting being a silver-edged dagger," Ser Wardius said, holding up the find. "Nice workmanship, your grace."

He tossed the dagger to Aefric who caught it. No magic to it. But then, he didn't expect any.

"The other stuff I collected on a bunk, for whenever your grace wishes to see," Ser Wardius finished, while Aefric examined the dagger.

Ebony sheath, carved with the likeness of a raven. Straight dagger, about as long as Aefric's hand. Double-edged, with most of the blade being steel, but the edging done in silver.

"Make an excellent noble's dagger, your grace," Ser Beornric said.

The noble's dagger was a tradition in Armyr. Every noble carried a dagger at all times. No matter how elaborate their clothing, or formal or informal the circumstance.

Aefric had been so accustomed to carrying a dagger on his belt from his adventuring days that, at first, he hadn't even noticed that no one suggested he stop.

Aefric suspected, though, that Ser Beornric made his observation to keep Aefric from offering the dagger to Ser Wardius, as a gift for finding it.

That seemed like the sort of thing that Aefric the Adventurer would do by reflex, but Aefric the Duke wasn't supposed to. After all, this was all his castle, and everything in it was his, and so on.

Certainly he could make gifts later, after everything had been inventoried. But giving gifts in the moment was probably not the way to go.

So Aefric fixed that dagger to his belt, and nodded thanks to Ser Wardius, who rewarded Aefric with a pleased smile.

Aefric looked the question at Sers Arras and Leppina.

"Hallway was better decorated on this side," Ser Arras said.

"Paintings, and little alcoves for busts of the former lords of Hrafnvigi."

"As for the rooms," Ser Leppina said, "first, were a couple of common rooms."

"The kind of rooms where one might take a break from a feast," Ser Arras said. "Couches and chairs arranged for private talks, small stage for musicians to help cover conversation, alcoves for more privacy, that kind of thing."

"Hollow spots along the walls of those rooms," Ser Leppina said. "Likely hidden doors or spy holes or both."

"After the common rooms, meeting rooms," Ser Arras said.

"Three of those," Ser Leppina said. "Each a different size. The first one only large enough for two. Second, maybe a meeting this size" — she gestured to the current grouping — "and the last for about thirty."

"Thirty?" Ser Yrsa asked. "Truly?"

"Big oval calinwood table," Ser Arras said, "with seating for thirty. Maps on the walls. Kivash, of course, but several of Malimfar, a few of Caiperas, and one of southern Armyr."

"They hadn't cleaned up properly after their last meeting," Ser Leppina said. "It's pretty clear that the Hrafntonn family was heavily involved in the attempt to invade Armyr this past spring."

"Might be worth packing that stuff up and shipping it to his majesty," Ser Arras said.

"I might at that," Aefric said, then looked at Ser Yrsa. "We'll have to take a look first, of course."

"Thank you," Ser Yrsa said, relief evident in her voice. "I was half-afraid you'd just pack it up in your hurry to make this castle your own. Your grace."

Aefric chuckled.

"The furnishings in those meeting rooms are all quite good," Ser Leppina continued. "High quality. Each also has a small stash of alcohol, as well as writing materials and such."

"We found what might be secret doors, in the small and medium meeting rooms," Ser Arras said. "Might also be spy holes."

"Nothing like that in the large meeting room though," Ser Leppina said.

"After that," Ser Arras said, "a military library, with a marvelous section about weapons."

"Nice furniture in there too," Ser Leppina said. "Comfortable. If I had to guess, I'd say the former lords of this castle spent a lot of time in there."

"Finally," Ser Arras said, "stairs going up."

"Should definitely be worth a look," Aefric said. "Though the secret doors and spyholes can wait until we've figured out the secret passages."

"No magic down that hallway," Ser Deirdre said, sounding disappointed.

"Not even a scry ward on the meeting rooms?" Aefric asked, surprised.

"Not even warding the big meeting room," Ser Deirdre said, shaking her head.

Aefric nodded, and turned to Sers Vria and Temat.

"We had the double-doors on this side," Ser Temat said. "Wide hallway. Series of paintings that look like a history of Kivash. How the city evolved around this castle and one other."

"One other," Aefric said. "Not two?"

"No," Ser Temat said. "And if I had to guess, I'd say the largest castle on this side of the river is also the newest."

"Interesting," Aefric said. "Go on."

"The rooms were offices," Ser Vria said, "though we can't be sure about a couple, because they were locked."

"The offices we did see were pretty well appointed," Ser Temat said. "Quality furnishings and the like. Well-kept records."

"Didn't see any hidden or concealed doors along there though," Ser Vria said, "except for the one we mentioned in the office that holds most of the castle's accounts."

"And we couldn't get it open," Ser Temat said.

"Odd that the office was left unlocked," Ser Yrsa said. "If others weren't."

"Depends on whose office it was," Ser Beornric said. "Could be that a few were locked because the people who used them weren't here when the surrender order was given."

"I'd be shocked if there weren't a number of Hrafntonn family members up at Frozen Ridge," Ser Arras said. "Given what we found in that large meeting room."

Aefric gestured at the gory décor. "Hardly need to see that meeting room to guess that. I'd expect this family to find their way into any war that breaks out within a thousand miles."

"Other than that, two small meeting rooms, The kind with room for a round table, four chairs, and a supply cabinet. That's about that."

"At the end of the hall, stairs going both up and down."

Aefric frowned. Shook his head.

"Wait," he said. He pointed to the concealed door at the back of the dais. "There's about sixty feet of passage on the other side of that door, leading to the garden. Which means there's about sixty feet of *castle* above that passage. But I didn't hear about any of you finding hallways going that direction?"

The knights all shook their heads, looking puzzled.

"Perhaps behind one of the locked doors?" Ser Vria asked.

"Doesn't seem likely," Ser Yrsa said. "More likely whatever's in the back half of the keep, on the first floor, is intended for family only. Maybe with its own set of stairs."

"Well," Aefric said, "we'll have to figure out how to get to it." He stood. "But right now, let's see what we've found."

———

WHILE AEFRIC AND FOUR OF HIS KNIGHTS WENT INTO THE SMITHY TO check it out, Ser Yrsa led Sers Vria, Temat, Leppina and Arras to check out the stairs down at the end of the hall.

Aefric didn't know much about forges. He'd never trained at blacksmithing, silversmithing, or any other kind of smithing.

But he'd been in many smithies over the years, and what he saw around him now was unusual.

The furnace was going, for one thing. He'd expected it to be cold, but no, he could see the reddish glow of the coals the moment he entered the room. Could smell the burning coals.

Couldn't quite feel any heat though…

"Did one of you start the furnace?" Aefric asked. But both Sers Micham and Wardius shook their heads.

"That furnace wasn't hot when we were in here," Ser Micham said.

"Only magic I sensed from it was the air elemental work I mentioned," Ser Deirdre said, sounding curious. "Nothing that would create fire."

She cocked her head at Aefric. Pawed the air briefly with her fingers moving. "I believe there's a fire elemental in there too. And it's responding to the Brightstaff."

"Possibly," Aefric said, frowning. Hoping it wasn't responding to *him*, instead.

The room looked too small to be a proper smithy. Only a half-dozen strides across. Tools all over the white stone walls, and a closet filled with stock for making armor and weapons. Two anvils. Cooling barrels. One long worktable.

All of it looking cramped.

No ventilation in the room, either, save for a few tiny arrow slits.

Aefric approached the furnace.

Here it was, late summer. A hot day outside. Not so hot inside the castle, behind all that stone, but still reasonably warm.

And yet, this room didn't feel particularly hot. Even though that furnace was raging.

Aefric opened the furnace door with a gesture. He could see the waves of heat within it. But still, even inches away, his hand could barely feel the heat.

Aefric stretched out his senses. Chuckled.

"You were right about the air elemental, Ser Deirdre," Aefric said.

"But it's balanced in there. A little fire, a little water, a little earth and a little air. Each doing their job."

At his silent command, the furnace fell cold. As it did, even the feel of its magic retreated, leaving only a hint of the air elemental behind.

There had to be ... compartments, of a sort, within the furnace, housing each of the small elementals. That would—

A shout came from down the hall.

"We're under attack," Ser Beornric said, drawing his sword.

Ser Deirdre was already past him into the hall, sword and dagger in her hands.

Sers Micham and Wardius drew their swords and moved to guard Aefric.

"Keep his grace here until I know the situation," Ser Beornric said, and stepped out into the hall.

"You're kidding," Aefric said, but Ser Beornric didn't answer.

At least he didn't close the door behind him.

Aefric started forward.

"Please, your grace," Ser Micham said, putting one hand on Aefric's shoulder. "This is why you have us."

Aefric gnashed his teeth. If the Brightstaff weren't already lighting the room, its yellow diamond would have started glowing from Aefric's sheer frustration.

He could hear the sounds of fighting now, down the hall. Clash of steel. Shouts.

Aefric drew a quick, deep breath. Didn't help with his frustration. He could feel the tension in his muscles. Feel his heart speeding.

Those were *his* knights out there. Fighting some unknown foe, while Aefric was "asked" to stand aside and do *nothing*.

He'd never been good at doing nothing.

"You both understand that I can enter a fight and help out, even while standing safely behind the two of you," Aefric said. "It's kind of how we spellcasters work."

"He does have a point," Ser Wardius said, and Aefric suspected that at least half of that concession was intended to get them out into the hall to at least *see* what was happening.

"And Beornric knows that," Ser Micham said.

Wait. That was *magic* Aefric was sensing from somewhere down the hall. Ser Deirdre's, yes, but not *just* hers...

"There's magic involved," he said urgently.

"Your grace," Ser Micham said, reasonably, "General Yrsa is already on the front lines. If she needs magical support, she'll call for it."

Ser Micham was right. But knowing that didn't make waiting any—

"Your grace!" Ser Yrsa's voice.

Aefric didn't wait to hear what else she might say. He pushed right between his knights and out into the hall.

Sers Micham and Wardius stayed on his heels.

In the hall, Aefric saw the kind of fight he hadn't seen in a long time.

Skeletal warriors. At least six or eight of them. Armed with swords and shields. They'd clearly pushed Aefric's knights back up the stairs — or Ser Yrsa had ordered a retreat to a pinch point.

Sers Temat and Arras were on the floor, bleeding beside the doorway.

"Down!" Aefric bellowed.

His knights dropped.

Aefric thrust the Brightstaff forward and sent white lightning crackling down the hall.

The skeletons raised their shields.

The shields didn't help. The skeletons were blasted apart in a flash of light and a *boom* of thunder.

Aefric rushed down the hall, while most of his knights came to their feet.

"Ten more," Ser Yrsa said quickly. "Coming up. Ser Deirdre is still down there. Our weapons are useless against them."

"Correction," Ser Deirdre said, sauntering through the doorway, dusting her hands. Her rapier and dueling dagger were back in their scabbards. "*Zero* skeletons remaining. And *your* weapons were useless against them."

She looked at Aefric. "Whoever created them had made them proof against regular weapons. But they fell to magic weapons — and magic — just fine."

"Ser Wardius," Aefric said, "fetch that gladius and spear. Just in case we face more of them."

"Yes, your grace," Ser Wardius said. He ran off, sword in hand.

Sers Vria and Leppina were already baring the wounds of their two fallen comrades.

"There are field kits in the guard post," Ser Micham said. "I'll get them."

"How bad are they?" Aefric asked, stepping closer.

Ser Temat looked to have taken a stab wound that slipped between the plates of his armor around his left armpit. Ser Arras' wound was lower, closer to her waist.

That had to have been a stab that got *under* her breastplate. How?

"Can't tell yet," Ser Vria said, working quickly on Ser Temat.

"Not ... too deep," Ser Temat said, though he was covered in sweat and bleeding more than Aefric liked.

"Then the scar on your throat won't get lonely anymore," Ser Vria said, hushing him.

Silly statement that. Likely a jest to calm him. Ser Temat already had a scar across the right side of his chest.

"Flesh wound here," Ser Leppina said. "Cut along the waist, just above the pelvis." She smirked at Ser Arras, who was doing her share of sweating too. "Finally a *real* scar on that pretty skin of yours."

"Jealous." Ser Arras sounded strained, trying to smile through gritted teeth.

"Are you kidding?" Ser Leppina said, catching a field kit that Ser Micham tossed her. "Once it's healed I'm going to lick it. You don't know how much fun it can be to have a big scar. Those little things on your hands and wrists hardly count."

If they were teasing each other, they'd live, Aefric decided. Which was good. He'd considered bringing down a healer for this, but he'd listened to the assurances that one wouldn't be needed.

He moved past the knights, then to examine the skeletons...

...but they were already crumbling to dust. And their magic had already faded away.

Soon nothing remained of them but their weapons.

Soon Sers Temat and Arras were wrapped in bandages and resting on cots in the nearby guard quarters. Both were sleeping, thanks to a soothing powder in the field kit, mixed with some water from the kitchen.

Ser Beornric had posted two soldiers from Aefric's personal guard to stand beside the closed door to the room where they rested.

Aefric suspected those guards were there as much to make sure Sers Temat and Arras rested, as to keep them safe from any other threats.

However...

"What happened down there?" Aefric asked.

He was standing now at a small guard post on the landing at the top of the stairs that led down to the cells below. Sers Yrsa, Beornric, Deirdre, Vria, Micham, Leppina and Wardius were with him.

"We were checking out the cells," Ser Yrsa said. "One by one, using keys we'd found on a hook here."

She pointed to a hook just inside the door.

"Two dozen cells down there," she continued. "First twenty-three were empty. The last had those *things* in it. Moment the door was open, they started attacking."

"So a trap, then," Aefric said. Shook his head. "I should've sent Ser Deirdre with you, watching for magic."

"Ser Temat took his wound opening the door," Ser Yrsa said. "Ser Arras took hers pulling him back. After that, we fought a defensive retreat to the pinch point at the top of the stairs."

"By that time," Ser Deirdre said, "I'd already leapt over the main part of the skeleton force, to present them with a second front to worry about."

"Yes," Ser Yrsa said. "We'd've been worse off without Deirdre. We might not all have made it up the stairs."

Wow. Admitting she'd needed Ser Deirdre's help was probably physically painful for Ser Yrsa.

"I just don't get it, though," Ser Yrsa said. "Swords having trouble with a skeleton, that I could see. Maybe the blade slips along a rib, instead of biting into the spine or something. But my maces?"

She held up both her great, heavy maces. "I've broken more bones with these than I'd care to count. And I got past their shields at least four times. Hit them squarely each time. *Each time.*"

"Fell magic," Ser Deirdre said. "Made them invulnerable, so only more magic could hurt them. Either spells or enchanted weapons."

"Never heard of that before," Ser Beornric said.

"Can't be cast on living beings," Aefric said. "The magic doesn't stick. But the undead, or those stone men we faced in the Dragonscar. They're functionally enchanted items themselves. And they can take magics that we can't."

Aefric had only seen that kind of invulnerability once himself, when he was hunting down that undead wizard Nevca. But as Keifer, he'd known the spells well from several sourcebooks over the years. Even knew the creatures most likely to have them.

But that conversation would be counterproductive.

"Anything else down there besides cells?"

"One large room," Ser Yrsa said with a frown. "Would your grace care to guess its use?"

"Torture chamber?" Aefric asked, hoping he was wrong.

"Very *well used* torture chamber," Ser Yrsa said.

"Lovely," Aefric said with a grimace. "All right. I think we can leave the hall of meeting rooms alone for now. Let's see about the offices."

They went back through the great hall, and then passed the double-doors on the right-hand side.

Aefric checked each locked door for traps before allowing Ser Beornric to try his keys.

Each locked door opened to a key.

A historian's office. A couple of offices for records of various types. No magic to speak of. Not until they got to the office Ser Vria had mentioned earlier.

The office where the castle accounts were kept. The office that had both a trapdoor tunnel escape route, and a secret door in the corner behind the desk.

The furnishings in here were marvelous. Or would have been, without all the dust. Ornately carved calinwood for the desk, chairs and filing cabinets. A beautiful seascape on one wall, and a sedate painting of river traffic on another. The plaster of the walls and ceiling had even been painted a gentle, spring green.

This room had a dormant light spell, easily triggered. Aefric left it unlit at the moment, as ample still light came from Ser Beornric's sword and Ser Yrsa's mace.

"Desk has a calendar," Ser Yrsa said, flipping through a book. "Dates involving war preparations from last spring."

"Good," Aefric said, checking out the trapdoor that Ser Vria was showing him. Once the carpet of stale rushes was moved aside, it wasn't hard to spot. It was white stone like the rest of the floor, but the grooves were visible enough, as was the handle.

Ser Vria opened it. Sure enough, the shaft looked to taper down and away in the same direction as the one in the great hall.

"All right," Aefric said, closing it. "Now, where's this secret door?"

"Here," Ser Deirdre said, indicating the wall behind a pair of filing cabinets. She reached behind the left-hand cabinet, flipped something.

Nothing happened.

"Unless I'm mistaken," she said, "that *should* have opened the secret door."

"That's what *I* told you," Ser Vria said, "when we asked you to check for magic."

"Yes," Ser Deirdre agreed. "But I was mentioning it because I sensed—"

"Magic on the other side of the wall," Aefric said, finishing the sentence for her. Now that he had his attention that direction, it seemed clear as day.

And yet, he hadn't noticed until right now.

"Subtle work," Aefric said.

"Yes," Ser Deirdre said with a nod. "And I think some of it is being used to keep this door closed."

"Well, let's see about that then," Aefric said.

First things first. He brought up the Brightstaff and checked first that it was a real door, not a false door — it was real — and then for traps.

It was trapped. That was part of the magic holding it closed. If the door were opened the wrong way, a blast of ice would freeze everyone in the room.

But only the living. Interesting. That would protect their records.

Ice magic, eh?

Aefric smiled. He set the Brightstaff to stand beside him, and drew the wand Garram from its scabbard on his belt.

The wand Garram. A gift from King Colm Stronghand himself, the wand was noted for its power over the magics of ice and fire.

Aefric kept the wand at the ready, and shifted his attention outside his body, through the flows of Qorunn's magic, and into the spell-trap on the door.

First things first. The trap wasn't what kept the door closed. That was a simple spell lock. The magic-user who'd cast it didn't even try to make the spell lock difficult to open. Likely, hoping that anyone who did would trigger the trap.

The trap was cast by the same magic-user who'd put the trap on the castle's front doors. The same one who'd cast those light spells in the museum rooms.

Sadly, that magic-user seemed to fall into patterns. Which meant that this one would be removed the same...

No...

Oh, that was *devious*.

This trap *looked* at first as though it had the same flaw as the one on the castle's front doors. That all that would be required to disarm it was a pulse of power just behind the moving keyword.

But that would trip the trap.

The structure had a kind of stickiness to it. Not enough to grab and hold Aefric as he investigated it. That couldn't be done without a good deal more power.

But if any magic *touched* the spell in the wrong way, it would seize a sample and trigger the trap.

It was the same quality that would trigger the trap if Aefric tried to simply open the spell lock.

So how could he disarm this trap?

The keyword?

That sounded plausible, but Aefric didn't trust it.

He studied that moving keyword for a time.

Good thing he did.

The keyword kept changing.

Just a hair. Just a little at a time.

The keyword looked at first like *gullinvatn*. But as Aefric watched, the "u" sound shortened and shortened until it became *gollinvatn*. But then it began lengthening back to a "u" sound, while the "i" sound shortened to an "e" sound so that it became *gollinvatn*, then *gullinvatn*, then *gullenvatn*.

Changes that seemed to imply that the keyword would shift, and that whoever wanted to open the door had to track the exact pronunciation and get it right.

That was a trick for magic-users who'd grown too reliant on their magic. The sort who would forget that keyword wards were meant to be used by people who *couldn't* study the wards to get the current pronunciation.

There was no true keyword here at all.

Which suggested that this trap was never meant to be disarmed.

It was a parting shot at the invaders of Kivash. Must've been cast last thing by whatever court wizard the Hrafntonn family kept, before they left.

All right then. No point in trying to disarm it at all.

"Everyone out," Aefric said.

Sers Yrsa and Beornric looked up from where they were going over that calendar book. Sers Vria and Deirdre frowned from where they'd been discussing something, over by the cabinets. Sers Micham, Leppina and Wardius looked up from their own conversation.

"Will I have to repeat myself?" Aefric asked.

His Knights of the Lake immediately began filing out. Ser Deirdre frowned as though she wanted to argue, but saw the look in Aefric's eye, nodded abruptly, and left.

Sers Yrsa and Beornric hesitated.

"Your grace," Ser Beornric began in reasonable tones, "whatever it is you intend, I'm not sure—"

"I'm sure," Aefric said. "You have asked that I trust my experts. Well, the only one more expert than I am in matters of magic is Karbin, and he's not here. So trust me, and wait in the hall."

Ser Yrsa opened her mouth to object, but Ser Beornric shook his head and whispered something to her. She gave him a glare, but snorted, picked up the desk calendar, and the two of them left the room.

That left the room dark, so Aefric lit up the yellow diamond atop the Brightstaff, standing beside him.

"All right," Aefric said, more to encourage himself than anything else. He hadn't done anything this dangerous…

Well, not in the last aett or two, at least. Maybe not since Frozen Ridge.

He held up the wand Garram like a shield.

He blew a pulse of power at the trap.

The spell-trap roared, spitting an avalanche of ice at him.

Aefric, roaring defiance, countered the ice with fire from his wand. Forming a shield before him. As powerful as he could make it, and as fast as he could conjure it.

Ice and fire clashed. Steam hissed loud as a dragon.

Shunting this much power locked up every muscle in Aefric's body. But he kept going.

So much ice came out of that trap. So very fast.

A relentless assault. Pressing his will to the breaking point.

He held that shield with everything he had.

Aefric's entire existence focused down to holding that shield. Conjuring fire, fast as he could.

Nothing else mattered. Only the shield between himself and icy death…

Finally, he felt a hand on his shoulder.

Aefric jumped. Lost his footing. Fell hard on the stone floor. His shield vanished in a puff of smoke.

His knights stood over him, looking down in amazement.

Aefric just lay there. Exhausted. Drained. Soaked in sweat. Panting. Trying to get his heartbeat to slow enough that he could tell one beat from the next.

"Not even a drop of water on the floor," Ser Deirdre said, her jade green eyes full of wonder.

AEFRIC SAT ON THE SURPRISINGLY COMFORTABLE CALINWOOD CHAIR IN that fancy little office. His knights brought him rye bread that wasn't quite stale, fresh water from a pump in the kitchen, along with a fresh-ish green apple.

For the first time since his trek into the Dragonscar a few aetts back, Aefric found he could actually eat an apple without cringing.

He'd eaten *so many* apples on that trip.

While he rested and gathered himself, his knights also checked on Sers Temat and Arras, reporting that they were still resting peacefully.

By the time Aefric finished explaining what he'd done, he was pretty sure Ser Yrsa wanted to take him by the shoulders and shake him. Or maybe just slap him.

She did neither, though her major scar was purpling with anger. And her red eye looked darker.

She closed her eyes. Forced down a deep breath.

Ser Beornric started to say something, but Ser Yrsa stilled him with a raised hand.

She needed one more steadying breath before she opened her eyes and spoke.

"Your grace," she said in a remarkably calm-sounding voice that Aefric didn't buy for a moment, "is telling me that he put his life in jeopardy when there was no need to."

"There was a need to. None of the rest of you could've done what I did."

"I sure couldn't," Ser Deirdre said, still looking at Aefric with amazement in her eyes. "I don't think Karbin could've either. Hells, I'm not sure the great *Kainemorton* could've done that."

"Kainemorton would've found another way," Aefric said.

"And perhaps," Ser Yrsa said, her voice still both careful and dangerous, "your grace could've found another way?"

"I'm no Kainemorton," Aefric said with a shrug. "And I don't think there *was* another way."

Ser Yrsa handed Ser Beornric both her maces, and the dagger at her belt. He had to sheathe his sword to take the weapons.

She flexed her hands a couple of times, as though she wanted to wring Aefric's neck.

"Your grace," she said, still in that same tone, "I have a question. Was that trap on the door or on the whole of the chamber on the other side?"

"The door," Aefric said. "But there are no other doors leading in there. I checked."

Ser Yrsa's mouth opened as though shouting should've followed, but she clamped it shut hard enough that Aefric heard her teeth clack together.

She flexed her hands another couple of times. Flared her nostrils in another breath.

"Your grace," she said slowly, "*does* remember that he has masons in his employ?"

Aefric blinked. Comprehension seeped into his tired brain.

"You mean—" he started, but Ser Yrsa finished.

"I mean that we could have brought in stonemasons to cut your grace a new door without risking his life!"

"You're right," Aefric said, frowning.

"*I*— excuse me, your grace?"

"I said, 'you're right,'" Aefric said. "I want to investigate this whole castle as soon as we can, but there's no real time pressure."

Ser Yrsa narrowed her eyes suspiciously.

"I'm not used to being someone who can casually bring in stonemasons for a problem like this," Aefric said. "I saw that trap and approached it like an adventurer, not a duke."

Aefric shook his head. "I'm sorry, Ser Yrsa. In fact, I'd like to offer all of you my apologies. I got caught up in the moment. I could blame the skeletons, or the sheer skill with which the trap had been designed, but that's no excuse."

He sighed. "I shouldn't have risked myself that way. Even though I was sure I could handle it, I could've been wrong."

"Thank you, your grace," Ser Yrsa said, taking her weapons back from Ser Beornric and fixing her dagger and her unlit mace back on her belt.

Ser Beornric drew his sword again, to add more light from one of Aefric's spells to the room.

Huh. The Brightstaff, still standing beside where Aefric had warred with the trap, had lost the light from its diamond. When had that happened?

"Oh," Ser Yrsa said, drawing back Aefric's attention. "I trust your grace will understand—"

"If you ask anytime you think I might be doing something that puts me at risk," Aefric said, dragging his tired body to his feet and calling the Brightstaff to his hand. "And yes, I'll understand. For a while, at least."

"Thank you, your grace."

"Now," Aefric said. "Let's see what all the fuss was about, before we see about dinner."

Aefric undid the simple spell lock with a gesture, then started to move toward the cabinets.

Ser Yrsa cleared her throat.

Reluctantly, Aefric nodded.

Ser Vria tripped the catch.

The whole section of wall behind the two file big cabinets came swinging soundlessly open.

The room on the other side was lit by magic.

Ser Yrsa started to step forward.

"Wait," Aefric said. "Safer to have me check one more time for traps first."

Ser Yrsa nodded and stood aside.

Aefric cast his spell, and gazed into the room through the diamond. And it was a tribute to either his discipline or his exhaustion that he looked only to see if he spotted the telltale red glow of a trap.

He did not.

"Go ahead," he said with a sigh, and stepped back.

"Treasury," Ser Yrsa said, sounding more matter-of-fact than anything else. "Chests full of ... gold ... silver ... copper ... even some platinum."

Several of the knights whistled. Platinum coins were rare, and more valuable than gold. Five, even ten times as valuable, in some places.

"Stacks of bars, too, like the jewel smiths use. And chests of gemstones." She poked her head back out. "The only threat in here is bad organization. Would your grace care to have a look?"

There was a time when Aefric would have *run* into that room. This sounded like the kind of horde an adventurer saw no more than once or twice in a lifetime.

But the truth was, Aefric was richer now than he'd ever expected to be. Rich enough that a little more treasure simply couldn't excite him the way it used to.

Nevertheless, he felt his tired heart pound a little faster as he stepped into the room. It *was* an impressive sight.

Open chests so full of coins and gemstones that they spilled over onto the floor. Stacks of gold and silver bars as tall as Aefric.

A bookshelf along one wall, with six large, heavy tomes...

Aefric called one to him with a gesture. Flipped through it. Aefric chuckled as he realized it was a ledger.

There were ledgers in the office he'd just stepped in here from, but he suspected that these ledgers were more accurate.

"Looks as though someone was cheating his taxes," Aefric said with a smirk, and sent the book winging back to its place on the shelf.

"Might be worth keeping up the same system," Ser Yrsa said softly. "This castle's in Merrek, after all, and I doubt your grace wants to pay Duchess Ashling more taxes than he must."

"I won't be paying her a copper," Aefric said. "She didn't just give me the castle, she gave me the land beneath it. The paperwork was quite clear. For all intents and purposes, we're in Deepwater right now."

Ser Yrsa whistled appreciatively. "She does want to curry favor with you."

"Or show her appreciation for last spring," Aefric said. "Deirdre? Would you come in here?"

"You want me, your grace?" Ser Deirdre asked, stepping up with a smile.

"Fighting that trap wore me out enough that I don't trust myself not to miss anything. Would you mind checking for magic?"

"Of course, your grace," she said, and began looking about.

"The light spell," she said, a moment later. "And a scry ward. That's everything."

"Good. I didn't miss anything then. Thank you." Aefric turned to Ser Yrsa. "All right. Let's close it up. I'll spell lock the treasury and its office, and then we can see about some dinner."

4

AEFRIC AND HIS KNIGHTS HAD ONLY JUST REENTERED THE GREAT HALL when one of his soldiers came in through the double-doors.

An abrupt enough entrance, in fact, that every one of Aefric's knights raised a weapon, which made the soldier stop moving and drop his spear.

He showed empty hands.

"Your grace," he said. "I did not mean to disturb—"

"That's all right," Aefric said, gesturing for everyone to calm down. "What do you have to report?"

"A messenger awaits at the gates, with two large carriages. From her grace."

That could only mean Duchess Ashling. So she *was* here in Kivash.

"Allow the carriages past the gate," Aefric said, pondering, "and escort the messenger up here."

"And good work, checking first," Ser Yrsa said, while the soldier retrieved his spear and trotted back out of the castle and down the hill.

Aefric dismissed his light spells as he and his knights stepped outside for the first time in hours. Clear skies above. Winds blew in from off the Risen Sea, moderating the late afternoon heat. The sun looked to be no more than an hour or two from setting.

No wonder Aefric was so tired. He'd had a long day, even before the fight with the skeletons and his outright war with that trap.

One of the advantages of being known to carry the Brightstaff everywhere. Gave him something to lean on, in moments like this.

"I'd say your grace is about to receive an invitation," Ser Beornric muttered, as the gates opened and two large, enclosed, ebony carriages entered. Each flew Merrek's flags, and each was pulled by a team of six horses.

"Can't just be me," Aefric said. "There'd only be one coach."

The messenger escorted up the hill by two of Aefric's soldiers looked to be one of Ashling's pages. She wore Merrek livery, and had the coltish look of a young woman who has grown much in a short period of time. She now stood no more than a handspan shorter than Aefric himself. She had the fine-boned and pale beauty of Armyrian nobility, emphasized by the way she wore her light brown hair bound in a complicated braid.

She stopped a respectful distance away, and bowed deeply. She held that bow.

"Greetings, messenger," Aefric said. "What word do you carry?"

"Greetings, your grace," she said, rising from her bow to stand with perfect posture. "On behalf of her grace, Ashling Fyrenn, Duchess of Merrek and Vanquisher of the Third Skull, I am come to welcome your grace to Kivash. I have further instructions to invite your grace and his knights to dine tonight at Ottarvigi, her grace's nearby castle, and to provide transportation if your grace is good enough to accept."

Aefric was too tired for politics tonight. He just wanted to have a simple dinner with his knights, and turn in early.

But the title came with responsibilities.

"I am most grateful for her grace's kind invitation, and quite happy to accept."

"Marvelous, your grace. As your grace can see, I have two carriages ready, and we can leave whenever your grace wills."

"I have a concern about…" Aefric shook his head. "What is your name?"

"My name is Cyneswith Ol'Cynerstan," she said with another bow, "and I am entirely at your grace's disposal."

"Cyneswith, two of my knights were injured in the course of our exploring Hrafnvigi. Does her grace have a physician at Ottarvigi?"

"Your grace, she has nothing less than a cleric of Nilasah," the page said, looking concerned. "And I know her grace would be eager to be of assistance to your grace's knights. Can they be moved? Or should I return with the cleric?"

Aefric looked at Ser Yrsa.

"We can move them," she said.

"Good," Cyneswith said, looking relieved. "Then with your grace's permission, I shall have the carriages brought up the hill, to ease the transportation of his wounded knights."

"Please do," Aefric said. "And thank you."

"The action is unworthy of thanks, your grace," she said, "but the sentiment is appreciated."

She turned and hurried down the hill, leaving the soldiers of her escort to trail in her wake.

Ser Yrsa didn't let them go. She called them over and began quietly issuing orders.

Meanwhile, Ser Beornric sent the remaining Knights of the Lake into the castle to carefully retrieve their wounded fellows.

Ser Deirdre nodded at Cyneswith, down the hill where she was giving orders to the drivers.

"That's no ler's daughter," Ser Deirdre said quietly. "Too precise in her formality. I'm betting she's the daughter of a count. Or at least a baron."

"The eldest daughter of Countess Siburh Ol'Cynerstan," Ser Beornric said, joining the conversation. "Duchess Ashling's most powerful vassal. Makes her an interesting choice for a messenger."

"Is Kivash in Ashling's direct lands?" Aefric asked. "Or those held by a vassal?"

"I'm not sure," Ser Beornric said. "There are probably maps back in that meeting room that could tell us—"

"No," Ser Deirdre said with sudden confidence. "Kivash must be in the Ol'Cynerstan county. The duchess would want her future vassal to meet your grace, as your grace now owns a castle among her lands."

"Not quite," Aefric said, but stopped there as the carriages approached.

His knights had rigged a pair of litters using the skeletons' shields and a few straps of leather. They carried Sers Arras and Temat out and helped them into the rear carriage, despite complaints from both knights that they could walk quite well.

Aefric wasn't sure that was true of either of them. Ser Arras' wound had been low enough to impede walking, and they'd both lost more than there share of blood.

Ser Beornric locked up the castle, and presented the keys to Aefric, who fixed them to his belt.

Cyneswith stepped up and bowed again.

"If your grace wishes his wounded knights to have a carriage to themselves, there should be enough room for him and his remaining knights in the other carriage. Though it might be a bit tight."

"I'll ride with Temat and Arras," Ser Vria volunteered. "Make sure they're all right on the ride."

"I'll join you," Ser Leppina said.

"Should be plenty of room then," Aefric said.

The carriage wasn't as comfortable on the inside as the magic one Aefric had ridden in earlier, but it was more than comfortable enough for a short ride.

Cyneswith rode up top with the driver, which seemed strange. Aefric was about to invite her to ride inside when Ser Beornric leaned in and spoke softly.

"She'll be a countess one day, your grace, but today she's a page like any other. Riding inside would be inappropriate for her."

The ride was brief enough, and Castle Ottarvigi impressive, for

Kivash. Easily six stories of smooth white stone, with three towers jutting up at least four stories higher into the afternoon sky.

Nothing on Water's End, of course. And perhaps not as large as Behal, either. But it was certainly the largest castle here in Kivash.

Castle Ottarvigi sat on a hill of its own, and inside the inner of its two defensive walls were several small buildings in addition to the castle itself. The courtyard had been tiled to match the white stone of the castle, though space had been left for a series of flowering fruit trees.

Aefric spotted two dozen soldiers on duty, already buzzing even before his knights brought Sers Temat and Arras out of the carriage.

Cyneswith must've jumped down and run for the physician before Aefric even left the carriage. Because he didn't have time to so much as say a word before he spotted a dusky-hued older man in the telltale yellow robes and hand sigil of Nilasah, goddess of compassion. The cleric came running out of the castle's tall double-doors, with Cyneswith leading and six assistants trailing in his wake.

The cleric didn't stop for introductions. Just took over handling the wounded knights. He quickly made sure they were safe to move, then his assistants began bringing them into the castle.

Aefric burned to ask questions, but even without the cautioning look from Ser Beornric, he knew better. This was just the way things were done.

Sers Arras and Temat were now getting the best care anyone could get anywhere. They'd probably be leaving that night under their own power.

Once the wounded were clearly taken care of, Cyneswith bowed to Aefric, and gestured for another page to approach. Another who looked likely to graduate soon from page training. He was starting to gain some muscle, and looked more like a man than a boy.

He bowed.

"If your grace will follow me," Cyneswith said, "I will escort him to dine in privacy with her grace, while Bruric here escorts his knights to dine with those of her grace."

The quick way both Sers Yrsa and Beornric nodded, both where Cyneswith couldn't see them, made Aefric want to object.

He didn't.

"Good," he said. "I look forward to seeing Ashling again. It's been too long."

———

Cyneswith escorted Aefric into Castle Ottarvigi. She was talking a bit about the history of the area, but Aefric was paying more attention to the castle.

Ashling, clearly, had already settled in. She'd replaced any old tapestries with her own, commemorating events in Fyrenn family history. Servants moved about as though they'd lived and worked here all their lives.

She'd even had floorboards installed. Red cherry, from the look of the wood. Made a pleasant change from the white stone floors of Castle Hrafnvigi. And either the previous owners had favored lighter colors on their plastered walls, or Ashling had been painting as well.

Cyneswith led Aefric up two flights of stairs and towards the back of the castle, then up a smaller staircase that had been concealed behind a tremendous painting of Kivash and the Risen Sea.

When the stairs began to gently spiral, Aefric realized he was now in one of the towers. The walls here were rounded and of white stone, like the stairs themselves, though their smell was freshened by vases of daisies sitting on shelves every twenty steps or so.

The windows Aefric passed weren't large, but they were frequent enough that he could see just fine without lighting up the Brightstaff's yellow diamond.

Cyneswith wasn't talking about history now. She was talking in excited tones about the Battle of Frozen Ridge.

"...and I was frustrated that Mother wouldn't let me don my armor and at least *take part* in the planning meetings out there in the field. So I'd climbed to the top of our tallest tower, intent on watching with a spyglass."

"Where exactly were you?" Aefric asked.

"Oh, our county seat is on the north shore of the Indecisive, your grace," she said with a smile. "No more than a half-day from here by boat. Perhaps two days by horse."

"Kivash is now part of your county, then?" Aefric asked.

"That's ... a matter of some debate between Mother and her grace," Cyneswith said. "And alas, I should say no more about that."

"I understand."

Interesting. Was young Cyneswith here as a hostage, as well as a page?

"So, there I was, atop our tallest tower, watching a lot of nothing happening through my spyglass," Cyneswith continued. "Armies on opposing ridges, yes, but at that point those armies were just sitting there."

She smiled at Aefric.

"Oh, I'm sure there was a great deal of activity and planning going on, but I couldn't see any of it from my vantage point. Made the whole thing so much more frustrating."

Aefric smiled. He knew all too well the frustrations of forced inactivity. For her, it might've been the army on her doorstep, but for Aefric, it was that pirate queen Nelazzi.

Aefric had, back at Water's End, a pendant that would *allow him and the ship he sailed straight through Nelazzi's own wards.*

He knew he could take her unawares. If only the king would give him permission to hunt her down...

"But then," Cyneswith continued, "out of the corner of my eye, I caught the sight of something flying due south. Something too large to be any of our local birds."

"I suspect I know what you saw," Aefric said, as they reached a landing that led into a hallway. Both landing and hallway attractively paneled in white oak, floor, walls and ceiling.

White candles burned in sconces along the walls down that hallway, throwing off more light than candles ought to. Aefric didn't need to check to know that magic was involved.

Cyneswith smiled again, and the look in her soft brown eyes might've been flirty. If she were older.

"May I share with your grace my experience of what I saw that day?"

"You may," Aefric said with a nod.

"Would your grace mind if we tarry here while I do so?" Cyneswith looked a little uncertain. "Her grace awaits only three rooms away, but I'm uncertain when I'll get another private chance to speak with your grace."

"If Ashling asks, you may blame me for the delay."

"Thank you, your grace," Cyneswith said, positively sparkling with her smile.

Give that woman a few years to mature and her looks might bring even more suitors than her title.

"As I was saying, I saw something too big to be any of the local birds, but not shaped right to be a great phoenix or pyltenius, or dragon, or anything else I could think of. So I raised my spyglass."

She mimed doing so.

"Imagine how amazed I was, your grace, to not only catch sight of a wizard in flight, but *such* a wizard. Not some old graybeard like Sirondfar, but young and strong and ... quite pleasant to look upon."

"You don't need to flatter me, Cyneswith."

"I flatter not in the least, your grace," she said, bringing one hand to her heart to indicate sincerity, "but speak only my true thoughts at the time. And if I may be so bold as to say so, I find my opinion of that day only confirmed, here in the presence of your grace."

"Thank you," Aefric said with a chuckle, which got him another sparkling smile.

"Well, this flying wizard was far more interesting to look upon than those distant armies, so I watched as he came to a halt in midair, regarding the armies of our enemy."

She grew more serious now as she continued.

"The wizard held a staff in hand, but instead drew a wand from his belt and..."

She shook her head.

"I have witnessed magic before, your grace. As any noble must, over the course of our lives. And yet, what I saw that day."

She sighed.

"How to describe it," she said. "It was as though I were seeing one of the great heroes of legend, come to life before my very eyes. The way he — the way your grace — sparkled with that icy blue power as he called forth his magic."

Sparkled icy blue? Aefric hadn't been aware he'd done that.

"And then, that magnificent lance of power, blasting off into the skies. Oh, and the skies! How that icy blue power seemed to spread like lightning through the skies all along that southern ridge. How thick clouds formed faster and faster, black as a nightmare. And then, oh, and then, how those skies opened up! How they rained and sleeted and hailed frozen death down on our enemies."

She shook her head, looking sober and almost stunned by her memory of the sight.

"The sheer volume and power of all that heavy snow and sleet, your grace," she said. "It made for an overwhelming sight. Knowing what it was doing to those people. Even seeing some of it through my spyglass. Even though they were my enemies, I found I did not want to watch. And yet, I could not look away."

"It can be that way, with a terrible thing," Aefric said quietly. "And make no mistake. What I did that day was necessary. But it was still a terrible thing."

"And not the only terrible thing," she said, now looking at Aefric with wonder. "I saw how your grace overreached himself with that spell. How he fell from the sky. I did not see your grace hit the ground, but your grace must believe I sent riders to look for him."

"I do," Aefric said. "And I thank you for it."

"It is a thing beneath thanks, your grace," Cyneswith said dismissively, then focused back on her point. "But that your grace survived such a fall. That ... that was truly the greatest miracle of the day."

"I think so too," Aefric said, "and I thank the goddess Kalinda for it."

Aefric told Cyneswith then of the two silver eyes he saw as he lost consciousness. The sensation of a kiss on the forehead.

Cyneswith gave Aefric a warm smile. "The gods are right to save those who would offer up their lives for others."

Aefric snorted. "I wouldn't count on it happening for me again."

"Did your grace count on it that day?"

"No."

"Which might be part of the reason the goddess spared your grace's life. A true selfless act of sacrifice."

"Don't make me sound too noble," Aefric said. "A goddess may have spared my life, but I'm still just a man."

"Perhaps," Cyneswith said. "But your grace, my family's castle would have been one of the first assaulted by Malimfar that day. Given what I have heard of their siege equipment, our castle would have fallen. And then, your grace, I know what depredations Mother and I — as well as all under our protection — would have faced at the hands of Malimfari soldiers and mercenaries."

"I know," Aefric said softly.

"So, I trust it will come as no surprise when I say that if there is *ever* anything that I and mine can do for your grace, your grace has only to ask."

"That isn't necessary," Aefric said, feeling a little uncomfortable with her blunt honesty.

Cyneswith nodded slowly.

"I had been told of your grace's humility. But that day your grace saved myself, my mother, my sisters and brothers, my aunts, uncles, cousins and all the people of my county. Your grace saved our lives, our fortunes, our lands, and even our very persons.

"And so I repeat, and your grace must believe me. We all stand in your grace's debt. If there is ever *anything* I or mine can do for your grace, he has only to ask."

She offered her hand.

Shock made the moment dreamlike.

Cyneswith was Ashling's vassal. Ashling's. Not Aefric's.

But here the young woman stood, offering *Aefric* her hand.

This wasn't quite an offer of fealty, but it wasn't far off. The gesture was heavily tied up in the oaths of vassalage.

He didn't know exactly what it meant, for her to offer her hand to a superior noble who was not her lord or overlord. But from the way Ser Beornric had spoken of her, Cyneswith was of an old noble family.

Aefric had no doubt that *Cyneswith* knew exactly what she was doing. And that she had waited to do so until they were alone and unobserved could not have been coincidence.

Aefric could have denied her. Could have shaken his head, maybe. But he knew that would have been an insult, and he wasn't sure how severe an insult.

And Cyneswith had done nothing to make Aefric want to insult her.

So he held his breath and kissed her hand. She shivered.

Cyneswith then emphasized whatever statement she was making. Closed her eyes and pressed her forehead against his knuckles.

Aefric's heart pounded. He hoped he hadn't just done something very, very wrong.

"Thank you, your grace," she said softly. "And now, I believe Duchess Ashling awaits."

"A moment," Aefric said, and used again a spell to freshen both his clothes and his person, while Cyneswith stared wide-eyed.

Apparently she hadn't seen that spell before, which made Aefric wonder just how much magic an Aymyrian noble really saw in the course of her life.

"Now I'm ready," he said.

To Aefric's surprise, no guard or servant opened the ornate, red oak door to Cyneswith's knock. Instead, he heard Ashling's muffled voice.

"Come in, Aefric."

Cyneswith gave Aefric one more smile as she opened the door for him, then bowed him in, closing the door behind him.

This wasn't a dining room at all. Or at least, not like any Aefric had seen since coming to Armyr.

The room had at least as much window as wall.

The room was round, and perhaps six strides across. The inner ... about half of the circumference was plastered and painted a sky blue, with splotches of fluffy white clouds.

The rest of the walls, or rather windows, or rather...

Oh. Aefric was clearly more tired than he'd realized. Because only now did he sense the magic of what he was seeing. Which explained why there were no panels or shutters.

There *were* no windows. The outer arc of wall, as well as a curved wedge of the ceiling, had been rendered invisible by magic.

Ashling laughed, a pleased and amused sound.

"Leave it to the Hero of Frozen Ridge to enter this room and fixate on what he cannot see."

With a chagrined smile Aefric turned his eyes to his hostess.

She reclined on large, ruby red pillows on the other side of a low, wide teak table edged in gold-etched scrollwork. The floorboards beneath her were covered in thick rugs of dark reds and yellows.

She wore her raven black hair down and loose, hanging past her bare shoulders. Her clinging gown was of pistachio green chiffon that looked to be as soft as her skin.

Were it not for Byrhta Ol'Caran, Ashling and her sisters — Zoleen and Queen Eppida — would have been the most beautiful women he'd ever seen.

Ashling herself was tall, willowy and breathtaking. She had the same amazing sapphire eyes as both her sisters, and...

No. That couldn't have been heat in her eyes. It was well known that Ashling favored women.

But then, they *were* alone in this room. No guards or servants...

"Much better," she said in soft, intimate tones.

Aefric frowned. "Ashling, what are you—"

She laughed then, a sound so free and open Aefric couldn't help smiling, even though he was sure she was laughing at him.

She had to slap the table to control herself.

"Oh, Aefric," she said in much more normal tones. "If you could have *seen* your face."

Aefric shook his head.

"Seriously, Ashling?" he said, still smiling half-against his will. "After the day I've had you give me games?"

"Just a bit of fun," she said. "Sit, sit, don't make me crane my neck looking up at you."

She turned a critical eye on Aefric's clothing as he stood the Brightstaff and sat cross-legged on his own set of pillows.

"Properly speaking, you're overdressed for this meal. If I'd provided you with a robe that matched my gown, would you have worn it?"

Aefric snapped his fingers as comprehension dawned. "We're dining Akhiri style?"

Akhir. That marvelous trading city, known as the last shining light of civilization before one entered the Southern Wastes.

"Of course," she said. "You've traveled so much I thought you might be the only Armyrian noble besides myself to enjoy Akhiri food."

"Well, to answer your question, yes. I would have. If I'd been told we were dining Akhiri. But I have to admit. A lot of their food is a bit spicy for me."

"There'll be plenty of yoghurt," she said.

"Thank you," Aefric said.

Ashling clapped her hands, and two pretty serving women in long white tunics and small white caps brought out ewers of water and crystal goblets.

They poured a goblet each for Aefric and Ashling, before returning through ... a door in the invisible wall?

So the edges weren't sky, but illusion? Nice bit of work, that.

Ashling cleared her throat.

"Just because I'm not seducing you doesn't mean I want you to get caught up in the magic of my favorite room in my new castle."

"If you put beauty before me, I shall appreciate it," Aefric said, nodding to Ashling, who inclined her head at the compliment. He gestured at the invisible wall / illusion mix. "And if you put magic in front of me, I shall examine it."

"You're getting better at playing the noble," she said with a nod. "Good."

Aefric and Ashling raised their goblets, sipped, then exchanged goblets. They sipped again, then exchanged goblets once more, and sipped a third time.

"*Gindecha nes klinskaa,*" Ashling said. In Ahkhant, the ancient tongue of Akhir, her words meant "Water is life."

"*Splindacha nes gindecha jela,*" Aefric said, giving the traditional answer, which meant, "Friendship is true water."

They set their goblets down.

The same two servants brought in a selection of berries with cream. In the kingdom of Armyr, that would only be a dessert, but down in Akhir, the berries and cream were used to whet the appetite for the meal to come.

"Your pronunciation is quite good," Aefric said. "Possibly better than mine. Do you actually speak much Ahkhant?"

"The words of the water ritual, and a few dozen other phrases," Ashling said with a smile. "As the eldest, I used to accompany Father on trading missions twice a year, which always included Akhir."

"You must know the place better than I do," Aefric said. "I've only been there twice."

"Oh," Ashling said with a sparkle in her eye, "probably not. I was a young girl traveling with heavy escort, not an adventurous wildman wizard out seeking his fortune."

"Adventurous wildman wizard?" Aefric asked, popping a raspberry in his mouth that exploded with ripe perfection.

"That's my favorite of the phrases I've heard," Ashling said, tossing a blackberry in the air and catching it in her mouth. Once she swallowed, she added, "Makes you sound dangerous the right way."

"I'd rather hear about what you did in Akhir," Aefric said. "That is to say, when you *eluded* that heavy escort of yours."

"Are you suggesting that as a young girl I would risk myself in a dangerous foreign land by sneaking out and getting into trouble?"

"To suggest otherwise would be to impugn either your courage or your creativity."

Ashling laughed delightedly and gave him soft applause.

"Oh, well said," she said. "You *are* getting better at this."

And for a time, Ashling told tales of her own adventures.

THEY WERE FINISHING WITH THE BERRIES AROUND THE TIME THAT Ashling was finishing her stories about Akhir.

"I was never in any real danger, of course," she said with a sigh. "The street thief I'd befriended was more likely a girl hired by Father. Someone to tell me stories and keep an eye on me. Take me to safe places and call them dangerous, so I'd get a little thrill."

"What about the two men with scimitars who chased the two of you through the streets?"

"Oh, at the time it was terribly exciting," she said. "But looking back I can't help but notice that those men never got closer than a dozen paces from us. Even though they had longer legs, and plenty of open space down at least two of those streets."

"What was the point then?" Aefric asked.

"I think Father wanted me to know the feeling of risk," Ashling said. "And, of course, to give me a few stories to tell."

"Stories are better than money sometimes," Aefric said.

"Depends on the stories," Ashling said. "I imagine yours are quite valuable."

"Some of them," Aefric said modestly.

"Speaking of stories," Ashling said, "I take it Cyneswith told you her story about Frozen Ridge?"

"In detail," Aefric said.

"I'm not surprised," she said with a sigh. "She's spoken of little else since she learned you were coming down here. I pity the boys trying to get her attention for the next few aetts. Did she try to steal a kiss?"

"No," Aefric said with a chuckle.

"Smart girl," Ashling said. "A few of the other pages were daring her to, once it was announced that she would deliver my dinner invitation."

Ashling smiled and shook her head. "I could have told her that wasn't the approach she'd need with you. She did offer you her hand?"

The question came so unexpectedly and was delivered so smoothly that Aefric almost answered without thinking. And his eyes definitely widened.

"I thought she might," Ashling said, sighing even deeper. "I must admit, I'm impressed, Aefric. I wouldn't have thought anyone could manage to both save my duchy *and* undercut the loyalty of my vassals in a single act."

A wave of cold washed over Aefric and tightened his guts.

"No, Ashling," he said. "I never—"

"I know, I know," she said, waving away his objections. "You never intended any such thing. I *have* met you before, you know."

"What can I do to make this right?"

Ashling clapped her hands, and the same two white-clad servants brought in salad and the first real beverage. (The water was merely a ritual of Akhiri dining.)

The salad involved tomatoes, olives, dates, kale, arugula, two kinds of zucchini, and crumbled croutons, dressed with a spiced oil. The drink was a light apricot wine.

Once the servants were gone, Ashling gave Aefric a pensive look.

"The truth is, you did an amazing thing that day. Probably the greatest feat of magic seen in Armyr in at least two hundred years. And it was witnessed, to some extent, by the whole of my armies, which included all of my vassals."

She quirked a smile and shook her head.

"You saved us all, and everyone knows it. Without you, Armyr *might've* been able to avoid being conquered completely. Once Colm took the field, with his armies. And maybe brought down Wylyn with his. But by then Malimfar would have held the whole Indecisive River Valley, and likely beyond. My duchy would have been halved, perhaps quartered. And Colm wouldn't have been able to get that land back. Not anytime soon."

"To say nothing of the lives lost and the harms done in the process."

"Exactly," Ashling said, taking a bite of her salad and letting her eyes flutter closed with pleasure. "I do love the way the spices in the oil play with the zucchini and tomatoes."

How could she eat? Aefric's anxious nerves were trying to shunt fresh energy through his tired system to deal with this new set of problems *he'd* caused, and his stomach seemed to be closing down.

Not to mention that he wasn't sure he'd be able to swallow past the heavy beat of his heart.

"What all this means," Ashling continued, "is that I owe you a great deal for what you did that day. And so do my vassals, especially Cyneswith and her family. I'm sure she told you that her lands would have fallen first."

Aefric nodded.

"Did you kiss her hand when she offered it?"

Aefric nodded guiltily.

"Let me guess," Ashling said, cocking an eyebrow. "You thought you'd be insulting her if you didn't?"

"Wouldn't I have?"

"Insulted? No," Ashling said simply. "But she's young and besotted with you. You would have hurt her feelings." Ashling smirked. "And if you could bring yourself to hurt a young woman's feelings, Vercy Ol'Karmak wouldn't think she might 'prove' herself a fit bride for you. Despite her obvious drawbacks such as an unimpressive dowry, a small title, and a family name soiled by the treason of her brother."

Aefric opened his mouth to object, but Ashling gave him a very direct look, with one raven black eyebrow raised.

His objection died on his lips. Everything Ashling had said was true. Technically. Though Aefric hated to see poor Vercy tarred by the actions of her brother, when she'd taken many steps to stop him.

"As I was saying," Ashling said. "It would be petty of me to expect my vassals not to express their appreciation. Especially a pretty and clever young thing like Cyneswith."

"What exactly does it mean that she offered *me* her hand?" Aefric asked. "I know what it means when one of *my* vassals does it, but one of yours?"

"About what you'd expect," Ashling said with a slight shrug. "She's saying that she's yours to command, despite the fact that she owes her fealty to me." Ashling rolled her eyes. "At least her mother is still countess. If Cyneswith had been countess and done that, I wouldn't be able to overlook it."

"So she won't be punished?" Aefric said, as much as asked.

"No," Ashling said with a sigh. "And she has you to thank for that. If I thought for a moment that you were the kind of man who would use the goodwill of my vassals to build his power base at my expense, I'd have to do something that would make me look terribly ungrateful."

"I'm still trying to get used to the power I *have* now," Aefric said. "The last thing I want to do is lobby for more."

"I know," Ashling said. "You probably don't even know yet what to do with that new barony Colm has given you. Still. I'm going to ask you to decline any more offered hands from my vassals, if you would."

"Of course," Aefric said quickly.

"Thank you," Ashling said, taking more salad on her fork. "Word may spread that Cyneswith got her hand kissed by you, but I can counter that by saying you did it as a romantic gesture, because she's so pretty."

Aefric set down his fork. "All right. Stop."

Ashling set her fork down and raised curious eyebrows.

"Hand kissing here in Armyr. That's not a romantic thing. That's only the vassal-liege thing. Right?"

"Yes," Ashling said. "Or at least, it's supposed to be. Which is why Cyneswith shouldn't have offered you her hand. But when she did, you kissed her hand — accepting her offer — not because you want her fealty, but because she's pretty and you found her charming."

"I didn't want to insult her," Aefric clarified.

"Because she's pretty and charming, yes," Ashling said, smiling.

"But—"

"Don't you think she's charming?"

"Well, yes, but—"

"And don't you think she's pretty?"

"I think she *will* be, but—"

"Then this is the truth, or near enough."

"People will think I want to bed her," Aefric complained.

"I daresay they will," Ashling agreed. "And she'd be most eager for the pleasure, I'm sure."

"She's a *child*."

"Hardly," Ashling said, chuckling. "She's scarcely two years shy of her majority, and I'd be willing to bet she's already enjoyed her share of bliss moments. I know I had at her age."

"But—"

"Aefric," Ashling said, seriously. "This is near enough the truth. It would solve both our problems here. And it would give young Cyneswith a smile and some bragging rights."

"I'm not going to sleep with her."

"I don't blame you. Berries are always sweetest when given time to ripen." She pointed at his salad. "Do try that, or my cooks will be heartbroken."

Aefric didn't like the idea of leading Cyneswith on. But he *had* screwed up by kissing her hand. So maybe he owed this to Ashling, who was clearly trying to cement their friendship.

Maybe this would be all right?

Aefric calmed himself through a deep breath.

Took a sweet taste of apricot wine to settle his nerves and stomach.

His stomach responded by telling him he'd had entirely too little to eat that day.

So he and Ashling dined in an oddly companionable silence for a time.

———

THERE WAS SOMETHING UNEXPECTEDLY PLEASANT ABOUT DINING AKHIRI style with Ashling, there in that half-invisible tower room, so high above Kivash.

The view of the city below was splendid, and included the river, the harbor, the Risen Sea and even the afternoon sun, which would likely set before they reached the dessert course.

Aefric and Ashling had finished their salads in comfortable silence, seated on those large, ruby red pillows on opposite sides of the low teak table.

With a different woman, the intimate setting might've felt romantic. Especially given the cushions, and the way Ashling lounged, with that chiffon dress molding itself to her body.

But Aefric knew the last thing she wanted from him was romance.

The salad was followed by a lamb dish, served with cool mint that contrasted sharply with the lamb's hot spices in the best possible way. It was served on a bed of wild rice and ... two other small grains that resembled rice, but weren't.

The spice was strong enough that Aefric had to give his mouth a break every few bites for a taste of soft, flat bread dipped in mint yoghurt.

Just as well. The fine, strong red wine they shared over the main course was good enough that he didn't want to distract his tongue from it with spices. And it went well with the yoghurt.

They spoke about Kivash for a time. About its shipping. The troubles she expected from Malimfar that necessitated keeping six of her warships in the harbor. And Ashling's plans for north-side expansion and the like. Which brought up an interesting question for Aefric.

"Will you be renaming it?"

"The castle?" she asked, glancing about. "I haven't decided yet. My historians are still researching its origins."

"I meant Kivash. Now that it's entirely yours."

"Oh, no," she said with a smile. "Kivash was the name of the first city at the mouth of this river. Care to guess when that was?"

"Back when this region was part of the principality of Fyr?"

Ashling nodded with a smile and savored a bite of lamb.

"Does Merrek go back to Fyr as well? An old duchy or something?"

Ashling winced as though the lamb had gone sour in her mouth. Took a hard swallow of wine.

"I take it that's a no?" Aefric asked carefully.

"Merrek Stonghand was the first king of Armyr," Ashling said. "He named our duchy after himself so the name would serve as a constant reminder to my family of 'our place,' even while 'honoring' us with the duchy as 'thanks' for our help in establishing Armyr in the first place."

"I'm sorry," Aefric said.

"You didn't know," Ashling said waving it away, though her smile wasn't quite sincere again yet. "It's not a topic we like to talk about." Her smile got warmer again as she continued. "For the most part, we don't even think about it anymore. We've very much made the land our own again, and built it into a force to be reckoned with."

She drew a long, slow breath. Let it out with a chuckle. "You just caught me off-guard. Asking about its origin that way."

"Then let's talk about something else," Aefric said, bringing the subject back to Ashling's plans for Kivash. Which eventually brought them around to the question of Hrafnvigi.

"How did your knights come to be injured?" she asked. "Temat and Arras aren't exactly inept. Were they unarmored?"

"They wore their full plate," Aefric said, and told the tale of the skeletons hidden in that last cell. "The skeletons attacked from surprise. Near as I can tell, Ser Temat was caught under the armpit because his arm had been extended, opening the door. Ser Arras, under her breastplate, while she was heaving him back to safety."

"Two unlucky stabs then," Ashling said, shaking her head.

"Possibly," Aefric said. "But perhaps not. There was more magic involved than was needed to animate the skeletons. They'd been charmed so that only magical weapons could harm them. Which might—"

"That can be done?" Ashling asked, dropping her fork. "That's a spell you wizards know? Why aren't all nobles protected thus?"

"Because it isn't easy, because the spell isn't well-known, and mostly because it can't be cast on the living."

Ashling shook her head. "Surely you could find a way to overcome that limitation, as you have so many others."

"Perhaps," Aefric said. "With enough time, and the right research materials." He shook his head. "But even so, it would likely take me decades."

"Decades?" she said, sounding disappointed.

"At least," Aefric said. He tried for a comforting tone when he added, "If it were easily done, someone would have figured out how, by now."

"True," she said distractedly.

From the calculating look in her startling eyes, Aefric suspected that she would give the research task to her ducal wizard, Sirondfar.

She looked back at Aefric and frowned. "Still. This happened in a castle I gave you. I apologize for that."

"There's no need," Aefric said. "I allowed myself to be lulled beyond caution. I should have known better, and I won't make that mistake again."

Ashling raised her wine goblet. "To not repeating mistakes."

Aefric raised his glass in solidarity, and they both drank.

"You'll sleep here tonight, won't you?" she asked, suddenly enough that Aefric needed a moment to realize what she'd said.

"I would be happy to accept hospitality—"

"Oh, Aefric," Ashling said, waving dismissively, "I'm not trying to trap you into anything. Don't be so formal. It's apparent that your new castle will take some clearing before you can be assured of sleeping in safety there. I'd be happy to host you in the meantime."

"This isn't a way to get me to spend time with Zoleen?"

"Ah, Zoleen," Ashling said with a sigh. "I do apologize for her, Aefric. She's the youngest, and Mother spoiled her. I sent her to Water's End to charm you. I don't deny it. I'd love to see you married into my family. But it never occurred to me that she'd act as though you two were already promised to one another."

"Did she tell you what she did?"

"She told me her view of things, and I suspect I can guess the truth." She shook her head. "It doesn't matter whether I know or not. You're the one she wronged. Tell me. Do you think you can forgive her? With time?"

"Forgive her?" Aefric said. "Yes. But trust her? No. She still doesn't seem to understand where she went wrong, even though I've been pretty explicit in my explanations."

"Of course you were," Ashling said, shaking her head. "Mother really did Zoleen no favors. With Colm intent on finding a bride for Killian among the princesses of other kingdoms, and her bridges burnt with you, Zoleen's prospects are not great."

"Surely there are foreign nobles who would be thrilled to marry her."

"Of course," Ashling said. "Perhaps as many as want to marry me. But the issue isn't whether or not she'll marry, but whether or not we can make her the *right* marriage."

"So it's not just about title and land?" Aefric asked.

"She is a Fyrenn," Ashling said. "We have ... more considerations than most nobles require. Which is why I am now two years into my own marriage negotiations."

"That's right," Aefric said. "You're unmarried."

Ashling fluttered her eyelashes. "Why Aefric, should I consider myself a contender for your hand?"

"My advisers think you are already, after our conversation last spring. Even though I *told* them you were joking."

"I was," she said philosophically. "But I do think we'd make a good match, and produce children that could bring the world to its knees."

Aefric frowned, unsure if she was joking this time...

"Relax, Aefric," Ashling said with a smile. "I'm not proposing. But I do think it's an option not to be discarded out of hand."

"Even though you favor women."

"Oh, I think that would work *for* us," Ashling said with a smile. "Think of all the willing beauties we could share in the process of your getting me with children."

She tilted her head. "In fact, perhaps we should share the noble privilege sometime. The two of us seeking the bliss moment aided by a noblewoman or two. See how we are together."

"My point was," Aefric said, trying to drag the conversation kicking and screaming back where he wanted it, "you aren't married, either. *I'm* getting all this pressure to marry, so why aren't you?"

"Oh, that," she said, waving her hand.

She smiled with her eyes and made Aefric wait while she savored another bite of lamb.

He took the excuse to eat a little more of it himself. It really was good, if a little...

Aefric quickly grabbed a piece of flatbread, dunked it in the mint yoghurt and shoved it into his mouth.

He was already sweating by the time the yoghurt soothed his tongue.

Apparently that bite had been extra spicy.

"Now," Ashling said, taking a swallow of her wine. "You asked why I'm not getting pressure to marry. First, I have heirs."

"Mekel," Aefric said, referring to her younger brother, "and Zoleen?"

"Yes, them, but they're in line after my son Dives."

Ashling had a son?

AEFRIC WASN'T SURE EXACTLY WHAT HE LOOKED LIKE, AS HE SAT THERE, stunned by the revelation that Ashling had a son. Slack-jawed, yes. Wide-eyed, sure. But there must've been something more to it.

In the moments following that revelation, Aefric's mouth forgot the taste of the spiced lamb, the mint yoghurt, even the rich red wine.

He wasn't even aware of the softness of the pillows he sat on, or the first hints of approaching sunset, from out over the Risen Sea.

Ashling's eyes danced with mirth, and she quirked both a smile and an eyebrow.

"I never said you'd be the first man inside me, Aefric. I experimented quite a bit around my majority."

"That's not what surprised me," Aefric said.

"Oh, I know. You didn't know about Dives. I don't draw a lot of attention to the poor boy, because he'll have more than he can handle soon enough." She gave a wistful smile. "Gorgeous child, but then, so was his father. Skin like mahogany, and eyes like caramel."

She sipped her wine.

"I came into my duchy when Father died, early in the Godswalk Wars. So much was happening so quickly, that I decided I needed an heir more than I needed a husband. So I saw to it that I got pregnant, and made sure to acknowledge the bastard even before his birth."

"But..." Aefric shook his head. "Doesn't having an acknowledged bastard hurt your marriage prospects? I mean, your future husband will know that his own children will be in line for the duchy behind Dives."

"Thus," Ashling said, spearing some lamb with her fork, "two years of negotiations."

She frowned at Aefric as she chewed her lamb, while he sipped a little of his wine.

"You know," she said, "that wouldn't be a concern for you, would it? I mean, my bastard wouldn't have anything to do with Deepwater or passing down your own lands."

"If *we* married, you mean."

Ashling nodded.

"Well, I've had to hear a lot of talk about bloodlines—"

Ashling started laughing, but it didn't seem to be at his expense this time.

"Oh, very *good*, Aefric," she said finally. "The essence of nobility in a single statement. It's not about who rules now, but who rules tomorrow."

She chuckled a little more and said, "And you're quite right. If Dives lives to hold the duchy and sire his own heir, your children would be cut out of Merrek, but mine would be part of Deepwater."

"That *does* make you a less appealing marriage prospect," Aefric said, hardly able to believe that those words had come out of his mouth.

How different his life was here from Keifer's life on Earth. As Keifer, he'd married Andi for love alone, and nothing else...

"I know," Ashling said, shrugging one shoulder and bringing Aefric's attention back to the present. "Capricious youth. If Dives weren't so marvelous a son, I'd be tempted to declare him unfit to hold the duchy and make of him a knight or ler."

"Sounds a bit extreme," Aefric said.

"Oh, I'd never do it. Not to Dives." For a moment, Aefric saw what might've been the most sincere smile he ever saw from her pass through those eyes.

In a flash, it was gone.

"But since *I'm* no longer a prospect to marry you," she said. "If I can get *Zoleen* to really understand what she did wrong, and swear never to do it again, would you be willing to give her another chance?"

"If I can believe she's sincere, I suppose."

"Good enough," she said. "And I understand Eppi has promised to give a title and dowry to Sighild Ol'Masarkor, if you favor her over Zoleen."

"She has," Aefric said, remembering the queen's promise. "And I do like Sighild."

"I don't blame you. If she weren't a cousin, I'd probably have bedded her by now myself. Eppi would have to provide quite a bit to make her a worthier bride than Zoleen, though."

"She seemed confident that she could," Aefric said.

"Eppi has never lacked confidence," Ashling said. "I think that's part of what Colm loves about her."

She turned a shrewd expression on Aefric.

"But Sighild isn't Zoleen's major competition, is she? I imagine that that magnificent beauty Byrhta Ol'Caran is a leading the way right now. Even though she has *almost* as many drawbacks as Vercy Ol'Karmak, and no royal patron to see her titled or dowered well enough to make a match for you."

Aefric restrained himself from telling Ashling that King Colm had offered to give Byrhta a dowry, if Aefric wanted to marry her.

Fortunately, thoughts of Byrhta seemed to distract Ashling, and Aefric tried to change the subject.

"What was the second reason you don't get the pressure to marry that I do?"

"We'll get to that in a moment," Ashling said, digging around for more lamb. "First, I imagine you still have hopes of making Maev your bride?"

Ah, Maev. Princess of Armyr, and a wonder unto herself.

Alas, Maev. Down in Varondam, conducting alliance negotiations with their king that might involve her marrying him.

But there was no point in denying so obvious a truth.

"I do," Aefric said.

"Well. Then it seems that competition is thick on the ground for the hand of our dear new Duke of Deepwater." Ashling smiled. "But if I might add one more name to your deliberations?"

Aefric girded himself through a breath. "Who?"

"Cyneswith," Ashling said. "I know she's young, but she's heir to a county, and her family is *almost* as old as mine. She'd be a good match for you. Not as good as Zoleen, of course, but arguably better than Sighild. And if you married Cyneswith, that would make *all* my vassals happy and give them a connection to you that I can live with."

"I don't know..."

"Please, Aefric," Ashling said. "At least say you'll consider her."

Aefric cocked his head. "You don't care if I truly do consider her. You just want me to *say* that to help defray damage from my kissing her hand."

"You're quite right, of course," Ashling said, not even looking as though Aefric had caught her at anything devious. "Your expressed interest would only lend weight to what I was saying about your being charmed by her. And it wouldn't commit you to marrying her, if that's what you fear."

Aefric didn't like the idea. But he also didn't like the spot he'd put Ashling in.

"This won't hurt Cyneswith, will it?"

Ashling shook her head. "She's smart enough to know her chances would be slim, given her competition. But your *considering* her would make *her* happy, make her *mother* happy, and draw favorable attention to her. In truth, you might be helping her as much as me."

Ashling smiled winningly.

Aefric sighed. "So long as you don't send her or Zoleen to my rooms tonight."

"And if I show up myself?" Ashling asked, fluttering her eyelashes.

Aefric started to say something. Stopped. Started again. Stopped. Frowned. Shook his head.

"You know," he finally said, "I don't know what I'd expect, if you came to my rooms for the noble privilege. But I wouldn't send you away."

"Truly?" Ashling asked, as though surprised.

"Truly," Aefric said. "I find that I actually do like you, Ashling. And your beauty is certainly stirring. I'd be as curious to see what we'd be like in bed together as I suspect you would be. *If* you showed up at my door."

Ashling nodded, smiling.

"In that case, when we're alone, you can call me Ash, if you like."

***

THEY SPOKE OF SMALL THINGS AS THEY FINISHED WITH THEIR LAMB. AND the dessert that followed was truly a marvel.

Whipped cream and chocolate and juicy, nearly overripe raspberries, all held together by an almost airy cake that made Aefric feel as though he were eating a dream.

Reality was the good, strong coffee served with it.

Ashling slowed down about halfway through her portion of the dessert. Toyed with her fork among the cream.

"And now," she said, "I believe you were curious about the *second* reason you get pressure to marry that I don't."

Aefric nodded. Savored a slow, lingering bite blending the ripe raspberries with the chocolate and cream.

"In truth, I don't want to admit this," she said. "Doing so goes against everything I've been taught. But by Elbar's Blood, I find that I like you too, Aefric."

She frowned at him.

"I do hope that's not going to cause me problems," she said.

"I don't see why it would," Aefric said. "Surely we'll work together better if we like one another."

Ashling sighed. "You're too new to nobility to understand. If you remind me, we'll discuss the subject again in a decade or two."

"The second reason, you mean?"

"No," she said with an exasperated smile. "See? By reflex alone I was trying to change the subject."

She shook her head.

"Would it help if you wrote it down?"

"Are you joking?" Ashling asked, sitting up straight. "I'd *never* commit these words to paper. And if anyone asks, I'll deny I said them."

"What words?"

Ashling sighed heavily.

"The second reason is power. In your first year or so as duke, you'll make many decisions and commitments that will influence the future of your duchy. More than you can guess."

She shook her head.

"I was trained for my role, and I still made mistakes. I can only imagine how many you will make."

She held up a hand, before Aefric could say anything.

"Don't misunderstand me," she said. "I don't mean that as a slight or an insult. I mean only that you will make many decisions that look small, but will have far-reaching repercussions you could not imagine at the time."

Aefric thought about the tribe of borogs he had allowed to live in the Dragonscar, at the north end of his duchy.

Others had suggested his doing so might be just that kind of mistake.

Aefric still disagreed. Still believed it was just the right thing to do. But it did sound like the sort of thing Ashling was talking about.

"I do my best," Aefric said. "And I have good advisers."

"Do you?" Ashling challenged. "How do you know?"

"Well," Aefric said, "Kentigern, my seneschal—"

"Was chosen by Arinda Soulfist, from a family chosen by Arinda's forebears." Ashling shook her head. "Trained to run things the way the Soulfist family ran them."

"There is value to consistency," Aefric said, "so long as I approve of the direction."

"True," Ashling said, leaning forward a bit now. "If the duchy is a ship and you want it going east, Kentigern appears to be taking you in the right direction. But does he steer you *due* east? Or *easterly*? And how do you know?"

"I know unjust laws when I see them," Aefric said. "And—"

"Unjust laws are easily spotted. Move on from Kentigern. Who else?"

"Ser Beornric," Aefric said confidently. "He's been invaluable."

"An Ol'Sandallas, I believe," Ashling said, and when Aefric nodded, she continued. "An old noble family. Certainly. But not the only old noble family in Armyr. And he was chosen *for* you by Colm. Why do you think that is?"

"Likely because King Colm wanted Ser Beornric to ... mitigate some of my more ... adventurous tendencies."

"The obvious answer," Ashling agreed. "And likely a major duty for him. But also to maintain the status quo."

"Why is that bad?" Aefric asked.

"The status quo can be good or bad, depending on where it leaves you. But are *you* evaluating the status quo? Or allowing others to guide your evaluation?"

Aefric frowned and sat back. "I don't know."

Ashling nodded slowly. "Good. Something for you to think about."

"And this comes back to marriage?"

"Whom you marry, and when, will have a larger impact on your duchy than any other single decision," Ashling said. "And because you are without family here in Armyr, you have no one to protect you from the influences of others. Myself included."

"So the pressure for me to marry—"

"Is pressure from others to gain influence in your duchy. Both now and in the future. And the sooner you marry, the more and stronger the influence. Because your personality is strong enough that, given time, you will forge your own way no matter what influences others have. And you'll take Deepwater with you. So the earlier others can gain their foothold the better for them."

Aefric blinked as he absorbed that.

"So what you're saying," he said slowly, "is that even Ser Beornric's opinions about my marriage go back to ... what? King Colm's desires for my duchy?"

"Well," Ashling said, nodding her head back and forth, "I'm not suggesting that your knight-adviser is actively working as Colm's agent. I think he's likely quite sincere in whatever he's telling you."

"It's just that you think his sincerity was chosen by King Colm because it aligns with the king's own hopes for Deepwater."

"Just so," she said.

"I think I understand now why you were hesitant to explain this," Aefric said. "I mean, I knew that everyone who put forth a potential bride had ulterior motives, but I didn't grasp the *scope*."

Aefric frowned at Ashling, as she took another bite of dessert.

"I'm curious," Aefric said. "Do you have an ulterior motive in telling me the truth about all this?"

"I wish I could say I did," Ashling said with a grimace, then frowned. "Well, maybe I do. After all, the chances of your marrying Zoleen now are slim. Perhaps, given the influence I am about to lose, I see benefit in hurting the influence of others, and raising myself in your esteem in the process."

Aefric looked at her sideways. "Is that what you're doing?"

"No," she said with a sigh. "I'll spin it that way if I ever have to tell others about this conversation. But the truth is, I do like you. I've never had a friend among the peerage before. But I'd like to think that perhaps you and I could be friends."

"I'd like that," Aefric said. Toasting with coffee was unusual, but drinking coffee with dinner at all in Armyr was unusual. "To a lasting friendship between us."

"May it live on in our children someday," she confirmed, raising her own cup.

And together, they drank.

AEFRIC WAS GIVEN THE THREE UPPERMOST LEVELS IN A TOWER AS HIS rooms. The windows were large, and glass. They had no shutters, but the outside world could be closed away by heavy, velvet curtains of deep indigo.

All of his rooms had white oak floorboards, though the plastered walls and ceilings varied in color. A dark brown for the small library of local history books, as well as what appeared to be a decent-sized meeting room. A pale pink for the sitting rooms (there were three, of varying sizes and intimacy). A soft orange for the closet and dressing room, and pale blues for the bedroom, bath, and garderobe.

The closet had a good deal of fine clothing, much of which looked as though it would fit Aefric.

Fresh daisies in every room lent a pleasant scent to the air, even more so than the rugs of woven rushes, which were clearly fresh.

All of his rooms here were lit by magic, and he was pleased to see that the black marble tub was heated by magic as well. It would take forever for hot water to get all the way up here.

The garderobe, also, eliminated by magic. Which was good, because Aefric didn't want to imagine his waste raining down from this kind of height.

There was no balcony, but considering the height involved, he didn't expect one. Up here, the winds would be too wild.

Oh, the tower didn't compare to the Seven Great Spires of Water's End, but it was still higher up than Aefric had been recently, when he wasn't flying.

All the same, it was a pity there was no balcony. Aefric was more than a little wound up from his conversation with Ashling — and from three cups of coffee over dessert — and soaring off into the early stars of night would have been a good way to give himself time to think, as well as burn off some nervous energy.

Although he could just imagine the reactions of Sers Yrsa and Beornric, had he done so. Flying off over an unsettled city, without anyone guarding him.

Sers Yrsa and Beornric...

Aefric began pacing his largest sitting room as he thought. There was plenty of room here, between large, overstuffed couches, over near the large hearth.

The Brightstaff bobbed along in the air behind him, keeping pace.

Ser Beornric, as he'd discussed with Ashling, had been provided by King Colm. Likely because the knight's views were the sort that the king wanted to emphasize in Deepwater.

So not a spy, per se, but still an influence that Aefric needed to be aware of.

As was Ser Yrsa. She'd been Arinda's general. What did that say about her as an adviser?

Aefric tried to think about the kinds of advice he'd gotten from Ser Yrsa.

Most of it had involved his own security and safety. And she'd been right far more often than wrong. Aefric might never have learned about Zoleen's work against Byrhta, if not for Ser Yrsa.

Oh, this was the kind of thinking that was new to Aefric. Combats and tactics he understood. Making rulings and evaluating the fairness of laws, well, those he was new to, but he felt confident in his sense of morality and ethics.

But what about the more ... nebulous aspects of nobility? All the dozens of small decisions that Aefric made every day. How many of them did he really make? And how many did he allow others to make?

And of the latter, how many of those others were following the guidance of the Soulfist family, rather than Aefric's own guidance?

Would Aefric need to ... what ... he wasn't even sure what the word was for going over all of the laws and policies of Deepwater and reviewing them.

Was that auditing? It sounded like an audit, but there was probably a better term for it. A term that someone like Ashling, raised to be a noble, would know at once, while an up-jumped street rat like Aefric wouldn't even recognize the word.

A knock interrupted his pacing. The Brightstaff came automatically to his hand. He looked over at the dark red door.

This was the largest sitting room. Which meant he was on ... yes, the lowest floor of his rooms. That meant that the door he looked at led out into the hall, where two of his knights stood guard.

"Yes?" Aefric called over.

Ser Vria opened the door enough to poke her head in. "Two servants to see you, your grace."

"Send them in," Aefric said, frowning with puzzlement. He couldn't imagine what could bring two servants all the way up here without his having sent for them.

The servants were young women, fidgeting just a little as though nervous about something. One had short black hair, and the other long, blonde tresses.

"Yes?" Aefric asked.

They looked at one another, visibly fighting not to giggle. They couldn't have seen more than a single summer past their majority.

The blonde seemed to be the more assertive, because she was the one who drew a deep breath, bowed, and said, "We've come to offer your grace *leaba*."

Leaba, the custom of a bedmate, offered only to a visitor among the ranking nobility of Armyr. It had to be offered freely, by a member of the common folk. It could not be ordered or coerced or paid for in any way.

Aefric had been given *leaba* before. Even allowed it to be offered on occasion, when he was the hosting noble.

But always it had been *one* person offering *leaba*.

"I'm not sure I understand," Aefric said slowly. "Am I to choose between you?"

That would be a difficult choice. They both filled out their Merrek livery well, they both had smooth, lightly tanned skin, and pleasing features.

"No, your grace," the brunette said with a bow. "Her grace gave us permission to offer your grace *leaba* together."

"Together," Aefric said.

"Yes, your grace," they both said, bowing, and small, excited giggles fought to get out through their words.

Ah. So this was Ashling's way of teasing Aefric with the possibility of sharing the noble privilege with her and another noblewoman at the same time.

Well, far be it for Aefric to be a bad guest.

"Then I am most happy to accept," Aefric said.

5

EARLY THE NEXT DAY, AEFRIC AND HIS KNIGHTS RETURNED TO CASTLE Hrafnvigi to continue their exploration.

With the single exception of Ser Deirdre, who wore her maroon leathers, all his knights wore their full plate armor today. Even Sers Yrsa and Beornric, who must've decided that they didn't want the risk of facing more skeletons unarmored.

Aefric doubted there would be more skeletons, but couldn't blame them for playing it safe.

Aefric himself wore clothes that had been provided by Duchess Ashling. A navy blue silk tunic, quilted and embroidered with silver thread, over black hose. He wore low boots of soft leather that had been dyed black, to match his belt.

The wand Garram rode at his belt, along with his belt pouch and the silvered dagger that Ser Wardius had found the day before. And, of course, Aefric had the Brightstaff in hand.

Sers Temat and Arras had only a touch of pallor to indicate that they'd been wounded yesterday. Such was the power and skill of Ashling's cleric of Nilasah.

They were the ones chosen to carry the two somewhat magic

weapons found in the Hrafnvigi museum the day before. The spear for Ser Temat, and the gladius for Ser Arras.

In addition to the extra armor and weapons, the exploration itself was handled with a good deal more caution that day.

The Knights of the Lake began the day by moving as a unit through the secret passage they'd found in the first-floor guest rooms, intent on opening every secret door they came to as they worked their way slowly through the castle.

Ser Deirdre went with them, checking for magic.

Aefric, to his consternation, did not. But while Ashling might've given Aefric a good reason to question the advice of his advisers in general, he couldn't find fault with their reasoning this time.

The Knights of the Lake were there to protect him from hazards, and it had been proven twice yesterday that there were hazards in the castle.

So Aefric could either insult his knights, or let them do their jobs. While he did a job they could not and should not do.

While his knights were exploring the castle, Aefric returned to the accounting office with Sers Yrsa and Beornric, entered the treasury, and took a better look at Aefric's new wealth.

More specifically, they searched to see if anything lay hidden among those chests full of coins and gemstones, those stacks of jeweler's bars of gold and silver and even a little platinum.

And it was a good thing they did.

When spending that much time in a single room, Aefric would either have to tune out certain distractions, or deal with them. Normally he might tune them out. But that morning his stomach reeled with uncertainty over the influences in his life, and what he might or might not need to do about them.

He felt the need to eliminate whatever distractions he could.

Starting with the dust.

Dust lay thick all about him in the treasure room. Clearly no one had cleaned in there for at least a few aetts *before* Armyr took Kivash this past spring. To say nothing of since.

When Aefric had first entered, the day before, he'd been

distracted by all the glimmering treasure. Not to mention that he'd been more than a little exhausted after defeating that magical trap.

But now that he was to spend some time in this room, he wouldn't do it tasting dust and sneezing every few minutes.

Aefric kicked Sers Yrsa and Beornric out of the treasury. They could go through the accounts, if they wanted, but surely there were no dangers left in the treasury, and Aefric wanted to deal with the dust his way.

No *wizard's valet*. Not for this. Not thorough enough.

No, Aefric centered himself, and cleaned the room the way he used to clean the alchemy lab in Kainemorton's tower, back when he'd been apprenticed to the Mage of Marrisford.

Aefric went inch by inch over the chamber, cleaning it with magic. The walls, the ceiling, the floor. The chests. Their contents. All of it.

Cleaning this way, as he had so often, once upon a time, Aefric slipped into an almost meditative state.

All of his attention on what he did, as he moved slowly over the whole of the room.

The smooth repetition of the simple steps of the spell. A spell he'd cast so very many times. To clean and polish with magic that any apprentice could figure out.

Wiping away dust. Scrubbing away grime. Rendering pristine everything in his path.

And as he did this, he found himself slowly tuning out his sense of the light spells that brightened this room enough to make the freshly cleaned coins and gemstones sparkle.

He tuned out the scry ward next. A good, workmanlike spell that would keep magic from detecting this room, or its contents. But nothing that needed his attention.

Finally he tuned out the dwindling remains of the spell trap he'd defeated.

There was peace and clarity in this kind of work. Peace and clarity that kept apprentices sane under their intense workload. And right now, Aefric needed that level of peace and clarity.

He was about three-quarters of the way through the room — just finishing the third chest of gemstones — when he felt a spark, off to his right.

Unknown magic?

Could there be more magic in this room than just the light, the scry ward, and the dregs of that trap?

Aefric hadn't noticed anything more the day before, but he hadn't spent long in here. And he'd been more than a little drained at the time.

Ser Deirdre hadn't either, but she'd spent even less time in the treasury than Aefric had. Plus, she was a dweomerblade. Her focus was such that there were types of magic she might miss.

Aefric stopped cleaning. Stretched out with his senses, moving his attention slowly through the flows of Qorunn's magic to ease around the room until—

There.

Behind the small stack of platinum bars fit for jewelry making, Aefric could detect a touch of magic to the white stone wall.

Aefric moved the platinum bars aside by magic, then knelt before that section of wall.

Down near the bottom. Yes.

Couldn't be a door. He'd checked for doors yesterday. Couldn't be a trap, either, for the same reason.

Anyway, it was too small to be either. No more than the length and breadth of Aefric's hand. Right down where the wall met the floor.

Aefric set the Brightstaff to stand beside him. Rubbed his hands together. Murmured the right words, and pressed his palms to his closed eyes.

In a single movement, he drew his hands away and opened his eyes.

No change. So this was not an illusion then. That spell would have revealed an illusion cast by even the likes of Kainemorton himself.

What was it then?

Maddening. This whisper of magic.

Old magic. It felt very old indeed. Decades, at least. Possibly centuries. Aefric could tell that much.

But it was elusive. Difficult to grasp with his mind. This was like trying to gauge the feel of something his fingers couldn't quite grasp.

The spell hadn't been cast by any magic-user Aefric knew. He could tell that much. And that included those who'd done the spells he'd encountered so far in Hrafnvigi.

No, this was something different.

But what was it? A secret cache? A teleportation link? Something else entire—

Damnation. Why did he have to think of teleportation?

Aefric sat back and sighed.

"I've found something," he called out to the other room.

Sers Yrsa and Beornric entered quickly, weapons drawn.

"There's magic here," Aefric said, pointing out the spot on the wall. "Old magic. Not a door or a trap. Beyond that I'm not sure yet."

"We should send for Karbin," Ser Yrsa said at once.

"Wait," Ser Beornric said, his free hand raised. "How can you be certain it isn't a trap?"

"Because I checked for traps yesterday. I would have found this, if it were."

"But could your spell have found *this*? Neither you nor Deirdre sensed it then, so maybe your trap detecting spell missed it?"

"Not the way that spell works," Aefric said, shaking his head. "It will detect traps, even if they have other qualities I can't sense. Same with doors. So it's neither."

"Still—" Ser Yrsa started, but Aefric cut her off.

"And I'm not summoning Karbin to deal with this," he said. "I need him at Water's End, doing what he's doing. Besides, *I'm* here, and I'm not exactly a slouch at magic."

"I didn't mean to imply that you were, your grace," Ser Yrsa said smoothly. "Only that your grace selected Karbin to serve as court wizard because as skilled and knowledgeable as your grace may be when it comes to magic, Karbin is more so."

"Nevertheless. Unless it proves to be beyond my skill to figure out, I'll handle this without him. This is my castle now, and my mystery to explore." Aefric frowned, looking around. "In fact, this is my treasury now, and I want it organized."

Aefric cast the *wizard's valet*, and set it to properly sorting the chests of mixed coinage and gemstones.

Sers Yrsa and Beornric looked at each other, likely not quite sure what to make of Aefric's abnormal tone. But surely they couldn't expect him to simply defer to others for *everything*.

"And now," he said, "I'm going to figure out this strange magic I've found."

Investigating that little bit of old magic in the Hrafnvigi treasury was like...

It was like trying to look head-on at something Aefric could only see out of the corner of his eye.

It was like trying to hear a single soft sound in the middle of a battle.

It was like trying to smell a faint hint of roses in a field of manure.

It was like trying to distinguish between the tastes of two specific grapes, after he'd already bitten into a whole handful.

In short, it was a demanding effort.

A proper wizard would probably have had a very thorough and systematic method for sifting through what Aefric could tell about that strange magic, so that each detail added a small piece to a greater puzzle. Likely, with enough time, the wizard could then step back and examine the puzzle — mentally filling in any gaps — until he understood the image, and thus, the magic.

But Aefric was a dweomerblood. His approach to magic was far less rigidly organized, and far more intuitive and organic.

That was often a great help to him.

This time, it seemed to be a hindrance.

A wizard might be able to glean information from the position of the spell, its age, the precise amount of power. And likely a wizard could make subtle adjustments to his perceptions with each pass, eliminating possibilities to what he was seeing until what remained had to be the answer.

Alas, Aefric couldn't work that way.

In fact, for the longest time, all he could tell was that there was magic there. Filling the space of about the length and breadth of his hand, there, where the white stone wall joined the floor. Not much. Just a faint bit.

He passed his perceptions over and over and over that spot. Trying to gauge the structure of a spell his attentions couldn't quite grasp.

If he could discern even a single quality, he might be able to use that quality as a link to allow himself to learn more, and eventually puzzle through the whole of the magic involved.

When Aefric finally caught his break, he almost didn't notice it.

The spell had a temperature.

Magic could sometimes feel hot or cold to Aefric. Yes, often that had to do with the element of the spell involved — fire magic felt hot and ice magic felt cold — but sometimes it had to do with the amounts of power and the spell's purpose.

A spell cast to manipulate someone often felt warm. But a soothing kind of warmth. A spell intended to defend against attack, often felt a little cold. As though from the breeze created by a barely missed strike.

After a good deal of time feeling as though he were trying to clutch fog — albeit with magic and not his fingers — Aefric came to realize that the room about him was moderately warm, compared to what was likely a hot day outside.

And the spell, like the room, was moderately warm too. Room temperature.

That was unusual.

A spell that carried no sense of temperature was no less common than one that carried a sense of heat or cold.

But one that *felt* the same temperature as the room around it?

Only one kind of magic ever felt that way to Aefric.

The magic of clay and stone.

There was a whole branch of wizardry devoted to the magic of clay and stone. Its adherents were known as *vohlcairns*. Aefric knew only a little of that kind of magic, but he knew some.

And once he had a fix on that quality to his sense of that small bit of magic, he came to understand it a little. The walls, the floor, the whole of this castle was stone. The magic of clay and stone would need little power to do something here.

So long as that something were small. Innocuous. Something that wouldn't draw attention. Possibly something latent, waiting for a trigger...

A hidden cache?

No. Not quite...

Now that Aefric understood that he was dealing with the magic of clay and stone, he was able to refine his attention.

That frustrating little bit of magic wasn't like fog after all. No. It was like the finest grains of sand, and that was by design.

The natural way to understand a spell was to grasp it. But trying to grasp *this* spell would make it slip through Aefric's metaphorical fingers.

Now that he understood that, he was able to spread his focus and come at the spell as a whole, rather than trying to pick it apart.

Picking a spell apart element by element was *usually* the best approach. But now that he knew more about what he was dealing with, Aefric could discern *how* to approach the whole of the spell so that he could do something closer to the equivalent of scooping up a handful of fine sand, rather than clutching it.

Yes, the magic of clay and stone.

Yes, just a small amount here. Just enough to...

...to secret something away in this one stone?

No. This was not a cache. Aefric had encountered caches made with the magic of clay and stone. They tended to run just a hair hotter than their surroundings.

This spot, this was a *keystone.* For some kind of magic that underlay the entire structure of...

No.

Was this a self-destruct key? Could this spot be triggered to collapse the entire castle?

No.

Not *quite.*

That felt *close,* but the temperature was wrong. A spell that could do that, even using the magic of clay and stone, would feel colder than the room around it.

Besides, Aefric was pretty sure that the concept of "self-destruct keys" didn't exist in Qorunn. All of his referents to the idea were from Keifer's memories of Earth. And as Keifer he didn't recall anything about "self-destruct" options from the *Torn Kingdoms* campaign setting.

Of course, there was always the possibility that Del Baker was adding that to the sixth edition. But better to assume that this magic tied into something that already existed within the lexicon of Qorunn. Especially since it felt *old.*

And the closest thing that Qorunn had to that idea were certain magic items that could be broken, explosively unleashing all their power at once.

That ... would feel hotter than its surroundings. Even if only in pulses above room temperature, to indicate the restrained power.

So likely not a self-destruct option then.

All right. What did Aefric know?

He knew he'd found a place within his castle — a single spot within a hidden room — that contained a very old, very intricate, but apparently not very *powerful* enchantment. An enchantment of the magic of clay and stone.

Wait. *Was* it not very powerful? Or did it seem to be a relatively weak enchantment because it was *latent,* as opposed to active?

Any spell, while latent, could appear less powerful than it would while active. And if this was a *keystone* spell, as Aefric thought it, then perhaps it only needed enough power here to activate other key spots when triggered...

A possibility fluttered through Aefric's gut. Excitement tried to swell in his chest. He quelled both through a deep breath.

This was either the oldest castle in the area, or the second oldest. And yes, the spell he was sensing, that could well be old enough for its magic to have been woven in with the construction.

The word "construction" caused that flutter again, and Aefric suppressed it.

There was a vague, background sense of magic to the whole of the castle. He'd noticed it before entering, and convinced himself that what he was sensing were wards. Light spells. All the other little magics that a castle like this tended to have.

In fact, he'd started ignoring that background sense of the castle's magic when they entered the great hall yesterday, and even here, today, he'd been ignoring it by reflex.

But what if he'd been picking up a thread of magic woven through the whole of the castle itself?

And if so, what if this little spot along the wall in this hidden room turned out to be the key to magics woven all through the castle's structure.

It made sense. Oh, it made sense.

And if Aefric was right, then this whole castle was a brilliant bit of magic. An elaboration of Raend's famous work.

The great *vohlcairn* Raend had once developed an enchanted item he called the Instant Tower. It looked like a cube, no larger than a gaming die. But when activated, it expanded to become a four-story stone tower. Magical lights inside, enchanted servants, and the like.

All the comforts of home, in a tower that could be carried in a pouch at one's belt.

Could this whole castle be an extension of Raend's work?

Raend himself had vanished one day, hundreds of years ago. And he'd never taught the secret of the Instant Tower to anyone. He'd made a dozen or two himself, but he'd never allowed anyone else to make one.

But what if someone else had figured out the secret?

Then again, if that were true — and this castle were built the same way as one of Raend's towers — then there should have been magic light available in every room.

So why the light spells in places like the museum rooms?

Hrafnvigi was an old castle. Perhaps the keywords for the lights and magic servants had been lost?

Maybe.

Unfortunately, there were only two ways to know.

He could try to activate the spell — which could be dangerous if he was wrong.

Or he could try to compare it to one of Raend's creations. But where could he—

That tower here in town. The one where the wizard Relimmorea lived. Aefric had known there was something familiar about that tower.

Now he realized why. The triangular windows and crenellations. That was why that freestanding tower had looked so familiar.

Apart from the color of the stone, it was just like the Instant Tower he'd stayed three nights in down near Kesh, during the Godswalk Wars.

That one had been inherited by its current occupant —one Baroness Helva — and strangely she hadn't wanted to talk about how her family came to own it.

So one of Raend's towers was here in Kivash.

Aefric needed to pay this Relimmorea a visit.

WHEN AEFRIC RETURNED HIS ATTENTION TO HIS BODY, HIS BACK WAS stiff and his legs were asleep from sitting cross-legged before a wall for far too long.

Aefric rolled his neck around, listening to the pops and cracks of muscles and tendons too long inactive.

"Can your grace hear me now?"

Ser Beornric's voice, long-suffering, from somewhere over Aefric's left shoulder.

"I can," he said, rolling his chest now to ease the stiffness in his back. The tingling in his legs, he ignored for the moment. "All is well?"

"You tell me," Ser Beornric said. "Your grace has sat there staring at the wall for most of the day. We couldn't rouse your grace for lunch. I had to talk Ser Yrsa out of sending for Sirondfar, to make sure you were all right."

Leaning on the Brightstaff, Aefric made his way to his feet and began shaking sensation back into his legs.

"You were right not to. I was just ... heavily involved in a magical investigation."

"And if something had gone wrong?" Ser Beornric asked, with dwindling patience in his voice. "Suppose we'd found ten times as many skeletons waiting for us on the second floor. How would we have gotten your grace's attention?"

Aefric looked up at the glowering knight.

"You've covered the second floor already?"

The glower intensified.

"All right, all right," Aefric said, waving dismissively. "If you'd shaken me, I'd've come out of my trance. I wouldn't have been happy about it, though, unless there'd been a compelling need."

"So shaking you *would* have worked?" Ser Yrsa asked, stepping into the room. "Ser Deirdre said it would, but that might have been one of her jokes."

"No, she was right about that," Aefric said. The pins and needles were gone now, but he really needed a bit of walking, to get his legs feeling right again.

"Would slapping you have worked?" Ser Yrsa asked. "That was my idea."

It would have, but Aefric wasn't sure that confirming as much was in his best interests. Especially not if Ser Yrsa did the slapping.

"Shaking me would be better," Aefric said. "More certain." He raised an eyebrow. "And less likely to draw a ... protective reaction."

Ser Yrsa gave Aefric a sinister lopsided grin. "Fair enough, your grace."

"What did today's explorations yield?" Aefric asked, walking out into the main part of the accounting office, where the rest of his local knights all stood around by lamplight.

"No traps or battles, today," Ser Yrsa said. "Guest rooms, parlors, and the like. An armory, fully stocked, and so forth. But that wasn't the most interesting thing. Beornric?"

"Thanks to the hidden passages — which go all through the castle, your grace — we found the way into the back of the first floor."

Ser Beornric smiled. "It's ... a sybarite's paradise, your grace. Sumptuous, for the most part, but also..."

"Their tastes ran towards the kinky, your grace," Ser Deirdre said, grinning. "Apart from the tubs and pools and overdone couches and beds and rooms full of pillows, they also had rooms set up like torture chambers. Except that all the cuffs and chains were padded to prevent chafing."

"Still bloodstains on the floor, though," Ser Vria said, shaking her head.

"As I said," Ser Deirdre said with a shrug. "Kinky."

"But I thought Malimfar didn't practice the noble privilege," Aefric said.

"Officially, they don't," Ser Beornric said. "Publicly they look down on us for it, and claim to practice celibacy before marriage and strict monogamy when married. But apparently, in private, they play by very different rules."

"Even that door near the garden," Ser Yrsa said with a frown. "The unhidden door. It doesn't lead to a gardening shed. It's a separate entrance to the family ... playrooms."

"Convenient," Ser Deirdre said. "Someone could approach through the streets in secret, cloaked. They could knock on the small iron door at the foot of the hill. Be admitted, escorted by guards to that door, and then straight into the playrooms for a few hours, before being escorted out again."

"Assuming they were allowed to leave, afterwards," Ser Vria said. "Some of those bloodstains were ... prodigious."

"I'm sure I'll find other uses for those rooms," Aefric said.

"Your grace won't even try them out first?" Ser Deirdre asked.

"Deirdre," Ser Yrsa warned, and the dweomerblade bowed an apology that didn't quite reach her smiling eyes.

"I only meant that some of the tubs look as though they would serve your grace well," Ser Deirdre said. "Their temperature can be regulated by keywords. And the fireplaces light with the right command word as well."

"Do you know the command words?" Aefric asked.

"I'm not as good at ferreting such things out of spells as your grace," Ser Deirdre said. "But I sensed the magic of them."

She frowned. "In fact, there was more magic back there than I expected. Some of which I couldn't quite puzzle through."

That might make sense. If the castle were what Aefric thought it was, its heart would be someplace not easily accessible from the outside.

Of course, the existence of that one door at the back of the castle would seem to indicate that the heart couldn't be in the "family play-room" side of the first floor either.

"Ser Deirdre, have you ever stayed in one of Raend's towers?"

"Never had the pleasure," she said sadly. "I love the idea of them, though. A little cube you toss on the ground, then say the right word and *bam!*" She smacked her open hand. "Instant tower."

"What happens to whatever was there?" Ser Yrsa asked.

"It gets ... forcefully shunted aside," Aefric said.

"How forcefully?" she asked. "Positioned properly, such a weapon could bring a quick end to a siege. And if soldiers could already be waiting within—"

"Anything living inside it when it gets collapsed gets crushed," Aefric said. "And it's not a weapon."

"It is if used properly, your grace," Ser Yrsa said. "Does your grace possess such a tower?"

"No," Aefric said. "But I might just possess a version that is much, much larger."

Aefric looked around for emphasis.

All of his knights started talking at once.

Aefric stilled them with a raised hand.

"I know," he said. "This would be amazing, if true. But ... I don't know for certain yet. Which is why, this afternoon—"

"Evening, your grace," Ser Yrsa corrected softly. "We've been here quite some time."

"Evening then," Aefric said. "Either way, I need to pay a visit to Relimmorea and her tower."

ALL OF AEFRIC'S KNIGHTS ESCORTED HIM TO THE TOWER OF Relimmorea.

Honestly, it felt like overkill. After all, he hadn't seen or heard any fighting in the streets, nor seen any indications that any of the locals intended him harm.

Still, caution might've been the right watchword. Certainly Sers Yrsa and Beornric seemed to think so.

And Aefric had to admit that he cut a more impressive image, escorted through the cobbled streets by his knights. Sers Yrsa and Beornric by his side. Ser Deirdre following a few steps behind. And the Knights of the Lake in their shining armor, surrounding them all.

Technically it was evening, but the sun had not yet set over the Risen Sea. The worst of the day's heat was past, though. And the streets of Kivash were still alive with travel and business.

But all was quiet on the street of Relimmorea's tower. It was almost eerie, really. The nearest sounds of traffic were all at least a street away.

Even the songbirds seemed to avoid the area near Relimmorea's tower.

This street was curved, as though it had wanted to go three different directions at various points, but couldn't make up its mind.

Rather like the nearby Indecisive River. Aefric wondered if that was intentional.

Most of the buildings along here were small, and ill-kept. Not as though they were abused, per se. More as though they were getting on in years, and not aging gracefully.

Shingled roofs missing shingles. Tarred roofs with bald spots. Walls with bare wood showing because they hadn't seen fresh paint since before the Godswalk Wars. Doors with visible wear in the places where regular visitors tended to knock.

At one time, all the windows of these one- and two-story homes had framed glass, but many now had only shutters to keep out the wind, as well as prying eyes.

The people seemed honest enough though. A bit furtive, but that was to be expected around what they doubtless considered an invading noble and his knights.

No. Aefric had seen more than his share of bad neighborhoods in various towns and cities, and this wasn't one of them.

Bad neighborhoods didn't smell like baking bread and ... were those crullers? They smelled lovely, and Aefric's mouth watered and stomach growled, reminding him that he hadn't eaten since breakfast...

No time for that now. He focused his attention back on his surroundings.

In fact, Aefric doubted this neighborhood saw much crime at all. Likely because of that prominent, four-story, white stone tower, which was Aefric's reason for being here.

He nodded at the sight of the triangular windows, and the triangular crenellations at the top. He'd remembered those windows and crenellations from the tower he'd stayed in, in Kesh.

He remembered thinking how those crenellations looked like sharp teeth, the first time he saw them. They looked no more innocuous now.

Same height, that tower. Same design. In all likelihood, the one before him was one of Raend's creations. Unfortunately, Aefric needed certainty. And he couldn't get that. Not from where he stood.

He wished he'd taken the time to note the feel of the tower of Baroness Helva, magically. But at the time he'd been more worried about the baroness herself. And about that army of taroks just over the ridge...

Aefric shook his head. That was years ago, now.

This tower, like the one Aefric knew from before, had a single wide, tall oak door. Rounded at the top, and magically reinforced.

Ser Beornric looked the question at Aefric, but Aefric shook his head. As a noble, letting someone else knock for him was the way things were done.

But he wasn't coming to visit Relimmorea as a duke. He was coming to talk to her, one magic-user to another.

And that had protocols of its own.

Aefric raised his free hand, palm towards the door, while his knights spread out around him.

Aefric created the pattern in his head. The right seven-knock sequence, each with its proper relative position and amount of pressure.

He snapped his hand into a fist and shunted power through the pattern at the door.

Seven spots on that oaken door flared dark red, the vertices of a seven-pointed star.

Seven knocks followed, with alternating amounts of pressure — and thus volume — with the first, third, fifth and seventh knocks being the loudest, and the second, fourth and sixth being progressively quieter.

He was not kept waiting long.

The door eased open.

An imp emerged, and the door closed behind it.

No two imps looked exactly the same. They varied in size, coloring, smell, wing size and shape, whether or not they had horns, and the like. And yet, each imp was unmistakably an imp.

This imp was on the small side, perhaps four hands high. Given that, it looked somewhat like a sexless human with dull orange skin, two stubby horns, bat wings, and a nose the size and shape of a potato.

Some imps carried a whiff of sulfur. This one smelled more like hot iron.

The imp looked over the crowd.

"The wizard's knock isn't for groups," the imp said in a startlingly low voice.

"The knights are here because I'm a duke in an unsettled city," Aefric said. "But I come to visit Relimmorea not as a duke, but as a fellow magic-user. If welcomed properly, I will enter alone."

Aefric heard Sers Yrsa and Beornric shift uncomfortably behind him. He'd told them that this was how it would be. And that — if Relimmorea welcomed him properly — his safety was assured while in her tower.

But they still didn't like it.

The imp looked Aefric over, and he knew he was being examined by senses other than sight.

"Well, you qualify, there's no denying it. And it's easy enough to tell by that" — the imp nodded at the Brightstaff — "exactly who you are. But none of that tells me why you've come."

"I wish to discuss the Art with Relimmorea."

"A conversation that would last until the gods walk Qorunn again, I don't doubt." The imp raised a hairless eyebrow. "Unless you have a specific topic?"

"I was hoping to discuss the most famous works of the *vohlcairn* known as Raend. And what might just be his unknown masterpiece."

The imp bowed.

"Then you are as puissant as my mistress has heard," the imp said. "Unfortunately, although she would welcome the man known as Aefric Brightstaff for such a discussion, she cannot be seen to admit Armyr's Duke of Deepwater into her home. For her to do so would be taken as a political statement."

"As a fellow magic-user I am disappointed," Aefric said. "But as duke, I understand her position. And as neither would I wish to cause trouble for your mistress. As such, I will leave at once, not to return without invitation. Would it aid your mistress if I make a show of being rejected?"

"You are kind to offer such," the imp said, "but it would not. She cannot be seen to either help or hinder the Duke of Deepwater."

Unspoken words came to Aefric's mind then. The imp's words, in the imp's voice.

"But in light of your offer, and as a show of goodwill, my mistress bids me to tell you that you are on the right track, and that all the answers you seek can be found within Hrafnvigi."

Aefric met the imp's eyes and nodded to show both his understanding and his gratitude.

"Then I shall take my leave now," Aefric said, "and trouble your mistress no further. But I thank you kindly for your words and consideration."

"You are most welcome," the imp said, and flew off straight up into the air.

As Aefric led his knights back toward Castle Ottarvigi and dinner, they got as far as the second twist of the street before Ser Leppina spoke.

"Aren't imps scions of evil, your grace?"

"They have that reputation," Aefric said, "but it's ill-founded. In truth, imps have no temperament of their own. They reflect only that of their master."

"And can we trust the temperament of that one?" Ser Yrsa asked.

"I hope so," Aefric said. "Either way, we'll know within the next few days."

No simple dinner with Ashling that night at Ottarvigi. Assuming any meal shared with Ashling Fyrenn could be thought of as simple.

Thirteen hells, even just the one aspect of their conversation from the night before — the influences Aefric had in his life that he'd never chosen himself — had been haunting him all day.

Nevertheless, he would have welcomed at least the *quiet* of dining with Ashling, compared to what was waiting for him when he and his knights reached Ottarvigi that evening.

Dinner with Ashling's court.

Odd, that somehow Aefric had thought she would either have no court to speak of here in Kivash, or perhaps a handful of nobles. After all, though Kivash was technically part of her duchy, he kept hearing how *unsettled* the city was about that point.

Aefric had expected that most nobles would *avoid* such a potentially dangerous place.

Apparently not.

The great hall at Ottarvigi was full to overflowing with knights and lers, not to mention a broad cross-section of relatives from Ashling's titled vassals.

It seemed that every baron and count that owed her fealty had at least a handful of siblings or cousins — or a mix of the two — who wanted to be right here in Kivash.

"Helping."

Which likely meant trying to figure out how their families could most benefit from the current unrest, so that when Kivash settled down again, they would have that much more influence here than their rivals.

And they all had rivals.

When he thought about it that way, Aefric realized he should've expected this. Kivash was a port city, after all, with direct river access not only deep into Armyr, but into several other kingdoms as well.

In that sense, Kivash was a more important port than even his own grand port city, Ajenmoor.

Not that everyone dining in the great hall that night was a noble of some stripe. There were also plenty of representatives from powerful merchant families and trade guilds. Some of them new to Kivash, but many of them locals who didn't care who collected their taxes, so long as business continued uninterrupted.

And all of them looked at Aefric the way a manticore looks at a wounded lamb.

He felt the weight of their gazes as he walked past their dozens of crowded tables, escorted by Cyneswith to his place at Ashling's side, on the dais. He could hear the way conversations paused as he passed, then got faster and more urgent in his wake.

His knights couldn't protect him from this kind of threat. Although they would stay nearby, once the meal ended and the mandatory socializing began, they would only protect him from threats to his body. Not to his peace of mind, nor to his finances.

But attending this sort of gathering was part of his role now, as duke.

At least the group at Ashling's table was small. Only six, compared to the twelve at each of the other tables.

Ashling and Aefric sat side-by-side in the center of one long side of the table, looking out over the assemblage.

To Aefric's right sat Ser Yrsa, the only adviser he was allowed at the table, and selected in case Ashling wished to discuss military concerns here in Kivash.

To Ashling's left sat her new castellan, Ecgnoth. He looked to be about Ser Beornric's age, and held his age just about as well. A touch of gray at the temples of otherwise black hair, and the kind of penetrating gaze that made Aefric think he had to be a Fyrenn. Ashling's uncle or an older cousin, perhaps.

Taking the end spot of the table on Aefric's side, Cyneswith's mother, Countess Siburh Ol'Cynerstan.

If Countess Siburh was a preview of Cyneswith's future, the sight was impressive. Not just in her beauty, which would have stood out in many crowds, but in the confidence of her bearing and the determination Aefric saw in her eyes.

Perhaps this was a woman who could, indeed, go toe-to-toe with Ashling. In fact, watching them resolve the question of whose lands Kivash was now part of might well be a sight worth seeing.

Opposite Countess Siburh at Ashling's end of the table sat Zoleen.

Zoleen was dressed conservatively that night. Her long, copper hair wound into a complicated arrangement atop her head, leaving her long neck bare but for a simple gold chain, crowned by a single large diamond.

Her dress was a high-necked gown of maroon chiffon, that nevertheless looked grateful to be worn by her. But then, she improved most outfits by wearing them.

The same could be said of Ashling, of course, who wore silk tonight. A gown of sky blue slashed with red, and embroidered throughout in patterns of gold and silver thread, with only enough jewelry to accent.

Aefric and Ser Yrsa hadn't taken time to change, which might have made some people uncomfortable. But despite the efforts of his valets, Aefric had yet to develop any pressing need to change his outfit for a meal. Especially if doing so would make others wait.

But Aefric felt confident in his navy blue silk. And as for Ser Yrsa, the woman was so comfortable in her full plate armor that she could likely sleep in it and wake up refreshed.

Countess Siburh wore brown and gold chiffon. The kind of gown that looked simple at first, but was likely very complex, if one took the time to study it.

At least, Aefric gathered that impression at a glance. The last thing he wanted to do was spend time gazing at a woman's dress, here on the dais in front of everyone.

No doubt his doing so would cause ... interesting rumors.

This meal was served in the Armyrian style, beginning with a light, white palate wine.

Aefric was served that night exclusively by Cyneswith, which he thought was strange. Usually pages didn't handle dinner service. Servants did. And it was true that each of the other diners at the table had a specific servant, making sure they wanted for nothing.

And yet, instead of a servant, Aefric was served by Cyneswith. A message from Ashling to Countess Siburh? Or perhaps to Zoleen? Or was it some kind of statement to the assemblage of nobles and others?

Knowing Ashling, there was more than one purpose and message involved.

Cyneswith, for her part, didn't seem either happy or upset to get assigned to dinner duty. She waited attentively on Aefric, but held a neutral expression, and took no liberties.

On the other hand, Aefric noticed that Countess Siburh kept glancing at her daughter. And whenever she did so, her mouth firmed in displeasure.

If that displeasure was real, and not a misinterpretation on Aefric's part, it didn't show in her conversation. Throughout the salad course — a mixture of greens and sliced root vegetables said to be a local favorite — she maintained pleasant tones as she asked Aefric blasé questions about his visit to Kivash, how he was finding his new castle, and the like.

Aefric kept his answers blandly uninformative. A skill that was new to him but, back in Water's End, Kentigern had assured Aefric he was getting better at it.

During the soup course — a creamy chowder of local shrimp and mussels — Countess Siburh surprised Aefric by saying, "I understand your grace has asserted ducal ownership of the Threepeaks Mountains, over the claims of his vassals."

"The claims of my two counts were improper when they were pressed," Aefric said. "I only corrected this."

"Truly?" Countess Siburh asked, affecting disbelief. "Even though the two counts were allowed to fight a war among themselves over their relative rights to those lands?"

"That was during the stewardship of Duchess Arinda," Aefric said, forcing a smile. "And they were allowed to fight that war not because they had equal or valid claims, but because Arinda's forces were needed elsewhere."

"The pirate queen Nelazzi was causing Arinda problems, I believe," Ashling chimed in. "You know something of the problems she can cause, don't you, Siburh?"

"You know well I do, your grace," Countess Siburh said with a feral smile. "Which is all the more reason why my claims here should be acknowledged."

"Oh, let us not change the subject," Ashling said, smiling with much more evident pleasure than her would-be rival. "We were discussing the Threepeaks."

"Very well," Countess Siburh said. "The point stands that the people of two of your grace's counties shed blood defending their claims. Did they not object to your grace simply ... overruling them?"

Aefric sighed, and set down his spoon. Pity, because there was *just* enough spice to that chowder to give it a really tasty *zing* with each mouthful.

"Let me ask your excellency a question," Aefric said. "Does a duke owe his vassals protection?"

"Of course," Countess Siburh said, eyes narrowed suspiciously. "And obviously your grace knows this fundamental element to our entire structure of government."

"I do," Aefric said, before pressing on. "Now, while a duke is committing substantial resources to dealing with a threat — resources including time, money, and lives — suppose that one or more of his vassals use that threat as a distraction to ... for example ... lay claim to lands not their own. Is that proper?"

"Of course not, your grace," Countess Siburh said. "But the key there is 'lands not their own.' A proper claim is a proper claim, no matter when it's pressed."

"By that logic," Aefric said, "how much worse is it if those vassals press an *improper* claim at such a time?"

Countess Siburh frowned, but did not answer.

"Oh, but this is an easy one, Siburh," Ashling teased. "It takes a *villain* to press a false claim when her liege lord is not in a position to stop her."

"A *false* claim, I suppose," Countess Siburh said.

"Which is key here," Aefric said. "Neither of the two counts involved had any proper claim to the Threepeaks. Which they knew well. They acted because wanted to steal Arinda's mines. And so they moved when she couldn't stop them. And their greed was such that they warred with each other over who would steal the greater share."

"Your grace continues to assert that their claims were false," Countess Siburh said.

"They were," Aefric said. "Unquestionably. Elbar's Blood, one set of those claims were penned *while* the land theft was underway."

"But this was years ago. They took and held that land for quite some time," Countess Siburh said. "They mined its mines, paid their taxes, and defended those lands during the Godswalk Wars."

"All based on a false pretense," Aefric said.

"Nevertheless," Countess Siburh said. "It was done without objection or even complaint from their liege. Not at the time, nor in the years that followed. They took that land. Held, worked, and defended that land. For *years*. Even if the initial claim were later called into question — as you say you've done — they *earned* a claim by right of blood, did they not?"

"Tell her, Aefric," Ashling said, locking eyes with the countess.

"There are a number of ways I could address that question," Aefric said. "But I'm going to raise two points. The first is that, by your own logic, the Threepeaks are mine because I took them back and my vassals couldn't stop me."

Contess Siburh nodded, as though accepting that point, but otherwise unconvinced.

"The second is, in my opinion, even more important. And it's something I emphasized as I took back those lands." Aefric leaned a little closer. "Theft or abuse from my vassals will be punished. Such punishments might be delayed, if they act while my attention is needed elsewhere. But when the hammer falls, they will know who swings it."

"Couldn't have said it better myself," Ashling said, smiling at Countess Siburh. "Shall we move on to the main course?"

THE MAIN COURSE THAT NIGHT WAS BOAR. APPARENTLY THERE'D BEEN A boar hunt during the prior aett, and enough boars had been killed that — after given time to cure — they could feed even the vast assemblage of Ashling's court in Kivash.

The boar was finely roasted with spices that managed to bring out the flavor of the meat, without any of its gaminess. And Aefric didn't know what culinary magic those cooks had worked, but the flesh of that boar practically melted in his mouth.

Marvelous.

The boar was served with a delightful mixture of corn and tara, and a heavily buttered rye bread.

Although Aefric's time with his soup had been foreshortened, he got plenty of time with his boar, because Ashling and Countess Siburh seemed to be involved in their own conversation. One that involved only occasional words — apparently unrelated to anything else around them — interspersed with significant nods towards a noble here and a merchant there, throughout the main floor of the great hall.

It seemed to be half a verbal fencing match of sorts, and half a united front against some of the others in the room. If Aefric read the cues right.

Not to say that Aefric was left entirely to himself. He spoke of local military matters with Ecgnoth and Ser Yrsa. Enough to give him a sense that Kivash was more settled than he'd been led to believe.

The locals might still be finding their equilibrium under Ashling's leadership, but the two largest pockets of local resistance had been quelled in the last several days. And there were indications that, barring significant funding from outside Kivash, the back of the remaining resistance might be broken.

Nothing would be certain until early autumn, but Ecgnoth seemed to think that Kivash was finally coming to accept that it was part of Armyr and Merrek now.

Aefric even had the chance to exchange a few pleasantries with Zoleen, who maintained a reserved tone and expression.

She did glance speculatively at Cyneswith, though, every time the page refilled Aefric's wineglass, or brought him anything.

Still, compared to that discussion at the end of the soup course, the main course was downright peaceful.

Aefric even had time to appreciate the music.

Of course, the music hadn't actually started until the main course, but even so, he was glad of it. Six players, all with lutes. Two with lutes tuned well down into the bass range, two handling the middle ranges, and two working the upper registers.

As they played, the players sang wordlessly, letting their harmonies tell their stories for them.

The music they made was hauntingly beautiful.

Before Aefric knew it, the main course was finished, and followed swiftly by dessert: roasted apples, served with honey and cinnamon.

As Aefric was finishing his dessert, Ashling said to him — in tones loud enough to carry — "Properly speaking, I should welcome your grace to Kivash with a feast. Dancing. Perhaps a hunt."

"Certainly *I* would so welcome your grace," Countess Siburh said, "should he visit *me*."

"And so I would," Ashling said, smiling as though she'd expected Countess Siburh to say exactly that, "were these normal circumstances. But given the excitement your grace has been facing in taming the wilds of Hrafnvigi, needing spell and steel both. Well. I would have to be a selfish woman to demand that you *socialize* following a day of such trials."

Wait. Was Ashling letting him off the hook for the post-dinner gathering? Certainly she was performing for the crowd. There was no other reason for her to call him "your grace."

"No," she said, with sadness that Aefric could tell was entirely affected for the crowd's benefit. "Much as I would like to let my court have the chance to converse with you at length, to hear your astute opinions on whatever matters they find most pressing, I cannot bring myself to demand this of you.

"In fact," she said, voice getting a little louder now, "I believe I know you well enough to say that, even exhausted as you doubtless are from your efforts today, you are such a good guest that you would *want* to meet my court and laugh and drink with them late into the night. Or am I mistaken?"

She raised a sculpted raven eyebrow at Aefric, who knew a cue when he heard one.

He smiled and nodded.

"Your grace is most perceptive," he said, hoping he knew where this was going. "As your guest, I feel a responsibility to be available to your court. And as I now have a castle here in Kivash, I can hardly deny the local nobles and merchant lords some of my time."

"Ah," Ashling said, "I knew your grace would be so kind as that." She shook her head with mock sadness. "But may I give your grace some advice, from one who has held her title *just* a little longer than he has?"

A few of the nobles at the nearby tables chuckled appreciatively at her understatement.

"Of course," Aefric said. "Your grace knows I welcome her opinion. Even if I often plunge ahead along my own path all the same."

That got a few appreciative laughs as well.

"As do we all," Ashling said with a laugh. "But my advice would be, forgo gracing my court with your presence for this visit. Your grace has a great deal to do, and a castle that puts forth more resistance than it should. I would hate to see your grace's reactions slowed tomorrow because of his goodwill tonight."

Never before had Aefric honestly felt the desire to kiss Ashling. But she was letting him off the hook for a night of dealing a room full of manticora.

All right, they were only nobles and merchants. But they were certainly as deadly as manticora, in their own way.

He sighed. "I fear there is wisdom in your words. But I would not wish to seem a poor guest."

"Have no fear on that account," Ashling said. "My court will understand. They know that your grace's life and health must come first, for the good of all Armyr."

She stood and raised her wineglass. "Armyr."

Everyone in the room stood and confirmed the toast before drinking.

A clever maneuver of its own, since even the locals were forced to confirm that toast, or be seen not doing so...

Ashling made a show of draining her goblet then, so Aefric matched her.

She turned to him. Took his hands.

"When next you visit Kivash," she said, "we will feast and dance and hunt. We will play games, and talk late into the night."

She shook her head. "But for this visit, we must all put our selfish desires behind our duty to Armyr, and insist that your grace rest for the trials his new castle sets him."

Aefric forced a sigh.

"Then I shall look forward to the pleasures of that next visit," Aefric said. "And for tonight, I shall take my leave."

"I trust your grace won't be offended if Cyneswith here sees you safely to your rooms?"

That set the room buzzing with speculation.

But up at the main table, Countess Siburh gave Aefric a considering glance, Zoleen glowered at her sister, and Cyneswith blushed a pretty shade of pink.

"Not at all," Aefric said.

"Then I bid you goodnight," Ashling said, and kissed Aefric on both cheeks.

The first time she'd done that — this past spring — Aefric hadn't known what it meant. He'd since learned that it was a public declaration of friendship between nobles.

So he returned the gesture this time, which increased the buzz of the crowd.

Aefric then turned, took the Brightstaff in hand from where it stood beside his chair, and followed Cyneswith out of the great hall.

AEFRIC AND CYNESWITH WERE FOLLOWED THROUGH THE CASTLE BY ALL of his knights save for Ser Deirdre. She must've opted to stay behind and see something of Ashling's court in Kivash.

Aefric hoped she didn't cause too much trouble.

As Cyneswith led Aefric out of the great hall and down a hallway to the first set of stairs, she showed a marked contrast to the playful girl of the night before.

She was quiet. Subdued, even.

Could she have been nervous about Ashling's implications?

Did she think Aefric was expecting her to do more than escort him to his rooms? Perhaps even remain with him for the noble privilege?

Aefric considered that as they reached the first stairway. A broad, marble thing, with a calinwood handrail etched in gold. The echoes were bright as they started up those stairs. The hard soles of his knights' boots sounded like an entire company of troops on the march.

Aefric decided that the clamor would work as cover for conversation.

"Don't let Ashling's words trouble you," Aefric said. "I expect you only to guide me to my rooms."

Cyneswith shook her head and looked at him, eyes puzzled. She ducked her head in a quick bow.

"Please do excuse me, your grace," she said. "My mind was else-where, and I missed your grace's words."

Well, she didn't *sound* as though she were expecting Aefric to make sexual demands of her. That was good, at least.

"What troubles you so?" he asked.

"My mother," Cyneswith said with a sigh. "I should not admit this, but I fear she is overmatched against her grace."

"I take it that the Ol'Cynerstan family has an old claim to Kivash?"

"Mother says we do," Cyneswith said, "through a larger claim to this part of the Indecisive River Valley."

"And Ashling disputes this claim, I expect."

"Her grace..." Cyneswith sighed and shook her head. "Her grace has pointed out that if prior claims were being considered, then the Fyrenn family's has precedence."

"Of course," Aefric said, then lost his train of thought as they rounded a landing, and slipped through a small, side door into a narrow passage Aefric didn't recognize.

Walls, ceiling and floor were all bare white stone here. Well swept, but without any of the decorative flair that Ashling had been showing through the rest of the castle.

Not even the smell of flowers in the air here, but the vague scent of old stone, and oil from the lamps they passed every twenty steps or so.

"Where are we?" he asked.

"Forgive me, your grace," Cyneswith said with another duck of her head. "This is a more direct route to the stairs that lead to your grace's tower. It's less pleasant to look upon, but—"

"More direct is fine," Aefric said. "Especially if we're less likely to wander into, say, any wandering nobles who disagree with Ashling's decision about freeing me from social obligations for this visit."

"Another brilliant move on her grace's part," Cyneswith said, wincing slightly.

"How so?" Aefric asked. "I mean, obviously Ashling wanted me in front of her court when your mother raised the question of the Threepeaks, but what else are you seeing here?"

"Your grace," Cyneswith said, looking forward and not at Aefric, "has a reputation for honesty and directness. There are ... many small matters here in Kivash that remain in question."

"Ah," Aefric said. "And the locals all wanted to put their questions to me, in the hopes that I would see things their way, not Ashling's. And thus, weaken her hold. Which would open the way for your mother to gain more local support, helping her own claim."

"Just so, your grace," Cyneswith said.

Huh. Apparently Aefric *had* been learning a few things about politics over the last season or so.

"And now, even if any of the nobles or other locals get to speak with me, they won't get to do so publicly." Aefric shook his head. "If I didn't know better, I'd suspect Ashling gave me a castle she knew would be full of trouble."

"Oh, no, your grace," Cyneswith stopped just shy of a tight spiral staircase, urgency in her brown eyes. "Her grace was furious when she learned that your knights had been injured exploring a castle she gave you."

Aefric chuckled. "She just didn't let that stop her from finding a way to use that fact to her advantage."

Cyneswith sighed and began leading Aefric up those stone, spiral stairs.

"And that is why Mother will lose," Cyneswith said, sadly. "Her grace can find advantage in setback as no one else can. Everyone in the great hall tonight knew that she gave your grace Hrafnvigi. Her grace made sure of that. And then to have your grace's knights take injury there, most would totter and fall after such a mistake. But not her grace."

Cyneswith shook her head. "Never her grace."

They continued in silence for a time, but a question flitted back into Aefric's mind.

"The Fyrenn family claim you spoke of," Aefric said. "That goes back to the principality of Fyr?"

"Yes, your grace," Cyneswith said. "The whole of the Indecisive River Valley was part of Fyr, and under Fyrenn rule. As well as other lands north and south of it."

"But that was centuries ago, before Armyr existed," Aefric said. "Which is your mother's point, I take it? That this is Armyr now, and only Armyrian claims should matter?"

"Yes, your grace," Cyneswith said, turning and looking hopefully at Aefric. "Would your grace care to issue an opinion on the topic?"

Aefric's knights halted a respectful distance back, just far enough back down the spiral staircase that Sers Beornric and Yrsa could keep watch. Just in case.

"I can't," Aefric said, heart sinking to so disappoint Cyneswith's hopeful eyes. "But not because Ashling is my friend, or my hostess, or any other such reason."

"Then might I be permitted to ask your grace why your grace will not issue an opinion? For surely your grace is entitled to one."

"I don't know enough," he said. "This is the sort of question I would put to my historian, to find out what precedents have been established."

Aefric gestured for them to keep moving, and spoke again as they started up those stairs once more.

"You see, I know what my instinct would be. But this is not a matter of instinct. This is a matter of law. And I would rely on my ducal historian to tell me what rulings have already been made by the kings and queens of Armyr on the subject of the precedence of prior claims. Most importantly whether or not past kings and queens have accepted claims which predate Armyr itself."

"Your grace is as direct and honest as his reputation," Cyneswith said, and led them in silence for a time.

Up a great many flights of stairs, in fact, before one landing led to a door. This led to another hall that had not yet seen the blessings of Ashling's eye as a decorator. Plain stone and oil lamps in sconces.

That hall led to a door, though, and once through it, Aefric recognized the stairs they mounted as those that led up into the tower where his rooms were.

As they mounted those stairs, Aefric frowned at Cyneswith's silence.

"I hope I haven't upset you," he said.

"The situation upsets me, not your grace," Cyneswith said, giving Aefric a smile that didn't quite reach her eyes. "Mother is in a difficult position, and I fear I see no good way out for her."

"You make it sound as though she stands to lose more than Kivash."

"Mother has challenged her liege lord," Cyneswith said. "Does your grace understand what that means?"

Aefric thought about that for a flight of stairs.

"It means that she's staking her reputation on this issue," Aefric said. "If she loses..."

He shook his head. "She'll lose allies, won't she?"

"Not completely," Cyneswith said. "She'll still be countess, and our county is the greatest in Merrek. She'll remain a force to be reckoned with. But Mother *will* lose standing with her allies. And the loss will cost her in negotiations for at least a season. Perhaps a year or more."

She very deliberately looked away up the stairs to the first vase of fresh daisies Aefric had seen and smelled for some time on this walk.

"The loss will also set back my marriage prospects. The families of prospective husbands will insist on waiting to see if this error of Mother's is an aberration or indicative of a trend."

"I'm sorry to hear that," Aefric said softly.

"Your grace has no need to be," Cyneswith said, flashing Aefric a shy smile. "Your grace has already been a great help to me. Covering my ... impulsiveness with the flattery that I charmed your grace into considering me a potential bride. That will do more to draw interest to me than any factor other than my future title."

Aefric wasn't sure what to say to that. His instinct was to try to boost her confidence. To tell her how much she had to offer, and the like. But that impulse had gotten him into trouble before...

"Even now," Cyneswith continued, her voice calm and strong though she flushed bright red, "there are those down in the great hall who will believe that your grace intends to seek bliss with me tonight."

Aefric was deciding how to tell her that she was simply too young for him to think of that way, when Cyneswith spoke again.

"I know better, of course," she said. "Her grace has made clear that your grace is to be offered *leaba* each night while he remains her guest here at Ottarvigi. And while I qualify for the noble privilege, I could not, of course, offer your grace *leaba*."

They reached the door to Aefric's rooms then, and Cyneswith turned to face Aefric full-on. All of his knights — save for Ser Deirdre of course — stood nearby, watching.

"I know I stand only the slimmest chance of one day becoming your grace's bride," Cyneswith said softly. "But I should be most pleased to come to your grace's rooms one night."

Looking into those brown eyes, Aefric could only answer honestly. "A night I'll look forward to one day."

For a brief time after Cyneswith's departure, Aefric was joined in his first sitting room by Sers Beornric and Yrsa.

They sat on dark red couches, looking out through wide glass windows over the city below, and sipping on a dark beer brought out by a mousy, but efficient serving lad.

The dark beer was rich, and nutty, and seemed to round out the evening's dinner well.

"That was quite a display," Ser Yrsa said.

"Oh, I don't know," Ser Beornric said. "She didn't go in for a kiss, which I half-expected her to."

"I *meant* down in the great hall at dinner," Ser Yrsa said, arching the split brow above her red eye.

"Oh, that," Ser Beornric said with a smile in his voice. "Before we get into that, may I just say one thing?"

Ser Yrsa nodded for him to proceed.

Ser Beornric stroked his mustaches, then turned a broad smile on Aefric. "I'd say we have another contestant for your hand."

"Did you really kiss her hand?" Ser Yrsa asked.

Aefric only got as far as nodding before Ser Beornric grimaced and said, "Well, it's the girl's own fault for offering it."

"Still shouldn't've," Ser Yrsa said, shaking her head before taking another sip of beer.

"I know, I know," Aefric said. "Which is why I let Ashling spread the rumor that I did it because Cyneswith had charmed me."

"Knew it wasn't her charms," Ser Yrsa said. "Nothing against the girl, but the way your grace's social calendar has been since becoming duke, she's hardly enough to get your attention."

"Or *is* she?" Ser Beornric said teasingly. "Has your grace decided—"

"Oh, *enough*," Aefric said. "You both know me too well for that."

"Then can we talk about what happened in the great hall?" Ser Yrsa asked.

"What?" Aefric said. "Did you expect me to lie about the Threepeaks?"

"Of course not," Ser Yrsa said, "but did your grace know about the dispute regarding Kivash?"

"That Countess Siburh disputes Ashling's right to claim it as ducal land? Yes. But no details. I don't know the source of her claim."

"Did you know that Duchess Ashling has been saying that Countess Siburh's claim isn't just inferior, but entirely without merit?"

"No," Aefric said.

"It's true," Ser Beornric said. "Ashling's stance is that the papers that form the foundation of Countess Siburh's claim were forged."

"So my point about the Threepeaks..."

"Will be interpreted as siding with Duchess Ashling," Ser Beornric said. "Especially since no one can prove differently because she just cut off access to you."

"I'm not sorry about that part," Aefric said. "I'm too tired to deal with that rabid pack of werewolves down in the great hall."

"And before you departed the great hall, you kissed Ashling on both cheeks," Ser Yrsa said. "Powerful statement."

"Look," Aefric said with a sigh. "I know Ashling is getting some mileage out of all this—"

"Getting what?" Ser Yrsa asked.

Huh. Another of Keifer's sayings from Earth had slipped in without Aefric noticing. Odd.

"Sorry," Aefric said. "Old Sartis street jargon for covering a lot of distance with very little effort. Point is, of course Ashling is using my presence here to her advantage. That's what she does. Why should I begrudge her though?"

Ser Yrsa frowned. Sighed.

"Your grace," she said. "You must remember that Ashling plays a very long game. What you do to aid her now may come back—"

"—to haunt me later," Aefric said. "I understand. But I also understand something else. I'm better off with her as an ally than as an enemy. And so far, she's been a good ally."

"So *far*," Ser Yrsa said.

"And when the day comes that she gives me reason to doubt her—"

"It will be too late," Ser Yrsa said, "and she will already have completed the move you didn't see coming."

"Yrsa," Aefric said.

"Your grace," Ser Yrsa said.

"What is the purpose of scouting?"

Ser Yrsa frowned, then sighed. "I see your point, but—"

"*What* is the purpose of scouting?"

"To keep an eye on one's enemies," Ser Yrsa said shortly. "And of course it's easier to keep an eye when you know where they are. And of course it's easier to do this when they think you're allies. But do you intend to tell me that you're faking your friendship? Because I will find that very hard to believe."

"Of course not," Aefric said. "But my role is to be honest. To forge alliances and make friends. To guide in the best way that I can."

"Ah," Ser Yrsa said, understanding. "So your grace would not bind *me* from ensuring that a weather eye is kept on, shall we say, Fyrenn influence?"

"Bind you from it?" Aefric said, chuckling. "By the gods I *rely* on your doing it."

He raised his tankard in toast. "To each of us serving Deepwater and Armyr as best we can."

They drank to that, then. And they drank together for a while longer, discussing their plans for their continuing investigation of Hrafnvigi.

But as the hour grew later, the time came for his knight-advisers to seek their sleep.

Aefric mounted the stairs in his apartments to his bedroom, then, and began to undress. Sleep would be welcome, and Ashling had provided him a bed that was more than good enough for the job.

Not so large as his beds at Behal and Water's End, but the feather bed was still far grander and softer than anything Aefric had known during his adventuring days. Well-stuffed, with silk sheets, and a silk canopy suspended from four posts.

Aefric was in his closet, hanging up his tunic and about to see to his pants when Ser Leppina called up the stairs.

"Your grace," she said. "Two serving women ask for admittance."

Two again? If Ashling kept this up, and word got out, some nobles might never be satisfied with a single offering of *leaba* again.

But perhaps he was mistaken. Perhaps they'd come for some other purpose.

Aefric took the Brightstaff in hand, but didn't bother putting his tunic back on as he descended the white stone stairs to see about his visitors.

He found waiting for him in the pink sitting room the same two serving women from the night before. The one with long blonde hair, the other whose black hair she kept cut short. Both pretty and tanned and shapely, even in their livery.

And the way they smiled as their eyes devoured Aefric made clear why they'd come before either ever said the word, *"leaba."*

6

Not long after dawn the next morning, Aefric and his knights returned to Castle Hrafnvigi to continue their exploration.

Once inside, rather than taking the main stairs and expected doors, they traveled through the series of secret passages that began all the way down with the first floor guest rooms, and continued on up, seemingly through the whole of the castle.

His knights, of course, were keeping an eye out for threats, as well as helping him generally search the castle and get a sense of what remained from the previous owners.

Aefric, though, had an extra purpose now. One he didn't share with the others. Not because he felt the need to hide it, but because they couldn't help him.

Not even Ser Deirdre. For though she had a good nose for magic, to say that a dweomerblade's skill at finding and understanding the magic of clay and stone was *limited* was to understate the matter.

Such magic was practically a blind spot in her vision.

So it would be up to Aefric himself to find the clues he needed. Assuming that they existed. That that this castle was indeed patterned after the work of the great Raend. Or even built by that storied *vohlcairn* himself.

A wonderful idea. If Aefric could find proof.

Perhaps a heart to the keep. Something that would help Aefric unlock its secrets. Relimmorea's imp certainly implied as much.

But if so, the day's exploration began with little sign that this was anything more than an ordinary castle.

The third and fourth floors presented no challenges to their new owner, save enough dust to choke a small animal. So much dust here that even by the light of Aefric's spells, the air seemed hazy. He and his knights kept wet cloths over their mouths and noses to help their breathing.

These two floors were mostly living spaces, likely for family and important others. Very few single rooms, mostly apartments of two to four rooms each, as well as parlors, and a game room on each floor devoted to bowling.

While the rooms and apartments were finely furnished, and there were clearly personal possessions and moneys left behind, it was also clear that most of these rooms had been vacated well before Armyr had taken Kivash.

Ser Yrsa guessed that the denizens of these two floors had likely been off at the front, for the war. And thus, had likely been caught up in the events of Frozen Ridge.

The fifth floor looked to have been dedicated to storage. Extra furniture that might be needed for private rooms. A variety of games for the game rooms, and other such things.

Whole sections of that floor, though, had been emptied entirely. As though they might have served some purpose many, many years ago. But it was a purpose that the Hrafntonn family saw little need to perpetuate.

Searching that floor made for a pleasant variation in one sense. The secret passages were tight quarters, but the main hall along each floors was wide enough to fight a skirmish, if needed. And all those empty rooms had helped remind Aefric that he wasn't just sneaking through cramped passages, he was claiming a new castle.

That was easy to lose track of in those tight, stone passages full of dust, where he was practically tripping over his knights.

They stopped for water from their skins at the end of every floor. As much to remoisten their clothes and rinse the dust out of their mouths as because any of them thirsted.

Back in the secret passages, mounting the stairs to the sixth floor, they followed the same order they'd been following.

Ser Deirdre up front, keeping an eye out for magic, followed by Sers Yrsa and Beornric, then Aefric, then the Knights of the Lake.

Up the tight stone stairwell they went, until Ser Deirdre reached a landing.

"This door is locked," she said, sounding offended.

"How can it be?" Ser Yrsa asked. "Is there an actual place for a key?"

"I have the keys," Ser Beornric said. "If you two wedge aside, I'll—"

"There's no keyhole," Ser Deirdre said. "There *is* some magic to it. Yes. There's a spell lock. Shall I handle it, your grace?"

"Wait," Aefric said, then cast his spell to detect traps and checked the door.

Or tried to. There were three knights in his way, and two of them were fairly large individuals, even when they weren't wearing full plate armor. Which they were that day.

"I have to get past," Aefric said.

"This sounds like a bad idea, your grace," Ser Yrsa said. "Better to take the regular stairs up and come at this from the other side."

"She's right," Ser Beornric said. "Something goes wrong, your grace will be up front with none of us able to move to assist."

"I could move to assist," Ser Deirdre said.

"It's still a pinch point," Ser Yrsa said, "and still a bad idea."

"Let me at least see if it's trapped," Aefric said.

Sers Yrsa and Beornric tightened against the side of the stairwell as much as they could, while Aefric did his best to slip past them.

One advantage to silk, over armor. Though silk did show the dirt more readily than armor did. The brightness of Aefric's red silk shirt had been dulled by dust, as had the dark orange of his hose, though the effect was less visible there.

Aefric noticed that Ser Deirdre made little effort to move aside as he reached the small landing beside her. If anything, she seemed to press against him.

"Excuse me, your grace," she said softly, her jade green eyes smiling. "Have to stay near at hand, in case your grace needs me."

Interesting. Ser Deirdre smelled like violets. He'd never noticed that before.

Aefric cast his trap-detecting spell, but through the yellow diamond the oak door looked clean. Nothing reddened to indicate a trap.

"Clear," Aefric said, then frowned. "But there's more magic here than the spell lock."

"I stand by my course of action," Ser Yrsa said. "We should go back down and come up by the main stairs."

"I don't know," Ser Deirdre said softly, close enough that Aefric could feel the warmth of her breath on his neck. Which meant she'd removed the moist cloth from her mouth. "There's something to be said for close quarters work."

"Give me a moment to examine the spellwork," Aefric said, doing his best to ignore Ser Deirdre's flirting.

He quickly determined that the spell lock had been cast by the same magic-user who'd trapped the treasury.

But what was the other magic?

Something ... latent. Waiting. On the other side of the door...

"There's some kind of latent magic on the other side of the door," Aefric said.

"Please, your grace," Ser Yrsa said. "Come back down."

"It's not a trap," Aefric said. "But I think you're right."

"What about the spell lock?" Ser Deirdre said. "Would your grace disarm that first?"

Aefric turned to her. "Why? So you can open the door?"

Ser Deirdre's teeth gleamed with her smile. "The door must be opened at some point, your grace. Otherwise your grace will be creating ever so much more work for his servants."

"That's not an answer," Aefric said.

"Does your grace order me not to open the door?"

Aefric chuckled. "I know how well you take to orders."

"Depends on the order," she said softly.

"How about this?" Aefric said. "I'm going to *ask* you not to open that door, until we've seen what's there from the other side."

Ser Deirdre sighed. "Very well, your grace. Whether your grace disarms the spell lock or not, I shall leave that door closed until your grace asks to have it opened."

"Thank you, Ser Deirdre."

Aefric turned away.

"Your grace isn't going to disarm the spell lock?" Ser Deirdre asked.

"No," Aefric said, shaking his head. "Not until I know what that latent magic does. And I'm not going to take the time to try to examine it. Not with all of you waiting here on the stairs. It'll keep for now."

Ser Deirdre chuckled softly, as Aefric resumed his place in the marching order and followed his knights back down to the fifth floor.

BACK IN THE MAIN PART OF THE CASTLE ON THE FIFTH FLOOR, THE DUST was not so thick as it was in the secret passages.

Here the wide stairwell that continued from the lower floors on up to the sixth had clearly seen a lot of use right up until the time that the Hrafntonn family was required to vacate their castle with only the clothes on their backs.

Here, Sers Temat and Micham took the lead — each carrying a blade lit by Aefric's spells, followed closely by Ser Deirdre, who kept an eye out for magic. Sers Yrsa and Beornric came next, followed closely by Aefric, with the Brightstaff's diamond aglow. Then Sers Vria and Arras, with Sers Leppina and Wardius on rear guard, also with blades lit by Aefric's magic.

The stairwell led to more than just a landing. The area at the top of the stairs was wide and long, and clearly had seen a great deal of use in combat training for the family. Cabinets full of padded armor along one side, matched by others with blunted steel weapons on the other side. At the far end, a series of calinwood bookcases full of texts about martial theory, mostly dedicated to combat at the level of individuals and small groups.

The windows here stood a startling contrast to those below. From the first floor through the third, there were only arrow slits. The fourth and fifth had small but respectable arched, glass windows. Perhaps as wide as Aefric's forearm was long.

But here in the training area, the windows were large enough for Aefric and all his knights to stand abreast without any of them feeling crowded.

When they stood near the library, they could look down over the city and the river, with the harbor off to the left. When they looked out of the windows near the stairs, their view encompassed much of the city, as well as the city walls, and the foothills to the south.

A main hall split off from the center of the training area, and looked to travel the breadth of the castle.

"Which direction, your grace?" Ser Yrsa asked, with an expression that made clear Aefric shouldn't raise the idea of splitting the group.

Not that he intended to. As an adventurer, he'd learned the folly of splitting the party when exploring new territory. And as duke, he'd seen the same problems play out on their very first day here at Hrafnvigi.

He had no intention of letting his knights get injured again. At least, not in his own castle.

"Towards the latent magic, I assume?" Ser Deirdre asked eagerly, standing near the entrance to the hall that would take them that way.

"No," Aefric said. "That'll keep for last, just in case it's a false lead."

They started down the hallway the opposite direction then.

The main hallway here was as wide as Aefric had come to expect, after the fourth and fifth floors. But this one was far better appointed. Cherry hardwood flooring on the white stone, and plastered walls painted a red so pale it was almost pink.

A series of paintings depicted past Hrafntonn patriarchs and matriarchs. A vicious looking crew.

Small iron statues of warriors — each no more than two hands tall — graced marble pillars between the paintings.

Two sitting rooms, very well appointed. Then a series of guest apartments. Each with multiple chambers, and furnishings fine enough to house visiting royalty.

Some of his knights gave small whistles of appreciation at the furnishings in those apartments, and at the rich clothes in the closets. Even with all the dust, it still made an impressive sight.

At the end of the hall, a small, undecorated side passage ran from the back of the castle to the front.

A series of small rooms here were clearly for the favored servants. Or perhaps for the servants of those visiting nobles and royals who were staying in the guest rooms here on this floor.

Aefric and his knights did find doors leading from the sitting rooms and guest rooms of this floor into that network of secret passages. But Aefric didn't allow exploring of those passages here and now.

At each end of this smaller hallway, a door in the corner led to stairs up to the tower above.

"Shall we check the towers?" Ser Deirdre asked eagerly.

Aefric nodded.

They started at the front of the castle, going first up into that tower.

Two more small floors here, each perhaps five strides across. The first floor housed a guard station, and the second was split into two rooms. One held four bunks for those guards, in two bunk beds. The other stored a good deal of ballista ammo, which looked like arrows taller than Aefric.

Arrows big and sharp enough to test dragon scales.

More stairs let up onto the top of the tower, where they found the great ballista that needed such ammo. Its drawstring had been cut, and would need replacing. But when in good repair, this ballista could probably hit a target hundreds of yards away. Possibly reaching targets on the far banks of the river.

The whipping wind carried the saltwater scent of the Risen Sea. An impressive view, from up here. The whole of the city, and out beyond the walls, as well.

The second tower matched the first, both in contents, and in the way its ballista had been disabled.

No magic so far.

Aefric and his knights returned to one of the sitting rooms for lunch. They sat on thickly padded couches upholstered with fine silk in dark colors. They snacked on provisions provided by Ashling's kitchen. Leftover boar from dinner — not quite ready to melt in Aefric's mouth today, but still quite good — along with fresh nava fruit and honeyed oat bread, all washed down with water.

Thus refreshed, they started down the last hall.

No paintings or statues on this side. Tapestries. Old ones, that depicted scenes from what looked like Malimfar's history. One likely their discovery of the Indecisive River Valley. Two others were sea battles, and two more land battles. The last involved a castle that could have rivaled Water's End in its size and brilliance.

All of these scenes must've involved the Hrafntonn family. Otherwise, why have them? Or at least, why have them *here*? But if so, the scenes and the people in them were not identified.

Starting from the training room, they found one sitting room down this hall, just as fine as the others on this floor. Facing it, the family armory.

At least, Aefric assumed it was the family armory. The weapons and armor here were of much finer quality than any he'd found in the other armories, save perhaps for the hidden one, behind the dais with the thrones.

These weapons — swords and spears, maces and great hammers, longbows and crossbows and complicated recurve bows — were decorated with gold and gems. The armor was similarly embellished. The suits of chainmail were gold-washed, and the suits of plate mail etched with the Hrafntonn sigil in red gold.

Fine as those weapons were though, Aefric spotted no magic among them.

Empty spaces along the walls indicated that about half of the weapons and armor were missing.

"Likely the missing weapons were up on Frozen Ridge with the family members from the fourth and fifth floors," Ser Beornric said. "Probably their *best* weapons, too."

"That's the way to bet," Ser Yrsa said distractedly. "I know the Hrafntonns weren't allowed to leave with them."

"What are you thinking, General?" Aefric asked.

"This is not a family that surrenders, your grace," Ser Yrsa said. "Consider the artwork we've seen. The training room here that's clearly for family and treasured guests only. The sheer number of armories."

She frowned at Aefric. "They're very militant."

"I agree," Ser Deirdre said. "Must've driven them crazy to be ordered to surrender their keep and leave with only the clothes on their backs."

"That's just it," Ser Yrsa said, turning to Aefric. "I have a great deal of trouble believing that they accepted the surrender order and simply vacated."

"But clearly they did," Ser Beornric said. "They're not here now. And they did leave a few surprises for the next occupants."

"Nevertheless," Ser Yrsa said, gesturing vaguely around. "This is a very defendable castle. They could have held here. Sent for reinforcements. And they'd've had at least two great ballistae to use against occupying forces when Malimfar's armies arrived to retake Kivash."

"Perhaps they feared his grace's magic," Ser Deirdre said. "Frozen Ridge must've made quite an impression."

"Perhaps," Ser Yrsa said, unconvinced. "The problem there, though, is that word couldn't have reached them ahead of Armyr's armies. Or not by much. By all accounts, Armyr caught Kivash completely off-guard."

"Perhaps they feared retribution against the rest of the city, if they tried to hold out?" Aefric asked.

Ser Yrsa scoffed. "Your grace would consider that. These people would not."

"I see one possibility," Ser Beornric said. "Perhaps all of their best warriors and strategists were up on Frozen Ridge. Perhaps those who remained behind weren't up to holding off a siege."

Ser Yrsa nodded. "Could be."

"We know they had a court wizard," Aefric said. "And we know that court wizard had enough time to prepare a few traps."

"You think their wizard was in touch with whoever they had up on Frozen Ridge?" Ser Deirdre asked.

"They'd know reinforcements weren't coming," Aefric said. "They could fight and die — meaning more Hrafntonn dead, on top of whoever they lost at Frozen Ridge — or they could leave and live. Even the most militant family would put survival of their house ahead of any one piece of land."

"Told you he's starting to think like a duke," Ser Beornric said with a smile.

Several of Aefric's other knights joined that smile.

"That makes more sense," Ser Yrsa said. "It also suggests that the Hrafntonns had both some dead and at least one survivor up on Frozen Ridge."

"And that they'll come back," Ser Beornric said. "As soon as they can convince King Eadred to risk it."

"Possibly on their own," Ser Yrsa said. "We'll need to track the escape route down under the castle. Find where it comes out and make sure we control it."

Ser Deirdre whistled, low and long.

Everyone looked at her. She smiled at Aefric.

"Excuse me, your grace," she said. "I was just thinking. Mad as the Hrafntonns must be at us for taking the castle, how much angrier must they be at King Eadred?"

True. The loss of Kivash and Hrafnvigi went back to King Eadred's ill-fated attempt to invade Armyr.

"She has a point," Ser Yrsa said softly. "Not sure how it helps us, though."

"I have an idea on that," Aefric said, "but it'll have to wait. We've more castle to cover."

Beyond the armory and sitting room, down that side of the castle, there were only two more sets of double-doors before the small passage at the end of the hall.

Aefric checked them and pronounced them real doors, and free from traps. And while he was checking, he made sure that there weren't any hidden doors long the hallway itself.

There were not.

Ser Beornric found the keys then, and behind those sets of double-doors were the best appointed apartments in the castle. Even the floorboards in these apartments were of calinwood. Each had a sumptuous bedroom, a private bath with the tub filled and heated by magic, multiple closets — including one closet each just for jewelry.

Sitting rooms, with sets for chess and other strategy games. Private meeting rooms. Each even had a private, personal armory behind a hidden door.

Those two armories had been emptied, suggesting that the occupants had been at Frozen Ridge.

Frozen Ridge.

Aefric realized with a sigh, as he went through those rooms with his knights, that he'd come to accept that shorthand term for what he'd done that day this past spring.

Didn't mean he had to like it.

The secret passages had hidden doors in the sitting rooms of these apartments, but Aefric held off exploring them just a little longer.

Small bits of magic throughout these apartments, mostly involving comfort and convenience. Mattresses that could heat with a command word. Mirrors that could retain and display any image they'd reflected in the past ... half-hour or so. Possibly for comparing outfits.

Aefric did find an interesting twist off of the message spell he knew, on one of the nightstands in the bedroom nearest the river. It was a small statue of a servant.

Anyone could touch that statue and speak, and his or her words would be carried to another room in the castle. Likely a servants' waiting room, or similar.

Ser Deirdre spotted one bit of tactical magic in the apartments. One meeting room held a mirror and map of Kivash and environs that proved to be a scrying device.

Touching any spot the map beneath the mirror caused the mirror to show an aerial view of that region from about two hundred feet above the ground.

Nifty bit of work. Aefric would have to study it at some point, so he could develop something similar for Water's End. And perhaps Behal.

Otherwise, of course, the main magic through those two apartments was scry wards.

The bedrooms of these two apartments also had trapdoor shafts that looked to lead down to an escape passage beneath the keep. The shafts were angled and looked smooth, but Aefric hoped they had a lot of padding at the bottom.

The shafts could wait though. Something else was bothering him about all this opulence.

Aefric was looking over a cloth-of-gold bedroom curtain that shaded out the afternoon sun, when he asked a question.

"Could this have been the Hrafntonn family's primary residence?"

"I doubt it," Ser Yrsa said. "I'd expect their primary residence to be in their own lands, well south of here. Or perhaps near the capital at Svarturvigi. Why do you ask?"

Aefric gestured around him. "Magic for convenience and comfort. Furniture with gold scrollwork. Entire closets full of expensive jewelry. Elbar's Blood, there's a calinwood chest in here filled with enough gold coins to buy a warship. Who invests this much in a secondary residence?"

"Someone rich enough to afford more," Ser Arras said. "Or perhaps someone who comes here to make an impression."

"Why here?" Aefric asked. "We're a long way from Svarturvigi."

"Ah," Ser Arras said, smiling. And in that smile, Aefric wondered if he saw an echo of Duchess Arinda. "But *here* is where they can meet with merchant families from all over Qorunn. Without necessarily involving the royal family."

"Interesting idea," Aefric said.

"Suggests they might use that back entrance for more than just indulging their kinks," Ser Deirdre said.

"It makes sense," Ser Beornric said. "They'd been in Kivash for a long time. They'd want to maintain a strong level of influence here, and money and appearances help that."

"Suggesting," Aefric said, "that they lost more in the war than a castle and some lives. This castle may contain most of their family wealth."

"Yes," Ser Yrsa said, "but they can't recover *that* loss without getting Kivash back first. Coming after us here wouldn't help. Not as long as Duchess Ashling holds the city."

After a survey of those apartments that took longer than Aefric wanted it to — mostly to make sure they didn't miss anything important — Aefric and his knights continued down to the smaller, cross passage at the end of the hall.

More doors for more servants quarters here, each connected to the secret passages that networked the castle. Though one of those rooms was a waiting area with passable couches and simple pinewood tables. In the center of the main table in that room, a small statue of a servant. The delivery portion of that message spell.

At each end of the smaller hall, doors that doubtless led to the towers above.

One tower, the one nearer the harbor, was like the first two. Guard post, guard bunks, and a ballista with its drawstring cut.

The door to the other tower, though, was spell-locked.

"Now we're getting somewhere," Ser Deirdre said, rubbing her hands together.

Ser Deirdre, of course, wanted to go straight after the spell lock.

Aefric called her back. Made his knights stand aside.

He shifted his focus outward and into the flows of Qorunn's magic. From there, he shifted his attention to the spell lock, and past it. He could tell there was more magic nearby, but...

Not close to the door. Good. He'd been worried that there might've been more of that strange latent magic behind this spell lock as well, but no.

It was just as spell-locked door.

He quickly confirmed then through the yellow diamond of the Brightstaff that the door wasn't trapped.

"It's safe," he said.

Ser Deirdre gave Aefric a hopeful look. "May I, your grace?"

Aefric nodded.

For Aefric, picking a spell lock was a matter of mental effort and a small gesture. Apparently, the process worked differently for Ser Deirdre.

Her right hand seemed to wave bonelessly as she used it to trace a sigil in the air. Maroon power followed her hand, scorching the air in its wake, and carrying the scent of burnt berries.

The first one must've been wrong, because she swore softly, shook her head, and wiped away the sigil.

The second was no better. And this time, she gritted her teeth. The other knights made restless noises. Ser Yrsa did nothing more demonstrative than drawing a single breath, but it somehow felt impatient.

Ser Deirdre's gaze flicked quickly to Aefric, as though determined that he not see her fail.

She huffed a deep breath and tried a third time, sketching in the air a more elaborate maroon sigil. And this time, the burning berry smell had a distinctly blackberry flavor to it.

"Hah!" she said, thrusting her hand through the center of the sigil, which flared and broke apart, while the door itself echoed the maroon flare.

Sure enough, the spell lock was now gone.

"Tricky little bastard, but I got it," Ser Deirdre said, shooting Aefric a smile. "May I go first, your grace? In case there's more magic?"

"Slowly and carefully," Aefric said.

"Why should she start now?" Ser Yrsa muttered.

But Ser Deirdre winked at Aefric, drew her rapier, and opened the door.

Stairs going up. One flight.

Door at the top of the stairs. Not locked, because Ser Deirdre opened it.

"Next time let me check for traps first," Aefric said.

"Of course, your grace," Ser Deirdre said. "Plenty of magic here."

Aefric fought not to push past Sers Yrsa and Beornric, who used their armored bulk to make sure Aefric stayed on the stairs, while Ser Yrsa made placating gestures.

"Let her check it out," she said softly. "Deirdre's a good hand at this."

Waiting for Ser Deirdre seemed to take forever. And she didn't help the wait, by oohing and aahing at everything she found, without saying what she was finding.

If each second felt like an hour — and it did — Aefric felt as though he passed half a season waiting for Ser Deirdre to give the all clear.

Finally, she appeared on the landing, silhouetted by bright white light from the room behind her.

"We've found their court wizard's lab," she said. "Most of the magic in here is lingering from past spells, but there's an engraved circle on the floor, plenty of apparatus and..."

Ser Deirdre grinned. "Grimoires! Two shelves of them!"

"Yrsa," Aefric growled.

"Any wards we need to know about?" Ser Yrsa asked, keeping her arms up and ready to hold Aefric back, just in case.

"The grimoires are pretty heavily warded," she said. "More than one layer of wards, I think. That's it. I mean. Apart from the scry wards, of course."

Ser Yrsa nodded, but insisted on herself and Ser Beornric going up first.

The chamber was about five strides across, just like the other towers. No dust in here, though. Peaked windows that shuttered closed, and lacked glass.

Aefric immediately spell-locked them closed. Just in case the former court wizard had a talent for shapeshifting.

Ser Deirdre was right. There was a lot of magic here.

The elaborate circle engraved in the floor, and filled with ... was that topaz? Interesting choice. It wasn't enchanted, per se, but it held the magical detritus of hundreds, perhaps thousands of operations.

"Handy," Ser Deirdre muttered to Aefric. "Having a ready-made circle with that much power to it."

"I'll break it before we head back down," Aefric said, and smiled at the shock in Ser Deirdre's eyes. "For all I know, the wizard who used it can send things to it from a distance. Can't risk that."

"*Thank you,*" Ser Yrsa said sincerely, then checked herself when the other knights clearly fought down chuckles. "I ... appreciate your grace's ... caution."

Aefric chuckled. "I take risks sometimes, but I'm not a fool."

He turned away quickly, in case she might've debated that point.

Magical paraphernalia on the worktables, enchanted to ease and facilitate research, but not in any way that could be used against him.

"Good," Aefric muttered.

The stool beneath the workbench had been enchanted for comfort, but not excessively.

"My guess?" Ser Deirdre said. "That was one overweight magic-user who didn't like his butt getting sore while working."

Aefric chuckled before he could stop himself, which was met with a sparkle of approval from Ser Deirdre's eyes.

On to the library.

Excitement shivered through Aefric. Truly, was there any more wondrous discovery than new magic he could learn?

He was still working his way through the grimoires left behind at Water's End by Duchess Arinda when she passed. And he'd already learned a great many interesting things about the way the Soulfist family approached magic. And more than a few things about magic itself.

But Ser Deirdre was right. The wards on these books ran four layers deep.

"This is going to take time I can't spend right now." Aefric sighed. "In fact, I may have to send Karbin back here to work his way through these wards. I'm not sure I can take the time myself."

Ser Yrsa started to say something, but stopped herself.

Aefric chuckled. "You're welcome, Ser Yrsa."

Ser Yrsa's grin looked feral and slightly threatening. But Aefric knew there was no malice in it. Her grins always looked that way.

"One thing before we move on," he said. And Aefric added his own layer of wards over the top of those grimoires. "Just in case."

"Shall we move up upstairs?" Ser Deirdre asked eagerly.

"A moment, first," Aefric said, and cast his spell to detect doors.

He found a trapdoor on the floor, concealed by illusionary white stone.

"Upstairs can wait," Aefric said, smiling as he dismissed the illusion concealing the door. "We have something else to check out first."

***

There was no lock on the trapdoor in the wizard's tower. Not even a spell lock, which Aefric considered the price of using illusion to conceal a trapdoor.

On the one hand, using a spell lock would be a more certain way of protecting what lay beneath. Because magic-users were not exactly common to begin with. And spell locks could keep out even a fair percentage of magic-users.

Aefric had developed a good deal of skill at dealing with spell locks in the course of his adventuring. Not to mention that he'd been trained by Karbin, the Iron Wands, and Kainemorton himself, though the years.

Few spell locks could keep Aefric out.

Illusion, on the other hand, would be better than a lock, in the sense that most people would overlook it. And the illusion covering this trapdoor had been good enough to fool even Ser Deirdre, who normally had a good eye for such things, for a dweomerblade.

It hadn't fooled Aefric, because while the illusion deceived his eye, it couldn't deceive his door-detecting spell.

But the choice had to be one or the other. The spell lock or the illusion. Not both. Because hiding a spell lock under an illusion was much, much trickier than just making a trapdoor look like part of the floor.

Trying to cover both would require more senses, more approaches, and, in general, a lot more work than added benefit.

Of course, once discovered, most any illusion could be broken pretty easily.

Must've looked impressive, though, from the way his knights murmured about Aefric's calling their attention to a trapdoor that hadn't been there the moment before.

It was an iron door, that could be pulled up with a small, thin rope.

Made the illusion work all the more impressive. Any of them might've stepped on that cord and not noticed.

"May I, your grace?" Ser Deirdre asked.

Aefric nodded.

Rapier in hand, Ser Deirdre shot Aefric a grin and pulled back the trapdoor.

Stairs leading down into darkness.

Ser Deirdre shot Aefric another grin, and limned her rapier in a deep reddish glow.

"You can see by that?" Aefric asked.

"Quite clearly, your grace," she said, "and its light isn't visible from very far."

She drew her dueling dagger in her off-hand and descended the steps slowly, showing more caution than Aefric expected.

"Tight confines, here at the bottom," she said. "Cabinets and…"

She whistled. "Found the reagents, your grace."

"Any lingering magic?" Ser Yrsa asked.

"Nothing," Ser Deirdre said. "Not down here."

"I'm going," Aefric said, and without waiting for a yea or nay from his knights, followed Ser Deirdre down the stairs.

The confines *were* tight at the bottom of the stairs. It looked like a small room, made smaller by floor-to-ceiling cabinets full of drawers.

Tight enough down there that Ser Deirdre had to sheathe her weapons to make room for Aefric. Fortunately the Brightstaff afforded more than enough light.

Though he noticed she made no move to leave. Instead she "made room" in such a way that they were pressed together as soon as he reached the bottom of the stairs.

As her violet scent reached his nostrils, Aefric found himself uncomfortably aware of the way her chest pressed against his arm.

From the smile in her jade green eyes, he didn't think it was accidental.

"Excuse me, your grace," she whispered, slipping an arm between them so that her fingers could reach the handle of a small drawer. "I wanted to make sure your grace didn't miss this."

She pulled open the drawer.

It was a drawer full of diamonds, each of sufficient size, cut, and clarity to be worth the cost of a good set of full plate armor. Not to mention its enameling, engraving, and likely other adornments besides.

"Useful for enchantment," she said softly. "Wouldn't your grace agree?"

Aefric nodded. The dust of an expensive diamond, properly crushed in a mortar and pestle, was a key ingredient in many long-lasting spells and enchantments.

"Not all of these drawers hold such value in gold, of course," she whispered. "But this lab appears to be *very* well stocked."

"Very," Aefric agreed, checking a few more drawers. Rare herbs. A unicorn's horn. Some teeth that looked draconic…

Of course, checking the contents of these cabinets was difficult with Ser Deirdre pressed up against him.

He turned to her, their faces inches apart.

"Ser Deirdre."

"Yes, your grace?"

"Are you expecting something in these drawers to attack me?"

"Best to be safe, your grace."

Aefric verified that he could sense no magic down here, then added a quick check for doors and traps as well.

"I think it's safe enough," he said. "I can catalog it all later."

"Of course, your grace," she said, lips slightly parted now.

"Ser Deirdre?"

"Yes, your grace?"

"It's time for us to go back up the stairs."

"Must we, your grace?" she asked with a mischievous smile. "I find this position quite agreeable."

"Ser Deirdre—"

"As my duke, your grace can forgo my courtesy anytime he likes, I hope he knows this. In fact," — her gaze flicked to Aefric's lips — "I suspect I'll enjoy hearing my name on your grace's lips more if *not* preceded by my courtesy."

"Deirdre?"

She shivered a little. "Yes, your grace?"

"We're almost done exploring this castle. I'd like to finish."

Her eyes sparkled with mirth. "Of course, your grace. I'm always happy to help your grace finish."

He smiled despite himself, which made her grin.

"After you?" he said, nodding to the stairs.

"Oh, no, your grace," she said softly. "It wouldn't be proper. I am just a knight, after all."

"I doubt you're *just* anything."

Ser Deirdre smiled. "Your grace always knows what to say."

Aefric started up the stairs, with Ser Deirdre two steps behind him, weapons in her hands once more.

"Of course," she said softly, "if your grace ever offers me the chance to *finish* first, I'd be only too happy to accept."

When Aefric and Ser Deirdre rejoined the others in the wizard's lab, Ser Yrsa frowned at Ser Deirdre. Muttered something to her while Aefric put a spell lock on the trapdoor that led down to those wonderful cabinets full of reagents.

Aefric suspected that his general would have words with Ser Deirdre later about proper comportment around one's liege. And she had a point.

But Aefric had to admit, he enjoyed Deirdre's flirting. And more importantly, he'd hate to see anything dampen the woman's spirit.

Ser Vria moved to check the door at the back of the room.

"Wait," Aefric said. "Everyone back onto the stairs."

"Your grace?" Ser Beornric asked.

"Behind that door is likely a set of stairs leading up to the previous court wizard's chambers." Aefric pointed at the topaz magic circle on the floor. "It's not impossible to hide a latent spell behind the detritus of many castings over a long period of time. I'm not risking that something we find upstairs will trigger something coming out of this."

"I could break the circle if your grace would prefer," Ser Deirdre said brightly.

"I'm sure you could," Aefric said, "but I'd like to do this myself."

Ser Yrsa frowned.

Aefric cleared his throat.

Ser Beornric began herding knights back onto the previous set of stairs.

Alone in the wizard's lab now, though with his knights watching, Aefric tapped the butt of the Brightstaff on the white stone floor.

White lightning began to play along its length.

Aefric gathered the white lightning in a ball at the butt end of the white thunderwood staff.

What he did next was the sort of thing that drove wizards mad. After all, wizards took a logical, orderly approach to magic that produced verifiable results that could be duplicated by anyone with sufficient training.

But while Aefric was weak at the applied logic aspect of magic, his instincts as a dweomerblood made him very strong in the other two aspects: artistry, and his understanding of the interrelationship of forces.

So Aefric allowed his eyes to become heavy lidded as he looked over that magic circle. Perceiving it both magically and physically at the same time.

He let his attention sweep back and forth across the circle and its many symbols and sigils and inscribed words in different languages.

First one way, then another, then spiraling in and sweeping out...

On the fifth pass he found the key to the circle. A small sigil along the due eastern portion of its arc flared red to his sight.

His instincts told him that this sigil represented the wizard who cast the circle. Which meant that this wizard did, indeed, maintain a connection to it.

At Aefric's mental command, lightning leapt from the butt end of his staff, smiting only that sigil.

The circle died.

"Whoa!" Ser Deirdre said from the stairs. "Vria. Did you see that?"

"Yes," Ser Vria said, sounding astonished. "It was like ... it was like all the leftover magic in that circle was a damp fog, and *poof*. It's gone."

"But the circle's still intact," Ser Deirdre said. She shook her head as the knights entered the room. "Never seen anything like that before, your grace."

"There are two ways to destroy a circle," Aefric said. "One is simply to break it. The other is to break its tie to the wizard who made it. That's what I did. Now he can't use it against me. And when I have time, I'll be able to make it my own."

Aefric nodded his head back and forth. "Or maybe give it to Karbin. We'll see."

"Is it safe to move on then, your grace?" Ser Yrsa asked, sounding more respectful than Aefric expected. Perhaps she understood how careful he'd just been. For a change.

Aefric smiled and nodded. "We're ready to proceed."

That door at the back of the room did indeed hide stairs that led to the next floor up, which had clearly been the wizard's chambers. And those chambers hadn't been nearly as important to the wizard as...

...as the lab had.

The round chamber held only a small, simple bed. A very basic desk, with four drawers. A thick red carpet to relieve the tedium of the white stone, but nothing on the walls to do likewise. A small bookshelf full of nothing books. Poetries and histories, but not the sort he'd expect a wizard to keep.

Not a wizard who served this household, anyway.

"Something's off," Aefric said.

His knights immediately readied their weapons. Aefric frowned as he looked about. He wasn't sure what was bothering him. This room just didn't seem consistent with the impression he'd been gathering about this wizard.

Illusion, perhaps? Hiding the room's real contents?

About the time the thought occurred to Aefric, it must've occurred to Ser Deirdre. For she spun her dueling dagger in one hand, then slashed it through the air, leaving a maroon trail that faded quickly.

Illusion was right.

The room was now completely empty, save for a piece of parchment tacked to the door that would lead up to the roof of the tower.

Aefric checked again for traps, just to be safe, then pulled the parchment off the wall and read it.

Dear Usurper,

If you have found this note, then likely you have found my reagents as well. I congratulate you on your puissance.

No doubt you expected to find waiting for you my own tools and weapons of the Art. But those I spirited away before the family summoned me to prepare a few surprises for you.

No doubt you have already found those surprises. Most of them, at least. I hope you enjoyed them as much as I enjoyed leaving them for you. I hope that surviving them has cost you dearly.

Would that I had time to deny you my reagents and my grimoires, but that time is denied me. If you are an honorable man, contact me at Svarturvigi and I shall ransom my grimoires. In so doing I shall even provide the secret of the wards that guard them, so that even in returning them to me, you will still gain in magic.

I can be a reasonable man about such things.

But I cannot be reasonable about Hrafnvigi. It has been my home for too long, and the home for the Hrafntonn family for far longer.

Have you found the curse yet? I hope not. I hope these words are the first you learn of it, and that dread sours your stomach. As it should.

For whether you find the curse or not, it shall find you. And do not hope to defeat my curse. I have inscribed it in a tongue so old that it is forgotten by all but me and my master. And my master is dead.

Perhaps, if you prove honorable about my grimoires, I shall give you the key to defeating the curse. You may have stolen my home, but you took it in war. And the Hrafntonn family respects war.

I shall await word.

Larus Hrafntonn

"Curse?" Ser Deirdre asked.

"We should send for Karbin," Ser Yrsa said. "Just to be safe."

"And we will," Aefric agreed. "But not yet. I want to see the rest of the castle first."

"Might be better to wait," Ser Yrsa said. "Karbin could be here in less than a day, if necessary."

"We finish," Aefric said.

"I can't believe he took the furniture too," Ser Beornric said. "If he could do that, why leave the grimoires?"

"I only know the magic involved by reputation," Aefric said slowly. "But if my references are correct, it is a spell that will take everything in a room and reduce it into something that looks like a gold coin. Likely that he then hid in his boot."

"And your grace doesn't think his boots held enough room for two coins?" Ser Yrsa asked.

"More likely," Aefric said, "he only had time to cast the spell once, and hurriedly. He simply didn't have time for his bedroom and laboratory both."

"So you're saying," Ser Deirdre said, frowning, "whatever he kept in here was *more* valuable than his grimoires and his enchanted research equipment?"

Aefric nodded.

She whistled. "Makes you wonder."

"Question for another time," he said, and nodded to the door.

There were indeed stairs behind that door.

They checked the roof, then, but it was empty. Aefric and Ser Deirdre checked for illusions as well, but found none, nor anything that had been rendered invisible and left behind.

They trooped back down the stairs then, and after Aefric spell-locked the door to the roof, they began checking the secret passages of the sixth floor.

Aefric insisted they check the areas away from the spell-locked door that masked latent magic first, just to be certain that they missed nothing.

They missed nothing. The secret passages up here were just as tight and dusty as those of the other floors. And just as empty.

Finally, Aefric and his knights found themselves standing at a second spell-locked door. One that had to lead into the same room as the spell-locked door on the sixth floor landing.

Two doors among the secret passages. Both of them spell-locked, by the same wizard who'd trapped the treasury, and cast other spells that had been causing problems. A wizard Aefric now knew as Larus Hrafntonn.

Two spell-locked doors. Both leading into a room where Aefric could sense latent magic, but no details.

In the back of his mind, Aefric couldn't help wondering about the curse Larus Hrafntonn had left for him...

"Which door?" Ser Yrsa asked, breaking Aefric from his reverie about wizards and curses.

"Pardon?" he asked.

There was only the one door in front of him here, after all, in the cramped, dusty secret passage on the sixth floor.

"I've been keeping a rough layout of this castle in my head," she said. "And finding the secret passages has been a big help with that, I don't mind admitting."

She pointed to the spell-locked door in front of Aefric. It just looked like an ordinary oaken door, like so many others in this castle. Style was a bit archaic, but otherwise unremarkable.

"By my estimate," she said, "with the exception of the escape shafts, very little of this castle remains unexplored. And what little there is holds some kind of latent magic, and lies between two doors. This is one of those doors. The other is also among the secret passages, on the landing above the stairs from the fifth floor."

"You think there's a tactical advantage to choosing one door over the other?" Aefric asked.

"It stands to reason," Ser Yrsa said. "If we're expecting a physical fight, as with the skeletons, this is the better position. We won't be ceding high ground. But if the threat is magical, the stairs might provide a safe haven for your grace while we enter."

"I trust," Ser Beornric added softly, from beside Aefric, "that your grace won't dispute our entering first."

All around Aefric, knights were nodding agreement.

"The only question," Ser Yrsa said, "is what kind of threat we're expecting." She gave Aefric a frank look. "Your grace has had a chance to examine different spells cast by this Larus Hrafntonn. What manner of curse should we expect? How will it manifest?"

"I can't tell from here," Aefric said. He raised his free hand before

Ser Yrsa could object. "I'm not suggesting entering first. I'm merely saying that the best attack is unexpected, yes?"

Ser Yrsa nodded stiffly.

"Which means that Hrafntonn's curse won't be illusion, or skeletons, or anything resembling that fire trap he'd laid on the treasury. In fact…"

Aefric confirmed once more that the door in front of him was real, and untrapped.

"There's no trap on the door at all."

"Then may I open it, your grace?" Ser Deirdre asked.

"Not this time," he said, and over Ser Yrsa's rising objections he spoke louder. "I'm not arguing for entering first. But right now I can't tell anything about that latent magic except that it's there, and it's not a trap. I should undo the spell lock *myself*, to make sure that nothing in the spell lock has the chance to connect to or otherwise activate that latent magic."

"Or," Ser Yrsa said, "we send for Karbin and have *him* do it. Or does your grace not trust the skills of his chosen court wizard?"

"Of course I do," Aefric said. "But sending for Karbin would be an adventurer's solution, not a duke's."

"I doubt that a great deal," Ser Yrsa said.

Aefric chuckled.

"On the one hand, my general, you're not entirely wrong." He smirked. "As an adventurer, I'd likely try that spell lock myself."

"Then what does your grace mean?" Ser Beornric asked, before Ser Yrsa could reply.

Aefric thought he saw recognition in Ser Beornric's eyes. Perhaps he understood Aefric's point. Or was close to it.

"I have a reputation here in Kivash," Aefric said. "Frozen Ridge saw to that, if nothing else. What will happen to that reputation if I balk before a single spell cast by Larus Hrafntonn?"

"Word will get out," Ser Beornric said softly. "It always seems to."

"Pro-Malimfar factions here in Kivash will use it as a rallying point," Ser Yrsa said, disgustedly. "They'll try to dismiss what happened at Frozen Ridge as a fluke, or exaggeration."

"Exactly," Aefric said. "They'll make Ashling's life harder. They'll push to bring the Hrafntonn family back, which means fighting to keep my new castle. And it may make me a more likely target for assassins, if my enemies see me as vulnerable."

He put a hand on Ser Yrsa's shoulder and looked her in the eye.

"I need to be able to leave here, laughing at the 'feeble' magic of Larus Hrafntonn."

Ser Yrsa shook her head, and sighed harshly.

"Your grace is right, of course," she said. "Though it pains me to see him risk himself."

"I'll undo the lock," he said. "But I'll stop there."

"Wait," Ser Yrsa said. "The question remains. This door? Or the other?"

"This one," Aefric decided.

"Why?" Ser Yrsa asked. "I know it's the closest, but is there another reason?"

"We wouldn't start hunting for secret doors on this floor. We'd start as we did, on the first. Which means that we had five whole floors to find the hidden passages. And since those tend to be the best way into rooms, it stands to reason that we'd progress just the way we did, following the secret passages instead of the main hall."

"So we'd come to the other door first, on our way up from the fifth floor," Ser Yrsa said with a nod. "Meaning it's the door he expected us to take. This one would be precautionary."

"I believe so, yes," Aefric said.

"All right then," she said with another nod, but a quirked smile. "So long as your grace has a tactical reason beyond convenience."

"Don't knock convenience," Aefric said, smiling. "It definitely has its place."

Ser Deirdre stayed near at hand as Aefric approached the door, but she didn't crowd him this time.

"I have an idea, your grace," she said softly.

"What?" Aefric asked.

"I've disarmed one of this man's spell locks before," she said. "Should be easy for me to do now. Perhaps I could disarm the lock, while your grace studies its magic and prepares to counter anything it tries? Or, if necessary, severs any ties to the latent magic?"

"That ... makes sense," Aefric said quizzically.

"I take risks with *my* life, your grace," she said with a small smile. "Not yours."

"All right," Aefric said. "Give me a moment to prepare, then begin."

Aefric relaxed through a deep breath, and shifted his focus outward through the flows of Qorunn's magic.

Looking at the door this way, he could now see the structure of the spell lock as an ornate mandala of red and black coruscating energies.

It had no ties to anything outside itself. Whatever that latent magic beyond the door was — and the spell lock prevented Aefric from sending his attention past it — that latent magic was unrelated to the spell lock.

Ser Deirdre began casting then. Her hand, waving as though boneless. Her sigil burning the air maroon, leaving the smell of burnt blackberries in its wake.

Seen this way, Aefric gained a much stronger sense of Deirdre's magic. Its nature was as playful and clever as the woman herself. She used magic the way she used her rapier — even that sigil was, in its own way, a work of feints and tricks, setting up the kill...

"Hah!" Ser Deirdre cried out and thrust her hand through the sigil's center.

Its power rained down on the spell lock, hitting seven different weak spots at the same time.

The spell lock sparked, flared, and came apart in a trail of red and black.

"Anything?" Ser Deirdre asked cautiously.

"No," Aefric said. "The lock is gone, and it didn't trigger anything else. Well done."

But Aefric's attention was past the door now, to the latent magic that he could sense more clearly, without the spell lock obscuring it.

Aefric could tell now that the latent magic was the work of Larus

Hrafntonn. Which meant that on the other side of this door had to be the curse.

FOR SAFETY'S SAKE, AEFRIC AGREED TO RESUME HIS POSITION BACK down the secret passage and closer to the middle of the group. Thus, he allowed Sers Deirdre, Yrsa and Beornric to enter the room ahead of him, while the Knights of the Lake handled rear guard, just in case.

Didn't mean he had to like it. All the years Aefric had spent as an adventurer had given him a real taste for exploration. He didn't like having to let others make sure a room was "safe" before he entered it.

Cost of being a duke. At least the perks were nice.

A thought that made Aefric smile. After all, this very castle was a "perk," and one he wouldn't have gotten to explore at all, were he still just an adventurer.

At the front of the group, her rapier in hand and limned in that dark red light, Ser Deirdre opened the door and stepped cautiously inside...

Moments later, her disappointed voice.

"Empty," she said. Aefric could hear her scuff the dusty floor with her boot before continuing, "Just a servants' waystation."

Sers Yrsa and Beornric entered, their weapons shining with the white light of Aefric's spells, letting him see in as well.

Sure enough, it looked like a small servants' waiting room. A simple wooden couch. A bed. Two small tables with one chair each. Did have a small, enchanted stove in the corner, perhaps for keeping food hot without fire, and a cabinet full of different kinds of alcohols, along with glasses and silver serving trays and utensils.

"Seems safe enough, your grace," Ser Yrsa said, though she sounded uncertain on that point.

Aefric entered.

The room was small, hardly big enough for the four of them, while they had their weapons out. And it didn't look to Aefric as though it was intended for its current use. Too small. Too ... odd a location. Especially on a floor that had more than one servants' waiting…

On a hunch, Aefric tested the bed with a hand.

It was soft. Feather stuffed, with silk sheets.

He started laughing. "It's a trysting room."

"It is?" Ser Deirdre took another look around, then gave a chagrined smile and shook her head. "How did I not see that?"

"Doesn't matter," Aefric said, turning his attention back to a more serious matter.

The latent magic.

There was some kind of spell here, just waiting to be activated.

And it felt like Larus Hrafntonn's magic.

"All right," Aefric said, tracking the feel of the latent magic to the white stone wall across from the bed. "The latent magic is *here* somewhere. And it feels like Hrafntonn's work."

Ser Deirdre immediately interposed herself between Aefric and that spot on the wall.

"Deirdre?" he asked.

"It's latent, your grace," she said. "Which means the curse hasn't hit yet. Let it hit me first."

"Ridiculous," Aefric said. "Stand back, and let me figure this out."

"And if the trigger is someone investigating the magic?" Ser Yrsa asked.

"It's not a…"

Aefric made the mistake of speaking while casting, and discovered he'd spoken too soon. His trap detection spell seemed to be reacting to that spot on the wall, where the latent magic was.

And yet, the spell *wasn't* quite responding right.

Seen through the many images of the facets in the Brightstaff's yellow diamond, a trap *should* have looked solidly red in multiple facets.

But…

Some of the facets made the wall look innocent. Untrapped. But that was consistent with the spell, because the pattern of the facets —

which were red and which a normal yellow — helped differentiate types of physical and magical traps.

The images that glowed red this time, though, were the problem. They should've stayed red. Solidly. But they didn't. They seemed to ease in and out of red.

But that made no sense at all.

"Something's off," Aefric said, and before he could say anything further, Ser Deirdre twirled her dagger, leaving a maroon trail in its wake.

The illusions broke. And it was plural, because there were multiple levels of illusion here.

First, the "trap" responses to Aefric's spell all vanished, and that one section of wall looked clean in every yellow image.

Second, the sense of Larus Hrafntonn's magic was gone from the remaining sense of the latent magic.

Third, that section of wall was now etched with writing, some of which was covered by a parchment note.

Aefric had to give Hrafntonn this much. The man had a creative mind, when it came to illusions.

Ser Deirdre gave Aefric a proud smile.

"Noticed the illusions the same time your grace did," she said. "Hope your grace doesn't mind my taking care of them. Hrafntonn's illusions follow the same kind of structure as his spell locks. Easy, once you've handled a couple."

"Deirdre," Aefric said with a half smile, "I could kiss you."

"Your grace should, of course, follow his instincts in all things," she said with a playful smile.

Ser Yrsa cleared her throat.

"Killjoy," Ser Deirdre said.

"More important matters concern us than your libido, Deirdre," Ser Yrsa said.

Aefric turned his attention then to the note.

Dear Usurper,

Congratulations. You have found your doom. And it has been written by an even greater wizard than myself. My hands may have carved the letters you see before you, but my master himself inscribed the scroll I used to seal your fate.

Well, that would be consistent with the sense of the latent magic now. It had a vaguely familiar feel, but was definitely not the work of Larus Hrafntonn.

A spell scroll *would* explain that. They tended to carry the feel of the magic-user who created them, not the magic-user who used them.

Aefric continued reading.

If you've any skill at the Art, you'll note that the curse feels latent. As it shall, while it lingers above your head, becoming active only in the instant that it strikes.

As I cannot expect you to read a language so old and forgotten as that of the curse, I shall do you the favor of translating.

The words read:

"Woe to you, oh fallen.

How days wither you like years.

How your spells fail, as though forgotten.

How red now, your bloody tears.

Death circles you. Your body fails.

Your spirit weak. Your future pales.

Soon only foulness shall remain.

And forgotten be your deeds and name."

On Midwinter I shall activate this curse. You shall be dead before the new year dawns.

You possess one and only one chance to avoid your fate. Contact me at Svarturvigi. Deal fairly with me for my grimoires.

Do this, and I shall give you the secret to shattering the curse. Do it not and die. Painfully.

This I swear.

Larus Hrafntonn

Aefric read the note three times, but the message didn't get any better.

"May I, your grace?" Ser Yrsa asked.

Aefric handed her the note.

She read it aloud.

And suddenly all his knights were talking and shouting and at least one pair of hands grabbed Aefric and tried to spirit him away.

"Stop!" he shouted, though his voice went unheard over the din of ideas and concerns.

Aefric smacked the butt of the Brightstaff against the white stone floor, causing the hands to release him and a thunderclap to *boom* in the tight confines of that room.

In the echoing silence, Aefric said, "I'm not going anywhere."

SILENCE REIGNED IN THAT LITTLE ROOM FOR A MOMENT AFTER AEFRIC'S proclamation.

No wonder the little trysting room had felt so crowded. Sers Micham, Temat, Arras and Vria had wedged in among the furniture, and Sers Wardius and Leppina hovered in the doorway.

Sers Yrsa and Beornric were closest. Apparently they'd been the ones to grab him, one hand each, intent on hauling him bodily out of the room.

Ser Deirdre, meanwhile, had her weapons out and glowing red, over beside the words graven into the wall.

"Ser Deirdre, stop right there," Aefric ordered.

"But, your grace, perhaps I can—"

"I said stop."

She bowed her head and lowered her weapons. Though her expression was as determined as ever. Aefric suspected she'd already sworn to herself to find a way to save him from the curse.

"Your grace," Ser Yrsa said, "we must get you out of here. We must call for Karbin. Your grace cannot deny now that he needs aid in facing this curse."

"In fact," Aefric said, forcing calm against the rising panic of his knights, "I *don't* know that. Not until I have a look at the curse itself."

"Do you know how to contact Kainemorton?" Ser Beornric asked, urgently. "Maybe he could come help?"

"It's chancy at best," Aefric said. There were now five knights between himself and the writing on the wall, so he reread the note, looking for clues, as he finished answering the question. "He never stays long in any one place."

"Then surely," Ser Yrsa said, "we can find a way to—"

"Enough," Aefric said. He turned a level gaze on his knights. "I know that all of you are only trying to protect me. And I love you for it. But this is a matter of magic. And until I have the chance to examine the curse, I wouldn't even know what to *say* to Karbin or Kainemorton."

"But what if the note is a bluff?" Ser Yrsa said. "What if the curse is activated by studying it?"

"It isn't," Ser Deirdre said, and when everyone looked at her, she continued. "There were multiple layers of illusion concealing the note and the words on the wall. If studying activated it, why bother?"

"All right," Ser Yrsa said, "that's a fair point. But I have trouble believing he'd give you until Midwinter to find a way to defeat his curse. Why not activate it immediately?"

"Because he screwed up," Aefric said. "And he's trying to cover for it."

"How so?" Ser Beornric asked.

"He was planning to take the contents of both his bedroom and his lab. Maybe his reagents room as well. But the spell he used must be too time-consuming. Likely he'd barely finished the first casting, before the family was calling for him. Demanding that he come lay traps."

Aefric nodded toward the words on the wall. "Even the curse was something he read from a scroll, rather than casting on his own."

"But he had time to carve the words," Ser Yrsa said.

"I doubt he used a hammer and chisel," Aefric said. "But the point is, he had to leave behind his *grimoires*. For a wizard, that's like leaving behind an arm."

"Both arms," Ser Deirdre said.

"He's desperate to get them back. Desperate enough to give me a pass on the curse, if I deal 'fairly' with him for the grimoires."

"I hesitate to ask..." Ser Yrsa said.

"I haven't decided about the grimoires yet," Aefric said. "But I haven't ruled out ransoming them back. For the moment, though, I *will* see this curse. So if you'd all please."

His knights moved back to give him room.

Aefric crossed the room and looked over the words graven in the white stone before him. The words of the...

Aefric started laughing.

"Your grace?" Ser Yrsa asked.

"Laughing at one's fate is admirable," Ser Deirdre said. "But I think avoiding it is better."

"No," Aefric said, still laughing. "You don't understand."

He lost himself laughing again while the others came closer.

They all looked at him as though he were insane.

"You were right, Yrsa! It's a bluff!" he said, though his laughter. Forced a deep breath so he could get a whole sentence out. "A marvelous bluff, and one that would work on *almost* anyone."

"Maybe *we* can contact Kainemorton?" Ser Yrsa asked Ser Beornric.

"I might be able to help there," Ser Deirdre said softly.

"Yes," Aefric said, still laughing. "Kainemorton. He's the key."

"Of course, your grace," Ser Yrsa said, taking one of his shoulders in a strong grip, and starting to turn him away again. "We'll contact him for you and—"

"No," Aefric said, trying to pull his shoulder back, but not having much luck against her grip. "You don't understand."

"Then perhaps your grace could explain it to us?" Ser Beornric asked cautiously.

"All right," Aefric said, but he needed several deep breaths to stop laughing. It really was a brilliant bluff.

Once he had control of himself again, he gestured for his knights to come closer. At some point, he'd let the light on the Brightstaff lapse — likely just before checking for traps — but he lit it again now, so the letters graven on the wall would be clear.

"This isn't a curse," he said, fighting down another chuckle.

"But how do you know that?" Ser Yrsa asked.

"Because I both read *and* speak this language," Aefric said, and laughed again briefly. "Kainemorton insisted I learn it, when I studied with him."

"What language is it then?" Ser Deirdre asked. "Because *I* sure don't recognize it."

"Almost no one does," Aefric said. "Not in this world."

"Your grace," Ser Beornric said, sounding as though he might be questioning Aefric's sanity again.

"All right," Aefric said. "The explanation. Do any of you remember the name of the first human empire?"

"Rentiss," Ser Yrsa said quickly. "Back when we were a young race. Back before even the elves and orcs had finished killing each other off."

"That's right," Aefric said, and pointed at the words on the wall. "And *that* is Rentissi. Their language."

"Rentiss fell *thousands* of years ago," Ser Yrsa said. "Nothing remains of that empire but stories. And you're telling me you speak their language?"

"The language held on here *long* after the empire fell," Aefric said. "Mostly in a written form, used by wizards. Which was why Kainemorton learned it originally."

Aefric shook his head. "It fell out of fashion centuries ago, though. Became more fashionable to use common languages, and simply rely on cyphers, where needed."

"So why learn it?"

"Because the Rentiss Empire didn't just rise here," Aefric said. "Kainemorton told me that it rose and fell in *hundreds* of worlds. Some where the Rentissi are loved. Others where they're reviled. But in many of them, all that remains is their language."

"And that's why Kainemorton wanted you to learn it?" Ser Deirdre asked. "He wanted to take you with him to other worlds?"

"He thought I might want to learn about traveling the worlds someday."

To visit Earth once more was always implicit in those discussions, but only because Kainemorton knew that Aefric had once been Keifer McShane.

Elbar's Blood, it had been Kainemorton who brought Aefric to Qorunn in the first place.

"If your grace does so," Ser Deirdre said almost shyly, "might I accompany him?"

"I haven't worked through the magic of teleportation yet," he said, smiling self-deprecatingly. "Much less the spells that would carry me to another plane of existence."

He quirked his smile at her. "But if I go, and you're around, I'll make sure to invite you."

"Thank you, your grace," Ser Deirdre said, almost glowing with her smile.

"So what does it say then?" Ser Yrsa said, pointing at the words on the wall. "If it's not a curse, what is it?"

"These are the keywords to commanding the castle," Aefric said.

"You mean this *is* like one of Raend's creations?" Ser Deirdre asked, the only one as excited about this as Aefric himself.

"I mean Raend signed his work," Aefric said, pointing to the name at the bottom.

He sent his knights out of the room then, and read aloud words to claim possession of the castle, and its magics.

As he spoke those words, hot power flooded him. Swept through his body, as though scalding the aetheric part of himself.

The power of the castle, testing him. If he couldn't handle the power, he couldn't command it.

But Aefric had been through tests like this before, most obviously from the Brightstaff.

Here, it was a matter of asserting himself not as a magic-user, but as a liege lord.

Had Aefric still been an adventurer, he might have failed that test. But he'd been a duke now for more than a season, and growing into his role.

He had the poise. He had the confidence. And the power bowed to him. Yielded up its secrets, as it settled into an equilibrium within him.

He could now light any room within the castle with a thought. Call forth ghostly servants and warriors as needed. Seal the castle to intruders. Fill it with magical wards and traps far beyond anything that Larus Hrafntonn had left behind.

And much, much more. Including, should he choose to, the ability to reduce the whole castle and its contents to an easily portable cube smaller than his fist.

Oh, this castle was a wonder indeed.

AFTER AEFRIC FINISHED HIS FORMAL CLAIMING OF CASTLE HRAFNVIGI — which he resolved to rename, now that it was his — he allowed Ser Deirdre to break the remaining spell lock on the other door into what had been turned into a trysting room.

Aefric decided to cast an illusion of his own, before leaving that room. He wanted to cover the Rentissi words on the wall.

True, almost no one could read them, but why take a chance? He'd have the wall paneled later, or...

Aefric was halfway through casting that illusion, when he realized he didn't need one.

He dismissed his half-cast spell, and merely swept his hand through the air. As he willed it, the Rentissi words submerged into the stone. Unless he willed otherwise, those words would not be visible again until his death.

He turned to his knights.

"The nature of this castle must be kept a secret," Aefric said. "Let the world believe it's just an ordinary castle. If word gets out that it's one of Raend's creations — and portable, if desired — there are many who would kill to possess it."

His knights slapped their hilts, committing to keeping the secret.

From there, Aefric and his knights returned to the sixth floor master bedroom and tested the chutes to see where escape route led.

The chute Aefric took snaked its way down, but was smooth enough that the ride felt comfortable. He arrived at the bottom slowly enough to land on his feet without issue.

Several of his knights were already waiting for him, of course, with magically lit weapons raised.

Aefric chuckled and had the castle light the room for him, while more knights came out of two of the three chutes that led into this room.

This low, wide room of white stone. They were still in the castle. Aefric could feel it.

Ser Deirdre, arriving last, was the only one to *whoop* as he came.

"That was fun," she said, grinning, and her enthusiasm brought matching grins from several other knights.

Though Aefric doubted the ride was as much fun in full plate armor.

"Single door over here," Ser Yrsa said. "Leads—"

"Out of the castle," Aefric said. "They had to tunnel to clear the other side of that door. It's not part of the castle."

"Yes," Ser Yrsa said, as though she considered Aefric's statement a little too obvious for comment. "And I'm torn about this. On the one hand, Ashling will probably give us whatever building this tunnel comes out into. Gods know she's happy enough with you. But if we do—"

"If we do, she knows where the escape route comes out," Aefric said. "I'm not worried about that."

"Is your grace worried about assassins learning from Ashling's people where this entrance is?" Ser Yrsa asked dryly. "Because I am."

"It's not much of an entrance," Ser Beornric said. "I wouldn't fancy trying to climb back up one of those shafts."

"Wouldn't stop a determined assassin," Ser Yrsa said.

"Nevertheless," Aefric said, "there's no need to worry. That door is optional."

He waved his hand, and it became solid white stone.

"There are a few places in the castle where the doors are optional. For example, There are two subterranean floors currently not in use because access was cut off to them some time back. Oh, and each of the towers could have a trapdoor."

"Then why does just the wizard's tower have one?" Ser Beornric asked. "I could think of several uses for an extra room in those other towers."

"That was all the previous owner wanted," Aefric said with a shrug. "I think somewhere along the way, the Hrafntonn family lost the keywords. That's the only reason to have some of those unnecessary light spells. Not to mention, this place would have been much harder to clear. And I couldn't claim it, if it already had a living claimant."

"But you won it in battle," Ser Yrsa said.

"Raend didn't care about things like that. If the castle accepts you, it's yours until you die or give it away. And I'm pretty sure the Hrafntonns wouldn't agree to give it away."

"Maybe the castle rejected one of the inheritors?" Ser Beornric asked.

"Possible," Aefric said, "though it's a poor statement about the family, if so."

"Either way, it's your grace's now," Ser Deirdre said. "Sounds like the Hrafntonns are in for a bad time if they try to come back."

"They are," Aefric said.

Ser Yrsa cleared her throat.

Aefric gave her a questioning look.

"Well, as this room and that tunnel *can* be used for escape," she said, "we should still figure out where it goes. And either buy or get Ashling to give you that property."

"Fair enough," Aefric said.

Aefric brought the door back. They all passed through it into a moist, narrow tunnel that was lower than Aefric liked. He had to watch his head, and he wasn't the only one.

Fortunately, the light spells on his knights' weapons were still active, so they could see clearly the dripping, mossy gray rock around them.

He sent the door away again, once the last knight was through it.

Interesting that he could do that from outside the castle. He'd have to test and see how far away he could be and still effect changes within it...

The tunnel came out in the basement of a warehouse on the river. An empty warehouse, that looked as though it hadn't been used since Armyr took Kivash.

Stone foundation and basement, but otherwise wooden construction. Looked strong enough. And it had two rowboats and a small sloop tethered to a dock in the back.

Aefric was standing in the warehouse doorway, looking at those boats and blinking at the harsh, late afternoon sunlight, when Relimmorea's imp flew down and landed on the wooden dock in front of him. Its hot iron scent strong even over the sea breeze.

Sers Beornric and Vria were beside Aefric in an instant, weapons drawn.

"I come in peace," the imp said, empty hands raised.

Aefric nodded and gestured for his knights to ease back.

The imp bowed. "My mistress commends you on accomplishing in three days what the Hrafntonn family has failed to do for at least six generations."

That could only mean properly claiming the castle. Aefric made a small sound somewhere between disbelief and amazement.

"Your mistress *felt* that?" he said. "She must be even more puissant than I had been led to believe."

"You are most kind to say so," the imp said with a bow. "But it must be remembered that she, herself, has enjoyed a great deal of experience with just that sort of magic. You will find it lends you ... a certain sensitivity."

"I'll keep that in mind."

"My mistress also wishes me to assure you that she shall keep the secret of your castle, provided you keep the secret of her tower."

"I agree, of course," Aefric said. "Such matters are no one's business but our own."

"I thank you on her behalf."

"And I thank her through you," Aefric said. "May I ask a question?"

"You may," the imp said, "provided you understand that I may not have leave to answer it."

"Of course," Aefric said. "But this is what I'm curious about. If your mistress understood the nature of the castle, why didn't she claim it for herself?"

"There are many reasons," the imp said. "But foremost is this. My mistress has grown past the urge to seek out glories and treasures. She is satisfied enough to see such a castle for the work of art and Art that it is, without the craving to possess it for herself."

"Then she has grown in wisdom as well as power," Aefric said, giving the imp a small bow.

"You are most kind to say so," the imp said. "Farewell, Aefric Brightstaff."

"Farewell," Aefric said, as the imp spread his wings and took to the air.

"It seems you've made a friend," Ser Beornric said.

"Safer to think of this as a truce with a neutral third party," Aefric said. "With the possibility of becoming allies one day."

"If I heard the imp right," Ser Beornric said, "Relimmorea sounds more positively disposed towards you than negatively."

"Perhaps," Aefric said. "But you have to keep in mind. She's clearly hundreds of years old. She's probably slow to trust."

"Better neutral than an enemy," Ser Yrsa said, stepping out onto the dock. "Slow to trust doesn't mean slow to *dis*trust. You didn't make her angry, and that's not nothing."

"More than that," Ser Beornric said. He nodded at the warehouse. "Unless I miss my guess, she just told you she knows where the escape route comes out at, but she'll keep *that* a secret too."

Aefric chuckled. "Better to stay on her good side, then."

"Yes," Ser Yrsa said. "And to dig an alternate escape route. Can that escape door be moved?"

"I'm ... not sure," Aefric said. "I'll have to try."

"If you can, good," Ser Yrsa said.

"In the meantime," Ser Beornric said, looking over the warehouse and the dock, "this one is well worth having."

"I'll talk to Ashling," Aefric said, smiling. "It's time to head back for dinner anyway."

"Thank you," Ser Micham said, then quickly gave an abashed smile when he realized he'd said that aloud. "Excuse me, your grace. I should've eaten more at lunch."

"That's all right, Ser Micham," Aefric said. "I'm hungry too. Feels as though that boar was hours ago."

"It was," Ser Yrsa said.

"So let's go let Ashling feed us," Aefric said, "And use her rikas to tell Kentigern we're ready for the castle staff to come."

"They'll have a lot of cleaning to do," Ser Arras said.

"They will indeed," Aefric said. "It's time to make that castle feel like home."

AFTER THE BIG DEAL THAT ASHLING HAD MADE THE NIGHT BEFORE about giving Aefric time to rest following his long days at Hrafnvigi, he expected to be dining alone that evening. Or perhaps with his knights.

And yet, with the sun riding low in the sky, Aefric found himself sitting with Ashling on a balcony, high above Kivash.

The balcony was white stone, of course, but rugs of thick, blue and black carpets had been laid out. The handrail around the edges was highly polished brass.

The furniture was of greenwood, surprisingly simple, but quite comfortable. Reminded Aefric of his own greenwood furniture, on his balconies at Water's End.

The wind had grown gentle, but the air stayed warm and sultry.

Aefric had changed into a white silk shirt with loose sleeves, tight cuffs, and laces from the collar to about the breastbone. For leggings he wore navy blue hose. His belt was black leather, to match his low, soft shoes.

He also wore the small, gold brooch studded with sapphires that Ashling had given him in the spring.

He left the wand Garram in his rooms. But, of course, he'd brought the Brightstaff. It stood straight and tall beside his chair.

Ashling wore a clinging chiffon gown the color of rich cream, held up by the thinnest of straps across her pale shoulders, and cut just low enough to be considered daring. For ornamentation she wore a thin, gold chain around her neck that dangled a citrine down near her décolletage

She wore her raven black hair down and loose past her shoulders.

They were sharing that sweet, honey and caramel liqueur called honsach, while they waited for their first course to be served.

"So, tell me, Ash," Aefric said, one eyebrow raised. "How many members of your court 'just happened' to see that this is how you dressed for dinner with me?"

"Why, Aefric," she said, teasing a smile and leaning a little closer to emphasize her low neckline, "don't you like the dress?"

"The dress is a joy to see on you," Aefric said, "as you well know. But you didn't answer my question."

Her smile widened then, and she swirled the honsach in her small glass. She gracefully shrugged one shoulder. "A few."

"Was Countess Siburh among them? Or would that be too obvious?"

"One of her close allies might've seen me fussing a bit with my choice of necklace," Ashling said, playing with the citrine.

Aefric chuckled and shook his head.

"Maybe I just wanted you to see me at my best," Ashling said. "After all, I understand I am to host you only one more night."

"Just so," Aefric said. "One last night here, for this visit. So naturally you wouldn't miss the chance to confuse your allies by pretending to them that you're making a play for me."

"Why ever would I do such a thing?" she asked, fluttering her lashes.

"Oh, given that it's you doing it, you probably have several reasons. But the one that leaps to mind is this. Thanks to your rumor, your court believes I have interest in Cyneswith. Which means her mother can play that to her advantage. By letting your court believe you're making a play for me, you undercut her efforts."

Ashling laughed, and she had a good laugh. Sincere, yet suggestive at the same time.

"Very good, Aefric," she said, and raised her honsach in toast. "Confusion to our enemies."

She'd made the toast generic enough that Aefric saw no reason to hold back, so he confirmed the toast and drank down his honsach.

It felt like drinking liquid candy with a kick. Aefric was always surprised that it didn't taste *too* sweet. Some skill on the brewer's part, he assumed.

"Of course," Ashling said, "you're discounting the possibility that I wanted to look good for you. After all, you're a handsome fellow. Dashing. With an air of mystery from all your magic, and—"

"Come *on*, Ash," Aefric said, laughing. "Enough. Do you want me to tell you you're beautiful? You are. Breathtakingly so. But you don't need to play games with me."

"Maybe teasing you is fun," Ashling said, shrugging one shoulder again.

"Especially when it also teases your younger sister?"

"Close," Ashling said, more seriously now. "Especially when it teaches her a *lesson*. She's been lobbying me for the chance to spend time with you. In *fact*, she tried to push to have dinner with you tonight herself. I finally had to assign guards to get her to behave."

"Thank you for denying her," Aefric said softly. "I'm not ready for a meal, just the two of us."

"I know," Ashling said, just as softly. "But she's being dense about this, and I'm losing patience with her. If you weren't leaving soon, I'd have to send her back to Fyrcloch."

Alarm bells rang in Aefric's mind. "How *much* are you losing patience with her?"

"What do you mean?" Ashling asked, tilting her head enough to drape her long hair down one shoulder.

"Ash," Aefric said, "I can't help but notice that I've been offered *leaba* by not one woman here, but two. Together. Two nights in a row."

She laughed, that open sound again.

"And you thought I was preparing you to find me coming to your room tonight?" Ashling said with a smile. "Well, maybe I am. Maybe I have a woman all picked out for us to share. Someone eager. Nubile. Someone you'd quite enjoy."

"I think that if that were your intention, you'd be playing it very differently."

"Oh?" Ashling smiled, then waited while two young serving women brought out the palate wine.

The same two women who'd been coming to Aefric's rooms at night. And both gave him wicked smiles.

"How would I be playing it?" Ashling asked, affecting innocence.

"I'd believe the outfit," Aefric said, as the serving women withdrew. "More daring than your usual, and doing an admirable job of emphasizing your beauty."

"Thank you," Ashling said.

"But I don't believe the behavior," Aefric said. "I think our third would be here with us already, so that we'd all have time to get comfortable with one another. To make sure we all got along, before starting anything."

She chuckled softly. "I could kick Zoleen for blowing it with you." She shook her head. "You're right, of course. I'm just playing, because I know you're safe to play with. We're friends, after all. Aren't we, Aefric?"

"Yes, Ash," Aefric said, smiling more sincerely now. "We're friends."

ASHLING CONTINUED TO TEASE AEFRIC THROUGH THEIR DINNER, BUT HE was pretty sure it was just good-natured fun for her.

And he had to admit. Charismatic as she was, her attentions — even playful — felt flattering.

Aefric told her about most of his exploration of Hrafnvigi. The discovery of the secret passages. The first floor "family" section and the ... array of uses the Hrafntonn family had put it to. The spell locks, the warded grimoires.

He omitted only a few key elements. The quantity and variety of treasures he'd found — saying only that he was pretty sure the Hrafntonn family had lost a good deal of their wealth with the castle — the reagents, the ballistae. He mentioned the armories only in discussing how warlike the Hrafntonn family had been.

And, of course, he said nothing at all about the nature of the castle or the magic he'd found within it.

He was surprised, however, that she brought up the escape route.

"I presume they had a bolt hole of some kind?" she asked, over a bite of savory, slow-roasted rabbit. "A tunnel to the docks, or beyond the wall?"

"A warehouse on the river," Aefric said.

"Which one?" she asked. "I'll make a gift of it, and three other properties, so that its purpose won't be obvious."

Aefric paused with his dry red wine inches from his mouth. "You're sure?"

"Of course," she said with a dismissive wave. "I want you *safe* when you're here, Aefric. You need an emergency escape route. And no escape route is useful if anyone could guess where it leads."

Of course, she would choose other properties that either helped her allies, hindered her enemies, or both. Probably both. But that was her nature.

Just as Aefric was certain that the other properties would have value, if Aefric used them properly. Thus increasing his own investment in Kivash, and his interest in keeping it Armyrian.

That was fine, though. That was just the way politics was played.

The rest of the conversation was much more relaxed and friendly. Ashling talked about her new castle and the fun she'd had in claiming and redecorating it. She also had a great many recommendations about local crafters, tailors, and other workers.

Aefric considered asking Ashling to recommend a locksmith, but realized he didn't need one. He could change the locks himself.

Not something to announce to Ashling, though he did want to get word to Ser Deirdre, so she wouldn't spend her morning hunting down a locksmith for him.

They spoke more about Kivash. About Ashling's plans for the north side. About ways she hoped to improve trade.

When Aefric thought back on that conversation later, he marveled that she hadn't spent the whole time talking. But she hadn't. Despite the topics, she'd been quite good about soliciting his views and opinions, and seemed to give them real weight.

She even broke up the more serious topics with gossip about this local merchant family and that local noble house.

Aefric probably relaxed during that dinner more than Ser Yrsa would have approved of. But if he gave away any information that he'd intended to hold close, he certainly didn't recall doing so.

Of course, the fact that he was tired from the stresses of the day — not to mention the effort of overcoming his new castle's test — might have played a role in how he relaxed over dinner.

They were just finishing up their dessert — a whipped chocolate cream dish that was both light and tasty — and watching the sun set, when Ashling surprised him.

"I've decided I *do* want to share the noble privilege with you."

Funny how something so light and creamy as that dessert could suddenly grow thick as tree sap in Aefric's throat.

Caught between trying to breath, speak, and swallow at the same time, he started coughing. Ashling was saying something as he coughed, bent forward, but he couldn't hear it over the rush of blood past his ears, and the sound of his own coughing.

By the time he cleared his throat enough to take a good breath, his face felt hot and his head light.

"I'm *sorry*, Aefric," Ashling said, one soft hand on his wrist. Though the sentiment was undercut by the humor in her eyes. "I didn't mean to shock you so."

Aefric needed a few more breaths before he could respond.

"I thought we were just friends," Aefric finally managed, sounding a little hoarse.

"We *are* friends," she said, looking puzzled. "That's the point."

"I don't follow," he said, sipping some of the rich, fruity dessert wine, to help soothe his throat.

"I see that," Ashling said, one eyebrow raised. "What I mean is this. I like you, Aefric. I honestly do. If you were a woman, I think I'd be falling in love with you by now. But you had the misfortune of being born a man."

She patted his wrist.

"Don't worry," she said. "I don't blame you for it. It wasn't your fault. But there is one advantage to your unfortunate gender. Some of the women who might *want* to share my bed are hesitant, because they've never been with a woman before."

"I see," Aefric said, chuckling now. "And you think that my presence in that bed would coax them into ... trying new things?"

"I'm quite sure of it," she said. "Which would make the experience more fun for both of us. And since we're friends, I think we could share without making it a contest of some kind."

"I'd hope so," Aefric said, frowning. "Sex shouldn't be a competition."

"See?" Ashling said with a dazzling smile. "We're on the same page there." She trailed her gaze over him. "And who knows? Once things get going, we might have some fun together ourselves. I understand you have some scars I might find quite tempting."

"You've suggested as much before," Aefric said dubiously.

"Ah," she said, raising an index finger, "but I was only teasing then. I've come to gain a good enough sense of you, I think, to safely say that even if I bring you the bliss moment, you won't turn into either a fawning sycophant or an arrogant blowhard."

"I should hope not," Aefric said.

"You'd be surprised how many men do, if brought the bliss moment by a woman who prefers women. They seem to take it as a statement about themselves."

"I still can't believe we're having this conversation," Aefric said.

"I'd go further than that," Ashling said. "I'd say the point is settled. I shall come to your rooms one night."

"But not *this* night?" Aefric asked.

"Oh, no," she said, patting his shoulder now, and letting her fingers play over the muscles a moment before withdrawing. "No, you're tired. And anyway, I wouldn't want to think I was using our friendship to pressure you."

She shook her head. "No. Tonight, I suspect the young ladies who served our dinner will be eager to offer you *leaba* one more time before you leave us. However. The next time we sleep in the same castle, I shall come to your rooms. When I do, if you feel enough trust in me as a friend to share a night with me and the woman I bring, invite us in. If not, you may say no without fear of harming our friendship."

Aefric made a show of looking her over and smiled.

"Ash, unless I have a compelling reason to do otherwise, I can assure you you'll be invited in."

"Then I shall have to aim for a night when you have no compelling reason to refuse."

"And you do have skill at hitting your target, don't you," he said, not even pretending it was a question. He raised his glass in toast. "To friendship."

"May it last beyond our lives," she said, confirming the toast.

Together, they drank.

AEFRIC SAT WITH ASHLING FOR SOME TIME, AFTER DESSERT. JUST lingering over good, strong, smoky ishka and talking about the Risen Sea and shipping, and the problems of the pirate queen, Nelazzi.

Ashling even showed willingness to commit two warships to going after Nelazzi, if Aefric ever got King Colm's permission to do so.

Then, at last, the sun was down, and Aefric was escorted back to his rooms by Cyneswith, with a personal guard of Sers Temat and Wardius.

Cyneswith didn't make conversation this time, as she led him down an elegantly decorated spiral staircase and out of this tower.

She looked a bit subdued, he realized, after seeing the outfit Ashling had chosen for dinner with Aefric that night.

Aefric was torn between the temptation to reassure her that Ashling had no matrimonial designs on Aefric, and the knowledge that he shouldn't encourage the poor girl anyway.

The truth was, future countess or not, he couldn't take her seriously as a potential bride. Not until she was at least of age.

And given the pressures that Aefric felt to choose a bride, he expected to be married by that time.

So he let her lead him in silence through a short hall, then back up a less elegant staircase to what would be his rooms for one more night here at Ottarvigi.

She did give him a sad smile on reaching his rooms, and Aefric couldn't help but give her a hopeful smile back, that left her departing with a pensive expression.

Sers Wardius and Temat took up their posts outside his door, but before Aefric entered, he turned to them and spoke.

"I need you to send word to Ser Deirdre for me."

"Would you like us to summon her, your grace?" Ser Wardius asked.

"No," he said, with an abashed smile as he realized what the knight was thinking. "Nothing like that. It's just that I no longer need her to find me a locksmith tomorrow, and I don't want her hunting through the city for one."

"Of course, your grace," Ser Temat said. "We'll see that she gets the message."

"Thank you," Aefric said.

"Good night, your grace."

"Good night, Temat. Wardius."

Aefric then opened his door and entered his rooms.

Those two pretty serving women were already there and waiting for him.

Aefric wasn't the least bit surprised.

7

———————

Aefric spent another aett at Hrafnvigi, seeing to it that the new servants set about organizing the castle to his liking.

He settled one of the older knights in his service — a woman named Raedwaru Ol'Erresan — as castellan, to look after the castle and Aefric's local interests in his absence.

Ser Raedwaru had come of age when Duchess Arinda's grandmother ruled Deepwater, and had served honorably ever since. Despite her advancing years, she'd even fought for Arinda during the Godswalk Wars.

Though time had slowed her spear hand, it had done nothing to diminish Ser Raedwaru's loyalty or her spirit, and she proved quite eager to take charge of a new castle in a new city for her duke.

Hrafnvigi — or rather Castle Cairdeas as Aefric now named it, after an ancient word for "friendship" — was a simple castle with little in the way of lands. As such, with a good castellan in place, it didn't need a true seneschal.

So Aefric brought in a majordomo instead. A cousin of Kentigern's. A woman named Fedelm Ol'Klimath, who was small enough to be often underestimated, and clever enough to use those presumptions to her advantage.

In addition to the old Hrafntonn Warehouse on the Indecisive River, Ashling gave Aefric three other properties around Kivash, rather than just the two she'd promised. The Sunset Inn, a newer two-story white stone building on the north side of the river, near the docks. The Starlight Stones, a much larger inn on the south side, near the gate to the Malimfari road that paralleled the river.

Perhaps most impressive, she gave Aefric the Wide Sea Shipping Company, which had a pier of its own on the docks on the south side of the river, four very large warehouses at the foot of that pier, and a business office close to the town center.

Not to mention the company's trading fleet of twelve three-masted caravels, and sixteen two-masted schooners.

All these gifts.

Not so long ago, all of Aefric's wealth had been what he could carry on his back. Of course, that was not an inconsiderable amount, given a certain sack he possessed that could contain a great deal more than it appeared.

Nevertheless, the sum total of Aefric's wealth in those days — not quite two seasons past — might have been enough to purchase a decent tower, or a small keep on an unimpressive plot of land.

Now, his wealth was such that he could be given two inns and a *shipping company*, in a *major trade city*, just so that the escape route from *his new castle* wouldn't stand out.

The amount of wealth he had now was staggering, when he stopped to think about it. More than he could have *conceived of* as a street rat kid in Sartis.

Then again, in many ways, the wealth wasn't *his*. He held it in trust for the people of Deepwater, and for the future dukes and duchesses. Countless people relied on him to use this wealth the right ways.

Well, *most* of it wasn't his, at least.

Aefric couldn't help but notice that the deeds to the inns, warehouse and shipping company, were in his *name*, but not his *title*.

They'd been given to him as personal gifts, rather than gifts to the Duke of Deepwater, like the castle was.

"Why do you think that is?" Aefric asked his knight-advisers.

It was a warm morning in late summer as he asked that question, and the three of them sat in their seats on the afterdeck of the *Duke's Hand* once more, sailing across the beautiful, dark blue Risen Sea on their way back north to Water's End.

Aefric wore a lightweight, cotton tunic of Deepwater gray over navy blue hose, with the wand Garram at his belt, and the Brightstaff standing beside his wooden chair.

Trailing behind them, of course, was the *Swift Wave*, carrying the soldiers of Aefric's personal guard.

"Who among us can guess the reasons of a Fyrenn duchess?" Ser Yrsa asked, in return. She was wearing her tunic and hose of dark browns again, which always looked somewhat wrong to Aefric.

She looked most natural in her armor.

"I think I might hazard an attempt," Ser Beornric said. He wore tunic and hose today as well, though his were dark red over dark orange.

Though honestly, Aefric thought Ser Beornric looked more natural in full plate armor as well.

"Duchess Ashling seemed to want to emphasize your shared friendship on this visit," Ser Beornric said.

Ser Yrsa scoffed.

"No," Ser Beornric said. "It's true. She may be a Fyrenn, and all that comes with that, but she clearly made strong overtures of friendship to Aefric."

"For her own benefit, no doubt," Ser Yrsa said.

"Perhaps," Ser Beornric said. "She certainly benefits from the friendship. But she also knows her reputation, and she knows *we* know her reputation. Gifts directly to Aefric Brightstaff rather than to the Duke of Deepwater strike me as trying to say that they are personal gifts to a friend, rather than political gifts to an ally."

"More likely," Ser Yrsa said, "she didn't want to give up the tax base."

"No," Aefric said. "The taxes she gave up. That was quite explicit in the gift."

"I'm sure Kivash's new mayor *loved* that," Ser Beornric said, chuckling.

"I still don't trust it," Ser Yrsa said. "She may call them gifts, but there is a price tag attached. Mark my words."

"A price tag beyond friendship?" Ser Beornric said, philosophically. "After all, she has allies and she has enemies, but how many *friends* can she actually number?"

"So you think the novelty of having a friend might be coloring her actions?" Ser Yrsa asked. She ran one finger down the scar on her left cheek. "I could see that. But once that novelty has worn off, she'll be all the more dangerous."

"Ser Yrsa," Aefric started, but Ser Beornric exchanged a quick glance with Ser Yrsa and held up a hand to request that Aefric stop talking.

Aefric gave his knights a quizzical look.

"We've been meaning to bring this up for some time now," Ser Beornric said.

"We didn't, at first, because you were new to your title," Ser Yrsa said. "And emphasizing the titles and courtesies of others seemed like the best way to help acclimate you to receiving them yourself."

"We thought you might take a clue from the speech of other nobles," Ser Beornric said, "but that you haven't might indicate that you've been misinterpreting what you've heard. And I suspect it's begun to put some of your knights on edge."

"All right," Aefric said, cocking an eyebrow. "What have I been doing wrong?"

"It's not *wrong*," Ser Yrsa said, "so much as unnecessary."

"We're talking about your use of courtesies," Ser Beornric said.

"What about it?"

"You are a duke," Ser Beornric said. "One of the premier nobles of Armyr. When speaking to anyone who owes you fealty—"

"Or any knight or ler at all," Ser Yrsa added.

"—you are only expected to give them courtesies when speaking formally."

"So I should be calling you Yrsa and Beornric, most of the time."

"Exactly," Yrsa said.

"So when we go to Norra for the Feast of Dereth Sehk, I should greet Baroness Herewyn as 'your lordship,' but otherwise just call her 'Herewyn?'"

"I think she'll be happier for it," Beornric said. "Call her 'your lordship' all the time and she'll think you're being formal for a reason."

"Your instincts are good," Yrsa said. "Trust them about when you should switch to courtesies. But in general, you should feel free to forgo them, when addressing your vassals. Or any knight or ler."

"I'll try," Aefric said. "May take some getting used to." He cocked his head to one side. "So that's why King Colm sometimes just calls me Aefric."

"Exactly," Beornric said. "And he and Queen Eppida will probably take to calling you Aefric all the time, once it's clear that you're comfortable calling your lessers by their names and not their courtesies."

"I hate that term," Aefric said with a grimace. "Lessers."

"It's not a derogation," Yrsa said. "It's a statement of political and social position. Everyone in Armyr is your lesser except the king and queen, the prince and princess, Duchess Ashling, and Duke Wylyn."

"And arguments could be made about those last two," Beornric said.

"Fine, fine," Aefric said. "I won't argue the point. I just don't like the word."

"Then let us discuss something else," Beornric said. "Such as what you intend to do with all that art, now that you've stripped the Hrafntonn family museum."

"You're not just putting it in storage?" Yrsa asked, frowning. "I hope you don't intend to sell it in Kivash. The locals wouldn't take that well."

"Not at all," Aefric said, smiling. "This is my plan. I'll send Karbin down to Kivash to work through the wards on those grimoires. Then, before he leaves again, he will ship all the contents of the Hrafntonn family museum — excepting the magic gladius and spear, which I'm keeping — to the Hrafntonn family at Svar-turvigi."

"To be ransomed?" Yrsa asked.

"No," Aefric said. "Just a gift. Taking their castle is one thing. Taking their family history is another. I don't want the contents of the museum rooms — or the portraits and tapestries in that sixth-floor hallway, for that matter — so why not send them back to the Hrafn-tonns as a gesture of goodwill?"

"They should be ransomed," Beornric said. "If you give them as gifts, you'll insult the Hrafntonns."

"But ... I don't want these things anyway. What's wrong with simply giving them back? Why is that an insult?"

"Why must a knight ransom back his horse and armor when he's unhorsed in a joust?" Beornric said. "Because this is how things are done."

Yrsa nodded seriously.

Aefric blew out a sigh.

"Fine," he said. "Once Karbin finishes with the wards on the grimoires, I'll have him see about ransoming those things back to the Hrafntonns."

"But not the grimoires?" Yrsa asked.

"No, those are mine now," Aefric said. "That's why Karbin will handle contacting the Hrafntonns. I know he'll understand. Larus Hrafntonn had the choice between taking his tools and weapons, or taking his grimoires. He made his choice. He has no right to ask to keep both."

"Fair enough," Beornric said.

Aefric sighed. "I do hate ransoming a family back its history, though."

"Well, then here's something you might like," Yrsa said. "Would you *please* take Deirdre to bed before she goes *mad* from frustration?"

Aefric shook his head, sure he hadn't heard that right.

Whatever Aefric's expression was, Beornric laughed to see it.

"Don't forget," Beornric said, still chuckling. "Knights *are* nobles. Pursuing the noble privilege with knights is perfectly acceptable."

"For that matter," Yrsa said, "you might consider Vria and Arras. I'm pretty sure they'd both be happy for the chance."

"Knowing those two," Beornric said, "they'd be even happier if called to your bed together."

"Too true," Yrsa said. "They spend plenty of nights in each other's beds anyway."

"All right, all right," Aefric said. "Your point is made. I'll keep that in mind. Can we turn to another topic?"

"Of course, your grace," Beornric said with a wolfish smile. "Shall we discuss your matrimonial prospects?"

"It occurs to me," Yrsa said, "that Ashling's endgame for this new friendship of hers could be marriage."

"It's not," Aefric said quickly. "She knows you two have me too concerned about bloodlines, and she's already got an acknowledged bastard in line for Merrek."

"That's not just a rumor then?" Yrsa said, sounding impressed. "She's doing a good job of keeping attention away from him."

"Right then," Beornric said, rubbing his hands together. "Let's go over the list of *actual* possibilities."

It was a topic Aefric didn't love, but he knew he had to deal with. So he settled in, and let his knight-advisers lead the discussion.

Ashling may have had a point about Aefric's advisers. He hadn't chosen them himself.

But he'd come to know them pretty well over the past season. He understood their perspectives and their biases, and he was confident that they would respect and support whatever decision he made.

A duke could do a lot worse.

SIGN UP FOR STEFON'S NEWSLETTER

Stefon loves to keep in touch with his readers, and loves to keep you reading. The best way for him to do both is for you to sign up for his newsletter.

Sign up at http://www.stefonmears.com/join

If you sign up for Stefon's newsletter, you get...

- Monthly updates about his publishing and travel schedules
- His latest news, in brief, and answers to reader questions
- A free short story for signing up
- List-only offers and occasional specials
- Plus a free short story every month!

ABOUT THE AUTHOR

Stefon Mears has always wanted a castle like this one. Stefon has more than thirty books to his credit, and he never stops writing. He earned his M.F.A. in Creative Writing from N.I.L.A., and his B.A. in Religious Studies (double emphasis in Ritual and Mythology) from U.C. Berkeley. He's a lifelong gamer and fantasy fan. Stefon lives in Portland, Oregon, with his wife and three cats.

Look for Stefon online:
www.stefonmears.com
himself@stefonmears.com